English Ivy

*Also by Catherine Palmer
in Large Print:*

Prairie Fire
Prairie Rose
Prairie Storm
A Victorian Christmas Tea
A Dangerous Silence
Finders Keepers
The Happy Room
Hide & Seek
A Kiss of Adventure
A Touch of Betrayal
A Whisper of Danger

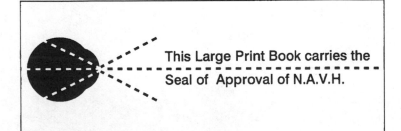

This Large Print Book carries the
Seal of Approval of N.A.V.H.

English Ivy

Catherine Palmer

Thorndike Press • Waterville, Maine

Published in 2004 by arrangement with Tyndale House Publishers, Inc.

Thorndike Press® Large Print Christian Romance.

The tree indicium is a trademark of Thorndike Press.

The text of this Large Print edition is unabridged.
Other aspects of the book may vary from the original edition.

Set in 16 pt. Plantin by Ramona Watson.

Printed in the United States on permanent paper.

Library of Congress Control Number: 2004105949
ISBN 0-7862-6781-X (lg. print : hc : alk. paper)

For Rhonda Maples with my love and gratitude for your abiding friendship.

As the Founder/CEO of NAVH, the only national health agency solely devoted to those who, although not totally blind, have an eye disease which could lead to serious visual impairment, I am pleased to recognize Thorndike Press* as one of the leading publishers in the large print field.

Founded in 1954 in San Francisco to prepare large print textbooks for partially seeing children, NAVH became the pioneer and standard setting agency in the preparation of large type.

Today, those publishers who meet our standards carry the prestigious "Seal of Approval" indicating high quality large print. We are delighted that Thorndike Press is one of the publishers whose titles meet these standards. We are also pleased to recognize the significant contribution Thorndike Press is making in this important and growing field.

Lorraine H. Marchi, L.H.D.
Founder/CEO
NAVH

* Thorndike Press encompasses the following imprints: Thorndike, Wheeler, Walker and Large Print Press.

Acknowledgments

If a book could be looked upon as a blossoming plant, this one has flourished in a greenhouse of warmth and sunlight. Many thanks go to the other "gardeners" who helped it grow. Audrey McIntosh contributed her ideas and listened to mine as the seeds of this story set around an English conservatory took root. Raoul Guise, a charming Englishman from Otley, went to great lengths to provide me with extensive information, both historical and contemporary, about the village. I cannot thank him enough for his assistance as this beautiful area of Yorkshire came to life in my mind and in my story. Kathy Olson, my brilliant editor, helped trim and prune it into shape. And Jan Pigott, my amazing copy editor, plucked away every last weed and brown twig. Of course, nothing can grow without regular feeding — and so I must also thank my tea-and-sympathy friends: Sharon, Patty, Kristie, Rhonda, Audrey, Lucia, BB, and Carole. Finally, I want to thank you, my dear readers, who welcome my small offerings into your hearts. Bless you . . . and may you grow in God's grace.

One

Brooking House, near the village of Otley Yorkshire, England, 1815

"At last," Ivy Bowden said to her three younger sisters as she placed the carefully penned instructions in her small beaded handbag. The printer in Otley would have plenty of time to prepare the invitations. In a few short months, she would celebrate her twenty-first birthday with a ball. By Christmas she would be wedded. Wishing for greater peace than she felt, she let out a deep breath. "And so — all is settled, and all is well."

"I should not say such a thing if *I* were to marry Nigel Creeve." Madeline gave a shudder. "And to have to live in Leeds in the same house with old Mr. Creeve and his wife. The pair of them give me nightmares."

"Maddie, you must not look on the dim side of things." Ivy tied her bonnet ribbons and wrapped a green wool shawl around her shoulders. "Nigel Creeve is a gentleman of the first order, and I am determined to be content with the arrangement."

"I think his eyes look like currants," said Clementine. At eight years, she was the youngest of the four. "They are small and black, and they sit in his head like two little raisins in a hot cross bun."

"Clemma, please!" Ivy laughed in spite of herself at the description of her intended husband. "How can you say such a thing? Nigel Creeve's eyes are perfectly ordinary."

"Indeed they are," said Madeline. "He has the most ordinary eyes I have ever seen."

"Oh, for mercy's sake, do come along — all of you — or I shall miss the mail coach altogether."

"But, Ivy, I cannot wear this bonnet!" Caroline, younger than Ivy by only eighteen months, had been sorting through the hat rack in the hall. "I must have my blue one. This one looks so ill on me."

"Nothing looks ill on you, Caroline dearest, and you know it. You are by far the loveliest of us all. Indeed, you will put us to shame in the village — blue bonnet or not."

"Oh dear!"

10

Caroline's lament drifted on the breeze as the four sisters hurried out of the house and into a fine spring morning. An early rain had washed away yesterday's gray clouds and left the sky the color of a robin's egg. The hedgerows were laced with spiders' webs, each tiny strand hung with a row of glistening dewdrops. Wild bluebells, yellow archangel, and white stitchwort had sprung up along the lane, and a pair of linnets were hard at work building a nest in the brambles and honeysuckle. It was, Ivy realized, the perfect day for the two-mile walk to Otley.

An ancient marketplace that had grown slowly into a village with cobbled streets and houses built of gray stone, Otley slumbered on the banks of the river Wharfe. Villagers proudly traced their history to the mid-eighth century, when "Otta" made his lea, or clearing, in the forest. No one was quite sure who Otta was or where he had come from, but it was enough to know there had been a beginning.

Ivy had lived all her life in nearby Brooking House, the ancestral home of the Bowden family. When the weather was fine — and sometimes when it was not — she took great pleasure in roaming the dales and fells that blanketed this rural triangle between the towns of Leeds, Harrogate, and Bradford. Countless streams and secret waterfalls provided perfect settings in which to read a book or watch sheep grazing the sweet moorland grass.

Immediately to the south of the village rose Otley Chevin. The rocky mount gave magnificent views over Mid-Wharfedale, and it provided much of the delicate golden stone from which the village had been built. Of all her family, Ivy alone made certain to climb the Chevin at least once a week. From its summit she could gaze out across the bracken and heather, and sometimes imagine that she saw the sea.

"Puddles," Madeline announced. "Our petticoats will be six inches deep in mud by the time we get back home."

"Yes, but all the rain means the heather may bloom earlier this year," Ivy reminded her. "I can hardly wait until the moors are covered in purple."

"Which serves to remind me — a soft shade of lavender would look fine on me, I think." Caroline grabbed the loose ribbons on her bonnet as a gust of chill air swept across the lane. "I mean to study every bolt of fabric in the shops this morning, for I am determined to have a new gown to wear to Ivy's birthday ball. I do so wish we could take a coach to Leeds and purchase our fabrics there, but of course we must make do with our own wee Otley."

"Leeds is a horrid town!" Madeline exclaimed. "I abhor it. To think that Ivy must live there simply appalls me. I fear she shall never have me as a visitor."

"Such a great loss," Caroline said. "How will she ever bear it?"

"Clemma, why do you dawdle so?" Ivy called to her youngest sister. "You must stay with us, for you know we are just at the edge of the forest."

"But, Ivy, look! The chimneys at Longley are smoking!"

"Come, Clemma, it must be the morning mist."

"It is not mist, for it is quite gray, and it is wafting straight up out of the chimneys. One, two, three . . . five chimneys are smoking at Longley."

"But that is impossible." Curious now, Ivy hurried back down the lane toward her little sister. "Mr. Richmond went to India ever so many years ago, and . . . upon my word, the chimneys at Longley are indeed smoking!"

"The house must be afire," said Madeline, who was peering around a tree trunk at the edge of the woods that surrounded Longley Park. "Indeed, it is in blazes and will burn down altogether before anyone can put it out. Such a shame, for I understood the furnishings were quite magnificent."

"But the house is not afire," Ivy said. "I feel certain someone has lit the hearths. Someone is staying at Longley!"

"I should imagine a band of forest gypsies has broken in. They will burn up the portraits for firewood and make bedding of the draperies. Longley Park is said to be full of gypsies, you know, and I understand the deer have been completely poached out."

"But what if it is the ghost of old Mrs. Richmond?" Caroline whispered. "Did she not die in India? Perhaps she has come back to haunt the house."

"Oh, do not say such things, I beg you!" Clementine grabbed Ivy's hand and huddled close to her sister. "Ghosts are horrid!"

"Ghosts are nonexistent," Madeline announced.

"Indeed," Ivy said, "they are altogether quite transparent, I am told."

"Oh, Ivy!" Clementine cried.

"Nonsense, Clemma, I am only teasing. There is no such thing as a ghost . . . while

14

that smoke is very real indeed. I wonder if Mr. Richmond has come back from India."

"Perhaps it is his son," Madeline said. "The pirate."

"A pirate!" Clemma gasped.

"Colin Richmond is not a pirate." Despite the damp soil, Ivy knelt and cupped her little sister's face. "Pirates and ghosts are only in stories, dearest. The scion of the Richmond family sails about in his papa's ship, that is all."

"That is *not* all." Caroline folded her arms and lifted her chin. "I am pleased to tell you a great deal more than that, for I have it on good authority that ownership of Longley Park was transferred to Colin Richmond upon his coming of age. He writes to his gardener, you see, who is married to our housekeeper's sister. Our very own Mrs. Bignell told me that the young Mr. Richmond was given letters of marque from the king of England himself, and he goes about attacking and looting ships — and if that is not a pirate, I do not know what is."

"It is not very gentlemanlike behavior, at any rate."

"Oh, Colin Richmond is far from a gentleman. They say he has a lady in every port —"

"Caroline!" Ivy stood. "It is not Christian to gossip."

"I am only telling you what I heard from our housekeeper."

"And that is —"

"He is said to be very rich, and a real rake!" Caroline rushed on. "He owns properties in India and America and Africa, and who can tell where else? How can he make such diverse holdings profitable unless he owns slaves —"

"Slaves!" Clemma cried. "Oh, he is very bad indeed!"

"And I should imagine he trades in opium, for how does a man become wealthy at sea these days unless he carries such a cargo? Opium and slaves and piracy and —"

"Caroline, please." Ivy pinched her sister's ear and dragged her back onto the lane. "You are every bit as wicked as you have made out Mr. Richmond to be if you choose to speak of such things without the assurance of them."

"Ow! But I have heard it from our own Mrs. Bignell, who is the sister of —"

"Do you suppose that a man of such vast fortune and such wide wanderings and such treacherous occupations would bother himself to write to his gardener?

Really, Caroline." Ivy released her sister and beckoned the others to follow. "No, indeed. If Mr. Colin Richmond is the sort of person who would take the time to correspond with a gardener, then it follows that he must be a gentleman of leisure. But if he is a pirate and a rake, then he certainly would have neither the time nor the inclination to write letters to anyone, least of all a lowly gardener. The information you have given us is all speculation and gossip, and it serves no worthier purpose than to fill your silly head with nonsense."

"I imagine he has killed people," Clemma said with a shiver. "Lots of them."

"Pirates are said to be dashing," Caroline murmured. "I should very much like to meet him . . . unless he wears an earring, for that I could not abide."

"It will not be young Mr. Richmond lighting the hearths at Longley," Madeline said with conviction. "I suspect it is old Mr. Richmond feeling very much colder than he did in India. He is the one who has all the chimneys smoking on a spring morning."

Ivy shook her head as she bustled her sisters down the lane toward Otley. Their sole pursuit in life was the accumulation of

17

trivial news. Who had worn that appalling violet bonnet to church? Which friend had been slighted by all the gentlemen at the recent dance at the assembly hall? Did everyone see the lace on Miss Bingham's gown? How can Mr. Desmond hope to marry when he has such teeth! Oh, it went on and on, and though Ivy loved her sisters dearly, she did enjoy the hours she spent away from them each day, tending to the sick and hungry in the village, or walking the moorlands, or reading in the family library.

Did the Creeves have a good library at their house in Leeds? she wondered as the party passed the massive iron gates of Longley Park. She sincerely hoped so, for reading and writing were among her greatest pleasures. The thought of Nigel Creeve gave her stomach a small twist, and she tugged her shawl more tightly around her shoulders. She had no reason to be uncomfortable with the arrangement her father had made to connect the two families, and she wished she could find greater joy in the coming nuptials.

Perhaps if she knew Mr. Creeve better, the matter would be resolved. As it was, they had spoken only a few times, and then he always seemed so stiffly reserved. But she had heard from more than one source that her future husband was upstanding and clever and very well respected. She hoped she would find him to be so once they were married.

"Papa has promised to give me a ball on my twenty-first birthday, too," Caroline was saying. "I am thinking of wearing red."

"Red!" Clementine gave a little skip. "I should never be as daring as that, Caroline! I shall wear pink when I am twenty-one."

"You and I are not likely to be given balls," Madeline intoned. "Papa will no doubt spend all his money on Ivy and Caroline. We shall have to content ourselves with nothing more memorable than a dance at the assembly hall in Otley. Or perhaps a tea in the garden at home."

"No, indeed! Do you really think so?"

"Papa is comfortable, Clemma, but he is not by any means wealthy. You know the Creeve family would not have taken Ivy for a pittance, and though Caroline is beautiful, she will require a good dowry, too. And that leaves only the crumbs for you and me."

"Crumbs?" Clemma frowned. "Well, then, I am determined to marry a very rich man who will allow me a ball whenever I wish."

"I am thinking of not marrying at all," Madeline said. "None of the men of our acquaintance can please me."

"Once Ivy has married into the Creeve family, we shall meet eligible bachelors of all sorts," Caroline said. "We shall go to visit her in Leeds and —"

At that moment, three ragged men leapt from the shrubbery beside the lane, cutting short her words. Their leader — a man with a gray beard and missing front teeth — raised a large, knobbed club as they approached the four young ladies.

Ivy grabbed Clementine. Madeline gasped, and Caroline let out a shriek.

"Yer bags," the leader demanded. "All of 'em, and we won't 'urt ye."

"Do as he says," Ivy ordered her sisters.

"But I —" Caroline clutched her handbag. "I want to buy cloth for my ball gown."

"Give it o'er!" the man snarled.

"At once!" Ivy shouted at her sisters.

Madeline cast her little purse onto the lane. Clemma, who did not have a bag, threw off her bonnet and shawl instead. Ivy tossed down her bag with the painstakingly transcribed instructions for the invitations to her birthday ball. As the men began to circle the four sisters, she could see they meant the worst.

20

"Caroline, give them your bag," she said. "I beg you!"

"No, they shall not have it. It is my money."

"Give it 'ere!" The leader lunged at Caroline, grasped her arm, and forced her down to her knees.

"Caroline!" Ivy screamed and leapt to her sister's aid. The man raised his club as Ivy wrestled the handbag from Caroline's arm. "Do us no harm, I beg you!"

"It is mine!" Caroline screeched.

"Lemme 'ave it!"

"Caroline, no!"

"Let go!"

As the bag flew out of Caroline's grasp, the robber brought his club down hard on the back of Ivy's head. She caught her breath, stunned and unable to focus, as the sound of running feet, shouts, and weeping filled the air. Fearing she might become ill, Ivy crumpled.

"You should have let him have your bag!" Madeline was crying. "Look, now he has tried to kill poor Ivy!"

"But it was *my* money! They had no right to it."

"Papa! I want my Papa!"

"Do stop wailing, Clemma." Madeline's voice rose above the others. "You and

21

Caroline must stay here with Ivy while I run back to the house and fetch help."

"Do not go, Maddie! The gypsies will come again and murder us all!"

"Of course not, silly girl! They have what they wanted. Now stay here."

Amid the ensuing cries and pleadings as Madeline left, Ivy tugged apart the bow at her neck. Slipping her fingers inside her bonnet, she gingerly touched the back of her head. A large knot was forming, and she felt an odd sense of confusion. In fact, the smallest movement sent the world spinning.

"Madeline has gone home." Clemma's tear-filled blue eyes came into Ivy's line of vision as the child laid her head on the muddy lane and gazed at her sister. "Ivy, are you quite dead, indeed?"

"I am not dead, dearest," Ivy whispered. "Calm yourself."

"Can you walk?" Caroline asked.

"I fear I cannot even sit up." She glanced at her fingers and noted that bright red blood stained the tips of her gloves. "I shall need a doctor, Caroline."

"Then I am resolved to go at once into Otley. I shall send the doctor to you directly, and I shall tell the constable the terrible thing that has happened to us all."

"But you cannot leave Ivy and me here alone," Clemma wailed. "Maddie told you to wait."

"Maddie will not tell me what to do, for I am a full two years older than she. It can do us no good to sit here with Ivy ill and the woods full of robbers —"

"Oh, dear me!"

"I shall run, though I am covered in mud and out of breath as it is. Stay with Ivy!"

As Caroline jogged down the lane, Clementine's small hand patted her sister's back. "There, there," she said. "Do not fear, Ivy, for Papa is coming, and so is the doctor and the constable. I wish our brothers were not away at school. Hugh and James would have accompanied us to the village, and then the gypsies would have been too afraid to attack. Ivy, you must rest until someone comes, and then you will be as right as rain before you know it. You will have your birthday ball and marry Nigel Creeve, and all will be well."

Ivy lay in the lane, wishing her head would stop throbbing and trying to find hope in the prospect of a birthday ball and a wedding to Nigel Creeve. When that did not help, she did what she realized she should have done in the first place — which was to pray.

God knew she was lying here, and her head was pounding, and her bag was stolen, and the thought of marrying a total stranger was making her more ill than ever. In fact, she felt almost desperate at this moment, and very close to tears. But her heavenly Father was more kind and loving than even her dearest papa, and surely he would not allow her to bleed to death here in the midst of the forest with none but poor little Clemma beside her.

"I shall tell you a riddle," the child said. "Elspeth, Elizabeth, Betsy, and Bess, each took an egg from a bird's nest. How many eggs were taken?"

Ivy smiled at the familiar rhyme. "Ooh, that is difficult indeed. What were their names again?"

"Elspeth, Elizabeth, Betsy, and Bess. That is four."

"Well, then they must have taken four eggs."

"No, only one! It was the same girl, you see, but four different ways of saying her name."

"How very clever, Clemma. Do tell me another."

Clementine was silent for a moment. "I do not know any more riddles. I cannot think . . . oh, Ivy, I am so frightened. Did you see how wicked those men looked? It is all Caroline's fault, for she should have given them her bag at once."

"We must not blame Caroline. I think they meant to do us harm all along."

"But if Caroline had not been so stubborn!"

Ivy reached out and laid her hand on Clemma's arm. "Do not be upset —"

"Oh, Ivy! Your glove is all bloodied! Did they cut your fingers?"

"I have touched the wound on my head, but do not fear —"

"You are bleeding, and you are going to die!" Clemma got to her feet. "Ivy, I must run down the road to Longley and see who has lit the chimneys, for it is the nearest help, and you are very ill indeed."

"No, please stay here with me."

"But, Ivy, if I do not go, and if you keep on bleeding, matters will be even worse than they are now."

"Papa will come soon."

"Not soon, for we were nearly a mile from home, and more than that from the village. It is a great distance, while Longley is just here. Truly, I must go, Ivy."

Though she meant to protest, Ivy found that she could not bring herself to utter any words. Somehow the entire scope of her vocabulary had deserted her, and she felt sure her tongue had turned to jelly.

"I am not afraid of pirates or ghosts," Clemma said. "And if it is gypsies who lit the fires, I shall tell them they have nearly killed my dearest sister, and they must give me bandages, or their evil deeds shall haunt them throughout all eternity!"

Ivy closed her eyes as her sister's footsteps sounded down the lane. As always when sleep came upon her, she sensed a swirling of silk around her face, golden silk, and the smell of spices. And coconut. And then words . . . words she had heard so many times before . . . gentle, comforting words . . . words that had no meaning at all . . . *so, jao* . . . *so, jao* . . .

"I beg your pardon, sir." The butler stepped into the large drawing room and coughed discreetly. "There is someone to see you. A lady. A very young lady."

Colin Richmond looked up from the ledger he had been perusing for the better part of the morning. "A young lady? And what is her name?"

" 'Clemma' is all she can say. Sir, she does seem very troubled. I understand there has been some misfortune near our gate."

26

Colin raked a hand through his hair and stood. "Very well, then. Send her to me."

He moved to the fire, took up a poker, and stirred the coals. Though it was early May and sunshine filtered through the long windows onto the carpet, the air held a chill he could hardly abide. It was no wonder his father had abandoned Longley for India so many years ago. The house was dank and dreary, a musty scent hung in every room, and the ceilings leaked.

"Miss Clemma, sir," the butler announced.

A small girl with bright blue eyes, pink cheeks, and tumbling waves of golden hair burst into the room and started toward the fire. But at the sight of the man standing before it, she stopped, breathing hard.

"You *are* a pirate," she said in a hushed voice. "Oh, dear me."

"I beg your pardon. I am certainly —"

"Never mind," she cried suddenly. "You must help us! My sisters and I were attacked on the lane. Gypsies took our bags, and knocked my sister down, and hit my eldest sister on the head, and she is bleeding, and she will die unless you come to save her at once!"

"Upon my word."

"Make haste, sir! There is no time to lose!"

Hardly able to reconcile the sight of so small a creature making such imperious demands, Colin motioned the butler for his greatcoat and hat. "Your horse, sir?" the servant asked. "Shall I have it saddled? Or perhaps you would prefer a carriage?"

"Is the scene of this calamity far, child?"

"Near your gate. The gypsies came out of the forest, and there were three of them, very wicked looking indeed! And one had a club, and he hit my sister, and now she is dying. My other sisters have gone for help, one back home and one to the village. I might have stayed in the lane, but I resolved I should come to you even though you might be a ghost!"

"Hmm," Colin said, setting his hat on his head and shrugging into his coat. "A moment ago, I was a pirate, was I not? Well, come along, Miss Clemma."

To his surprise, the little girl took his hand and began to pull him as they left the foyer of the great house. In moments, the two of them were sprinting down the drive toward the gate. It occurred to Colin that despite the urgency of the moment, he was rather enjoying the run.

"And then Caroline refused to give up her bag," the child was gasping out, "because she means to buy a length of cloth to make a new dress for the ball, but you see, that is why the man pushed her down. She should have given it up!"

"And then he hit her in the head?"

"Not her, my other sister. She went to rescue her, and then he hit her, and then Maddie hurried home, but Caroline went to the village!"

There were enough *she*s and *her*s in this tale to confuse any man. As they approached the gate, Colin spotted the figure of a slender woman lying at some distance down the lane. A bright green shawl had slipped away from her shoulders, and her muddied gown outlined the feminine curve of her form. Noting the crimson stain that had spread across the back of her bonnet, he left the little girl and raced on ahead.

"Madam!" Coming to her side, he knelt in the dirt and laid a hand on her arm. Unsheltered by the shawl, the woman's skin was delicate and pale, so velvety he could hardly sense its substance against his callused fingers. But when he touched her, something inside his chest clenched tight in a knot of deepest dismay, and he knew without a doubt he would do anything in his power to protect this fragile creature.

"Fear not," he said, drawing her shawl over her shoulder. "I am here for you."

A pair of large brown eyes flecked with gold fluttered open and gazed at him a moment. "Thank you," she mouthed.

His instinct to scoop her up and rush her away was quelled by the certainty that before him lay a true English lady, a woman so unlike the brazen doxies who plied their trade on the wharves of countless ports. She would never have felt the rough touch of male hands or known the intimacy of a man's close embrace.

"May I . . ." He paused, trying to construct the niceties of speech that had never been his manner. "May I have permission to carry you to my house?"

"Yes." The word was no more than a breath.

Before she could speak again, he slipped his arms around her and lifted her against his chest. She weighed no more than a sparrow, and he knew he must be careful.

"Go back again, Miss Clemma," he ordered the child as she arrived and took her sister's hand. "Run to the house, and tell my man to prepare a room. One with a fire already lit. Take my chamber, if necessary!"

"Yes, sir!"

As he set off up the drive, he could see the little blonde girl darting ahead on her mission. With all the running she had done, she would sleep well this night — if only she could be assured of her sister's health.

He looked down at the woman in his arms. Her lashes, long and black, lay on ashen cheeks, and her lower lip trembled a little with each breath. She was beautiful. And well loved. He sincerely hoped she would live to see the morrow.

Two

"Is it broken?" Clementine's voice filtered through the sheep's wool that filled Ivy's brain. "Her head, I mean?"

Though she felt the most intense headache of her life, Ivy was relieved to note that her senses were intact. She could easily make out the clean, white, monogrammed sheet on which she lay, an elaborately carved press cupboard nearby, and the red brocade chair upon which sat her youngest sister. She could also smell the most delicious mingling of leather and exotic spices — an intriguing mixture of lemon, cloves, and sandalwood. It was a warm, masculine scent that put her in mind of the library at home. Thinking of home set her to wondering where she was and who was pushing about on her head, making it throb worse than ever.

"Such head wounds as this generally do bleed a great deal," a deep voice said above her. "But I am quite certain the skull is not fractured. Indeed, there may be nothing more serious here than a bit of a gash and a rather large bruise. I am not certain it even warrants stitching."

Upon that pronouncement, a tall gentleman with a head of unruly black curls walked into Ivy's line of vision. As he rolled up the crisp white sleeves of his shirt, she was startled to see a pair of deeply tanned and muscular arms emerge. *My goodness,* she thought as the stranger began to rinse his hands at a washbowl near the door, *such prodigious arms . . . and such an extraordinary degree of . . . sinew . . .*

As he dried his hands on a towel, the man strolled toward Clementine. Tossing the towel on the bed, he installed himself in a chair near the little girl and propped his large, muddy riding boots on a fringed silk footstool. And now Ivy knew the source of the leather she had smelled. But was this gentleman also the wellspring of that mesmerizing scent? The very idea that the mysterious blend of spices arose from his heated skin sent a ripple of unexpected tingles up her spine.

"We shall wait for my man to return from Otley with the doctor, but I think you need not fear for your sister's life," he said, giving Clementine a smile that revealed a set of strong white teeth and carved the slightest of dimples into his left cheek. "A good rest and a strong cup of tea should set her to rights. Which reminds me — Steeves!"

The word came roaring out of his mouth with such volume that Ivy imagined it could be heard throughout the whole of the moorlands. A moment later, a smallish fellow appeared in the room, bowing up and down as if he were on a spring.

"Steeves, did I not order tea sent up?" the man in the chair inquired. "Upon my word, it is nearly ten o'clock."

"Yes, sir, t' kitchens are abustle, sir. But seein' as 'ow you came upon us all sudden-like yesterday, sir, t'cook is 'avin' quite a time of it downstairs."

"But tea — how difficult can that be? Surely the woman can find tea, milk, and a lump of sugar somewhere in the kitchens. Come, man, I am quite put out by this delay."

"Yes, sir. I shall see to it directly, sir."

As poor Steeves hurried out of the room, the gentleman folded that pair of brawny arms across his massive chest and studied Clementine. Though there was nothing menacing in his manner, he seemed to loom over the little girl. His squared jaw, slash of a nose, and great granite-hewn form gave him the appearance of a dark, shadowy crag towering above a small golden kitten. Ivy thought it might be a good time to speak up, but her tongue seemed to have stuck to the roof of her mouth, and her head was swimming so wildly that she could hardly stay alert.

"Are you not a pirate, then?" Clemma's voice asked. "You look like one."

At that, Ivy's eyes flew open. Good heavens, this man must be Colin Richmond, and she must be lying at the great house in Longley Park! Recalling the dastardly speculations that Caroline had put forth about the fellow, this could not be a good situation in which she and Clementine found themselves.

"I am not a pirate," Richmond said. "Nor am I a ghost."

"I am very glad of that."

"As am I. In fact, I am the owner of Longley Park, and at this particular moment, I find I am a gentleman of leisure — though I might dispute that. I have found little leisure since my return to England. My name is Colin Richmond, and I have lately arrived here from my home in India."

"India is very far away."

"Indeed. And now that you know me, may I be so bold as to ask your full name?"

"I am Clementine Jane Bowden, though we usually call me Clemma."

"Aha."

"Yes, and next up the line is Madeline, who ran back to the house to fetch Papa. We call her Maddie. And then comes Caroline. She would not give her bag to the robbers, which caused the problem in the first place."

"Let me see if I have this straight. Clementine, Madeline, and Caroline. I am almost afraid to ask the name of your eldest sister. It would not be Eglantine, would it? And you call her Eggy?"

Clemma giggled. "No, it is not that!"

"Rosaline? Adeline? Emmaline?"

"It is Ivy!"

At that, Richmond sat up straight, put his boots on the floor, and leaned forward to have a closer look at the woman he had rescued. Ivy had been observing him through half-closed lids, but now she opened her eyes and stared back. Though he might not be a pirate, he was clearly no gentleman, ogling her up and down that way with his dark eyes flickering.

"Ivy, did you say?" he demanded of the little girl. "And what was your family name again, Miss Clementine?"

"Bowden, sir."

"Ivy Bowden? No, that cannot be right."

"Indeed, it is right. She has always been called Ivy, and we never think of calling her anything else."

"Is it short for Evaline or some such thing?"

"No, it is only Ivy."

"And she is your eldest sister?"

Clementine let out a sigh. "All right, I shall tell you again, only the other way round. There are six of us in all. Ivy is the eldest. She is to celebrate her twenty-first birthday in the fall, though I am sad to say her bag was stolen away by the gypsies. She had worked on the instructions for the printer for days and days, and it will take her ages to write them all out again. At any rate, after Ivy is Caroline. She is eighteen, and Madeline is sixteen. Then come my two brothers. I did not mention them before, for they are away at school in Plymouth. Hugh is fourteen, and James is eleven. I am Clementine, and I am eight, but you may call me Clemma."

Richmond leaned back in his chair and raked his brown fingers back through the tangle of curls that tumbled across his brow, as though the room had suddenly grown too warm. "This is a fine matter," he murmured. "And you say she is soon to turn twenty-one?"

"Yes, I am," Ivy spoke up. It was time to put an end to this detailed discussion of the Bowden family. Until they knew Colin Richmond better, it was not advisable to give away too much of themselves. With some effort, Ivy pushed herself up onto her elbow. "Sir," she said, "I am most indebted to you."

"Nonsense. Any blackguard would have done the same. And any gentleman would be able to provide a decent cup of tea. *Steeves!*"

His bellow sent Ivy back onto the pillow, as Richmond rose and stalked to the door. Clemma bounced up from the chair and hurried to her sister's side. Ivy reached out and took the child's hand, grateful for the comfort of her presence.

"Thank you, Clemma. You did well to fetch help."

"I was very brave." She glanced over her shoulder at Richmond, who was striding out into the corridor. "He is nice. I do not believe he owns slaves. He cannot be as bad as that."

"Clementine!" Ivy clapped her hand over her sister's mouth. "He will hear you."

"Well, I cannot credit any of the things

Caroline said about him. He sent servants in every direction to fetch help, and now he is gone to see to our tea. I like him."

"True, he has behaved in a decent manner. He is somewhat gentlemanlike." She listened for a moment to the bellowing down the hallway. "Though rough around the edges."

"Caroline will think him handsome."

"Caroline thinks every man handsome."

"And herself beautiful." Clemma smiled. "You are looking pinker, Ivy. But your hair is a shocking sight. It needs a good wash, and all your curls have gone as straight as a pin."

"I am not surprised." Ivy touched the back of her head. Her hair had never been much to rave about, though it was thick and long, and she kept it glossy clean. But it was brown and straight, and how could that be thought lovely when all her sisters had managed to sprout curls and waves in every shade of gold? They had blue eyes, too, while hers were brown, and so she had resigned herself to being the mouse of the family.

"Ivy, dearest child!" Her mother rushed suddenly into the room, followed by her father, Madeline, Caroline, and Mr. Phillips, the village doctor. "Oh, you are looking ill. Very ill!"

"Mama, I am all right."

"No, indeed, for you are quite pale, and all covered in mud, and your dress is wet, and there is no telling what else."

"Her head is cut open — that is what else," Clemma said. "But I ran down the lane and fetched Mr. Richmond, who carried her here. I was quite brave."

"Yes, you were, Clemma." Mama sat at the edge of the bed and pushed Ivy's hair back from her forehead. "Oh, dear, are you in great pain?"

"I am a little dizzy."

"Dizzy! There, Mr. Phillips, she is dizzy!" Mama beckoned the doctor, who approached with his black bag and began to explore the back of Ivy's head. "We should never have allowed you to walk to Otley, for we had heard rumors that the gypsies were about again."

"Mama," Ivy said, "we walk to the village more than once a week, and we have never had cause for alarm until this day."

"You will not walk there again! Not unless someone cuts down the shrubbery around Longley Park, for it is a veritable forest and perfect for ambush. And the gypsies must be cleared out as well."

"I plan to tend to my property as soon as may be," Colin Richmond announced. He

40

walked into the room, followed by three kitchen maids bearing trays of tea things, cakes, and cold meats. A discernible gasp arose from the ladies in the room as he leaned one bare arm against the post of Ivy's bed and with his free hand began to flick open the row of buttons on his red brocade waistcoat. "Now then, sir, I suppose you are Mr. Bowden?"

Papa appeared startled by the unexpectedly forward address. "Yes, sir. Indeed, I am."

"Colin Richmond, lately of India. Pleased to make your acquaintance."

"He is not a pirate," Clemma piped up. "And I do not believe he has a lady in every port."

As everyone gasped, Richmond laughed heartily. "Not every port, I assure you. There are far too many ports, and far too few fine ladies, I have found. But here seem several. Will you introduce me, Miss Clemma?"

As Clementine pointed out her sisters, Ivy struggled to sit up on the bed. This would never do. Clementine was showing very poor manners, Madeline had her lips pinched in evident disapproval of their host, and Caroline was visibly blushing. Mama seemed determined to supervise the setting out of tea, as though this were her own home. And Papa, for some odd reason, was grinning from ear to ear.

"India, did you say?" he asked as he settled into a chair. "May I ask in which part of that great land you resided, sir?"

"My family owns a winter home in Bombay," Richmond replied. He shrugged out of his waistcoat, tossed it onto a nearby stool, and seated himself on a settee. "In the heat of summer, we retreat to Darjeeling in the Himalayan Mountains."

"The Himalayas, ah! Capital, sir!"

"You have been to India, Mr. Bowden?"

"No, indeed, but I profess a great passion for mountains. It is among my greatest pleasures to ascend the Chevin and make camp, whereupon just before dawn I awake to observe the rising of the sun. As one of England's own sons so aptly put it, 'Night's candles are burnt out, and jocund day stands tiptoe on the misty mountaintops.' A lovely image, do you not agree?"

Ivy closed her eyes and drew down a deep breath. Though the physician was snipping her hair and washing the painful lump on her head, her greater mortification lay in the fear that her father might subject their host to his vast reams of memorized verse.

James Bowden believed that a gentleman's time was best occupied in improving his mind by study and memorization. For Ivy, this had meant delightful hours seated in her papa's lap as he read aloud books on scientific exploration and discovery, novels of high adventure and romance, dramas filled with intrigue, and poetry from the Psalms to such contemporary versifiers as William Blake, William Wordsworth, and Samuel Taylor Coleridge. For her father, every social occasion provided opportunity to share from his storehouse of wisdom. And it looked as though Colin Richmond would not be spared.

"I have quoted to you from Shakespeare," Papa informed him, a pleased smile lighting his blue eyes. "I daresay a more illumined poet has never been born."

Richmond stared at the man for a moment. "You spoke from *Romeo and Juliet*, of course, but the Chevin is hardly the equal of the Himalayas, sir. The Chevin is but a mound of granite, while the Himalayas are the highest mountains in the world. How can you compare the two?"

"Ah, but from the crest of the Chevin, one is provided magnificent views of Mid-Wharfedale. As far as the moorlands are concerned, it is the top of the world."

Richmond lifted his cup in a toast. "To the Chevin, then."

Clearly delighted, Papa returned the toast and plunged ahead. "Not three years ago, sir, the noted artist Joseph Turner came to Otley and used the Chevin as the model for his painting titled *Snowstorm: Hannibal and His Army Crossing the Alps.* I urge you to view this work, Mr. Richmond, for it is magnificent. The interplay of light and shadow is truly remarkable, and though the observer may be aware that the soaring ramparts are only Otley Chevin in Yorkshire, he might easily mistake them for the great peaks of the world."

"I shall make it a point to study the painting at my earliest opportunity."

"Bravo. Very good, sir." Papa turned his attention to a crumpet. Ivy loved her father dearly, but she wished he would not so often wade into unfamiliar territory. Yet little could be done to curb his enthusiastic contributions to any and every subject under discussion.

Richmond propped one booted foot across his knee. "So, has your family lived long in Yorkshire, sir?"

"I am pleased to say we trace our ancestry to Otta himself, the founder of Otley village. Brooking House, my family

44

home, is nearly one hundred years old, though of course Longley Park predates us by several generations."

"You should come to visit us, Mr. Richmond," Clemma's little voice piped in. "We could have tea in the garden."

"Clementine!" Mama exclaimed. "It is your father's place to invite guests."

"Yes, but I like Mr. Richmond, and I want him to see our brook. We have got a brook at the bottom of our garden, Mr. Richmond, and there is a lovely bridge over it. We have little fish in our brook, and frogs and polliwogs, too. I think it is nearly warm enough to take off our shoes and go wading."

"Miss Clemma," Richmond said, "you have painted a picture of my very favorite sort of brook. I shall be delighted to wade in it with you."

Papa cleared his throat. "Well, be that as it may, Mr. Richmond, you must come to Brooking House directly you are settled here at Longley. We shall have you to dinner. By all accounts, our cook is among the most accomplished in the area. Indeed, sir, we shall feast together on fine food and enlightening conversation, for I believe a lively discussion can be as satisfying as a platter of roasted pork. John Milton put it so well when he wrote:

How charming is divine philosophy!
Not harsh and crabbéd, as dull fools suppose,
But musical as is Apollo's lute,
And a perpetual feast of nectared sweets
Where no crude surfeit reigns."

Richmond studied his guest for a moment. "Milton, eh?" he said. "I believe I should prefer the platter of roasted pork."

Papa laughed as though this were a good joke, and Mama and the others joined him. But as Ivy lay on the bed, she prayed that this moment might be ended as swiftly as possible. Clearly Mr. Richmond felt nothing of the awe and respect that Papa's verses incited in some men. Instead, it seemed clear that Richmond viewed his guests as bumbling country people who had seen nothing of the world and could say little to interest him. Though politely chatting with her father, to Ivy's great discomfort, he kept his focus almost entirely on her.

She supposed he wanted to know what Mr. Phillips was discovering during his examination of her head. Or perhaps he resented her family's intrusion on his time.

Maybe he found her appearance disturbing, for she knew she looked appalling in her muddy dress, tangled hair, and gloveless hands. But whatever the reason he kept staring at her, Ivy felt great dismay at the long, penetrating gaze of his deeply set brown eyes.

"Miss Bowden," the doctor said, drawing her attention, "you have suffered an alarming injury for a delicate young lady such as yourself. Are you feeling weak?"

"Hardly at all. Truly, I believe I'm quite fine. Certainly well enough to go home as soon as may be."

"Did you lose consciousness after the blow to your head?"

"Not for long. I was well aware of my sister —"

"In fact, Mr. Phillips," Richmond cut in, "she has been barely sensible for the better part of thirty minutes. When I carried her into the house, she was faint and unable to make clear responses to my questions."

"I see. And has she taken any food or drink, sir?"

"None at all."

"Has she been in great pain?"

"Indeed, for she cried out several times —"

"Excuse me," Ivy said, giving Richmond

47

a quelling look. "I have *not* been in great pain, Mr. Phillips. I have simply been resting, and I should very much like to go home now."

"I would not recommend that as being in the best interest of your continued recovery, Miss Bowden," the doctor said. "Though I do not feel that your wound is deep enough to require stitching, the loss of blood is a concern. Of greater worry, however, is the severity of the blow you received. Any injury to the head can be quite traumatic, and I believe you should not be moved from this place until I am assured that you are able to eat, drink, walk, and converse with the aptitude you enjoyed before your misfortune."

"Stay here? At Longley? But I —"

"That is an acceptable arrangement," Richmond announced, standing. "Mr. Phillips, you must return to examine the woman as often as you deem appropriate. Mrs. Bowden, you are welcome to stay at Longley for the duration of the young woman's confinement, or you may send her lady's maid if you wish. And now I thank you all for a most enlightening conversation, but if you will excuse me, I have matters to attend."

At that, he gave a curt bow and strode out of the room. After giving Mrs. Bowden a list of instructions and warnings regarding his patient, the doctor also took his leave of the family. The moment the door shut, a clamor arose.

"I want to watch over Ivy!" Caroline burst out.

"But I cannot stay here," Ivy cried. "Oh, Papa, please take me home."

"Do let me be the one to stay at Longley, Papa!"

"You think Mr. Richmond is handsome, do you not, Caroline?" Clemma asked. "That is why you want to stay."

"I find him very cold," Maddie said.

"I am not going to stay here," Ivy said.

"Such eyes!"

"He is prodigiously tall!"

"He believes himself superior to us all."

"I found the tea sorely lacking in amenities," Mrs. Bowden put in, silencing her daughters for a moment. "There was no jam."

"Do you think he is rich?" The excitement began again.

"More than ten thousand a year, I should imagine."

"He has good teeth!"

"But he does not smile enough."

"I like his hair."

"I like his boots."

"They were muddy."

"I want to go home," Ivy tried again. "Please, Papa —"

"He cannot know John Milton well," her father was saying. "Not if he would prefer a platter of pork to a reading of that man's noble works."

Fearful her father might launch into a lengthy rendition from *Paradise Lost*, Ivy forced herself to a sitting position and clasped his arm. "Papa, please do take me home at once," she said. "I am quite exhausted, and I should like nothing better than my own bed."

"Nonsense, child," Mama cried. "Did you not hear the doctor? Mr. Phillips has left explicit instructions that you are not to be moved."

"Yes, my dear girl." Papa laid his warm hand on Ivy's brow. "You must stay here and recover yourself, for I would not have any further harm befall you. Madeline will keep you company."

"Me? But I do not want to stay at Longley."

"Which is precisely the reason you must. Your lack of enthusiasm will keep you from exploring the house as Clemma might do and from trying to charm Mr. Richmond, as Caroline certainly would do. If you and

Ivy are unhappy, it will be a great comfort to you both to share your suffering. As Pubilius Syrus so aptly put it, 'It is a consolation to the wretched to have companions in misery.' And on that bit of wisdom, we shall make our departure."

"I shall have your clothes sent to you directly," Mama said. "Be mindful that this acquaintance with Mr. Richmond cannot be a bad thing. Indeed, I believe he has been sent from India to the great benefit of our family."

As everyone bustled out of the room, Madeline slumped into a chair and set her chin in her palm. "Mama believes God has brought Mr. Richmond to England for the sole purpose of forming an association with our family. As though he had no other business here at all."

"God is at work in every matter," Ivy said.

"She probably hopes he will marry one of us. Caroline, I suppose, since you are promised to Mr. Creeve."

At the mention of the name, Ivy groaned and lay back on her pillow. Why couldn't she feel better about her marriage to Nigel Creeve? Papa had worked out all the details, and the arrangement was certainly to her advantage. One of the very first verses

Papa had instructed her to put to memory assured her that God could make good come of all that happened to those who loved him — so Ivy should have great hope for happiness. There was no reason to feel afraid. Or restless. Or so terribly filled with doubt.

As Madeline let out an enormous sigh and wandered over to the window, Ivy shut her eyes in rest. All these ill feelings must be the result of her mishap on the lane. Or of the loss of her carefully penned instructions regarding the birthday invitations. Or of this confinement in a strange, cold house that had been shut up for years.

Her discomfort might even be the fault of Mr. Richmond himself, Ivy decided. Though his house was well furnished and his situation quite comfortable, he lacked the refinements of a true gentleman. He bellowed and blustered and stalked about in his muddy boots. He freely spoke exactly what was on his mind. And he stared . . . rudely stared at her with those large brown eyes.

She felt sleep slip over her with its familiar smoothness of rustling silk, the perfume of exotic flowers, the fragrance of spices . . . odd how Colin Richmond had

carried with him that scent . . . that warm
and spicy scent of her dreams . . . and then
the words came again . . .

So, jao . . . so, jao . . .

Three

Colin stood at the long window of his library and studied the intriguing young woman who strolled along the garden path below. Ivy Bowden had been at Longley for three days now, yet they had spoken but briefly. She had kept to her room until this morning when they passed in the corridor — she and her sister coming to the breakfast table and he leaving it.

"I am better, thank you," she had replied on his inquiry. "Mr. Richmond, sir, please know that I am deeply indebted to you for your kind and honorable assistance."

"It has been no hardship on my part," he had assured her, giving her a nod of acknowledgment. But as he walked away, he could only think how indifferent his response to her gratitude had sounded.

What should he have said? Which polite phrases and obsequious gestures would have assured her that she had been no trouble at all? And why had he not been taught these things?

In a small knot garden below the library, Ivy stopped to admire the budding pink roses on a bush. The hem of her pale blue gown skimmed her ankles, and the brim of her straw bonnet obscured her face. One slender hand stretched out and cupped a delicate blossom. Then she bent forward and dipped her nose into the petals.

At her movement, Colin's wayward thoughts instantly transformed the flower — and Ivy was leaning toward him instead. Her lips, soft and pink, lingered tantalizingly near. Her breath was sweet, the touch of her skin like the velvet petals of a rose. Pale and delicate, her hands reached to stroke his hair, and he ached to take her in his arms.

Discomfited by the allure of his unexpected response to the young woman, Colin took a deep breath. These thoughts were utter nonsense. He had come to England on a mission of short duration, and there would be no time for dalliance. Especially not with Ivy Bowden.

Besides, he had complete confidence that upon any lengthy encounter, she would find him rough and ill mannered. Miss Bowden was a true English lady, the finest sort of creature. Refined. Delicate. Articulate. Polite. Perfect in every possible way. She was uncommonly lovely, too. He had hardly a clue how to behave around her.

Reflecting on his early childhood, Colin could recall only the scruffy, half-naked Indian boys who had been his companions. Together, they had climbed mango trees, chased goats, and chattered away in Hindi as if there were no differences between them. Before her death when he was fourteen, his mother had been little more than a fragrant vapor in his life, a lovely phantom who kissed him once in the morning at breakfast and once in the evening before bed and then sent him away to be tended by his ayahs. His father appeared occasionally, always immersed in business or politics, and was scarcely interested in a grimy little boy with skinned knees and missing teeth. Why had his parents not taught him how to act properly around respectable young ladies? Dash it all, they should have!

As Ivy wandered toward the large glass conservatory that had once been the jewel of Longley Park, Colin jerked the curtains shut. Perhaps his parents had believed that sending him away to boarding school in England would provide him every proper instruction. And though rugby games, midnight escapades in the forest with his chums, and countless black-robed schoolmasters had given him memories both fond and painful, his education now seemed woefully inadequate.

Afterward, it had been back to India, back to rugged mountains and blistering heat and the astonishing poverty of the people around him. Why had he not noticed their utter destitution before? And why had all his boyhood friends suddenly become strangers?

Colin's father had put him on board one of his trading ships, the better to learn the family business. Had he stayed in England, the elder Mr. Richmond might have spent his days as Mr. Bowden did — reading and viewing paintings and memorizing reams of classical poetry. But on a visit to India as a young man, Colin's father had developed a passion for making money. Opening the family's coffers despite a tide of advice to the contrary, he had bought ships, built trading posts, financed expeditions, and sailed the globe with the sole object of enriching himself.

Colin was expected to follow in his father's footsteps, and so he had. And so he would. He liked the sea life, and he had a good head for business. Things might have carried on seamlessly had he not been summoned to his father's office one day and given a task. A simple task. Nothing complicated or challenging about it. Nothing the least bit difficult. Not until the day he had lifted Ivy Bowden from the lane and looked into her trusting brown eyes.

"Blast!" Colin slammed his fist on the mantel, sending the porcelain figurines into a shiver. There was no choice but to go and speak to the woman. But how? And what to say to her? And what would she think of him when it was done?

He stalked across the library and slammed the door behind him. Better to do it now. Have it over with. He would handle this thing just as he handled every matter that presented itself. Head-on. Straightforward. No mincing about. He had not been taught gentlemanly niceties, and he would not try to feign any behavior foreign to him. He would simply face the woman, say what had to be said, and be done with it.

"Oh, my goodness, I did not see you there!" Ivy started as an old man in a lumpy gray sweater hobbled toward her. Reaching for a clay pot she had toppled in her surprise, she asked, "Am I disturbing you?"

"Nay, nay, come along inside, if ye wish." With a gnarled hand, he beckoned her to step farther into the large glass conservatory. "Ye must be t' young lady from ower t' Brooking House wot got knocked in yer 'ead. Bad business that, eh?"

Ivy's slippers made no sound as she moved onto one of the many pink sand paths that had been laid out along the floor. The conservatory fairly shouted at her with a burst of green and growing things — ivies long overdue for a trim, rosebushes that had gone to cane, fallen pots of sprawling ferns, and topiaries so far out of form as to be comical. The scent of rich, black earth filled her lungs with the promise of summer. A fine, warm mist hung in the air, dampening the leaves, dripping from the rusty ironwork trim, and assuring Ivy that the hard-earned curls she had painstakingly pinned beneath her bonnet would soon hang straight.

"Do you live inside here, sir? In the conservatory?" she ventured as the old fellow paused to pinch a yellowed leaf from a camellia bush. "Are you a gypsy?"

"Me?" He chuckled. "I'm nobbut a Yorkshireman, lass. Born an' bred right 'ere. My cottage lies not a stone's throw from Otley. Name is Ian 'edgley, if ye please. I'm t' gardener at Longley Park."

"The gardener!" Relief spilled through her. After the encounter on the lane the other day, Ivy felt she was not quite ready to confront any more strangers. "And I am Ivy Bowden. I am pleased to meet you, Mr. Hedgley."

"Same 'ere, same 'ere. Nice to 'ave a lady about t' place. Sommat pleasant to look at, ye know. So, are ye takin' a bit of a tour round the grounds this mornin'?"

"Yes. It is my first day up and about. Longley is a lovely place."

He snorted. "Used to look a lot better, I can promise ye that. When I were a lad, t' current owner's grandpa kept twelve gardeners rushin' about 'ere at all times. *That* Mr. Richmond were a good man, but 'is son and grandson . . . well, they ain't t' same sort of fellows. In them old days, I were an undergardener. We 'ad every 'edge trimmed, every blade of grass neatly mowed, and every rose bloomin' so bright it would almost pop yer eyes right outta yer 'ead. Ye never seen such a sight in yer life, that. And this conservatory . . ." He shook his head. "It were a wonder to behold."

"It is a magnificent building."

"Gone to ruin."

"Surely not."

"Aye, lass, for there's only me to tend 'er, and I'm not 'alf the fellow I used to be when I were young and 'ealthy. If ye look close, ye'll see there's creepers settin' roots amongst t' marble stones, and moss spreadin' ower t' benches and tables, and 'oles in t' glass up there. Birds fly in, ye know, and they make such a mess it can 'ardly be borne. In its glory days, this conservatory were t' shinin' light o' Yorkshire. There was balls and parties and teas inside 'ere all t' time — ladies and gents lookin' like peacocks in all their finery. At night, filled with candles, she used to glisten like a diamond. We gardeners kept t' great 'ouse loaded with fresh and 'ealthy plants, too, brought in from t' conservatory even in t' dead o' winter. And bouquets of flowers bloomin' in every shade of t' rainbow."

"I wish I could have seen it." Ivy smiled at the little man whose returning grin was entirely toothless. "You have painted a lovely image, Mr. Hedgley. And now that Mr. Richmond has returned, perhaps we can anticipate a refurbishing of the conservatory."

"Not likely. Told the staff 'e's sailin' back to India once 'e's done what 'e came for."

"He has not returned to stay then? But why is he here?"

"That I canna tell ye, for I dunno myself. But I reckon 'e's got that India fever just like 'is father. Nay, I suspect 'e'll stay at Longley for a few months, tend to a little business in London, make sure t' old 'ouse ain't fallin' down on its ears, and then away 'e'll go again just like 'is papa."

"Do you think he will deal with the gypsies first?"

"Them ain't gypsies, lass. Them is nobbut poor Yorkshire folk what has no means of sustenance. They build camps in t' forests of Longley Park and shoot Mr. Richmond's deer and rabbits for their cookin' pots. Well, why shouldn't they? 'e don't care, sailin' off round t' world like that. Now, if a master would stay 'ere at Longley like 'e should and run things proper, there'd be plenty o' work in t' village and roundabouts. A good landlord keeps 'is people 'ealthy and 'appy and busy with honest work."

"Perhaps Mr. Richmond is not fully aware of his responsibilities here. I understand he has lived most of his life in India."

"Oh, 'e knows what 'e ought to do.

Writes me letters now and again, checkin' up on things. I write 'im back and tell 'im things is goin' straight down t' drainage pipe, if ye catch my meanin'."

"Is it the young Mr. Richmond who writes to you? Or his father?"

" 'im wot came in from India t' other mornin' without a word o' warnin'. Mr. Colin Richmond owns t' place, for it were give to 'im on 'is twenty-first birthday. Do ye suppose 'e's been 'ere once to look in on us, miss? No, not a single time till now, and we 'ad all give up 'ope of ever seein' t' fellow, when he suddenly appears and near frightens the lot of us half to death. There's only a handful of staff kept at Longley regular, ye know. Not like in t' old days."

He shook his head, bald save a few stray wisps of white hair around the ears. Ivy felt her heart go out to this dear fellow. Even the men who had attacked her did not seem quite so abominable now that she understood their plight. Indeed, she regularly visited destitute families in the village, taking from Brooking House what food, clothing, bedding, and shoes could be spared. She had great compassion for the ill and unfortunate, and she wished with all her soul that she might do more on their behalf. After all, she had been blessed with a warm home, a loving family, and plenty to eat. She took seriously the Bible's command to care for others, and she believed that in some small way she was doing these acts for Christ himself.

"Take a look at this pot, lass," Mr. Hedgley said. He led her farther into the conservatory to a large terra-cotta planter overgrown with vegetation. "This were at one time a magnificent lavender bush. French lavender, mind ye. T' scent could knock a man flat. But it's not cared for now. It's not tended. And see what's become of it? Around t' back, root rot 'as set in, and at least 'alf t' poor fellow is dead. On t' side, see, what do ye suppose moved in? Poppies!"

"Oh, dear."

He pointed out another pot down the row. "There's t' little trickster, that poppy there. Scatters 'er seeds all over, she does, and don't think twice about it." Mr. Hedgley tugged the vagrant poppies out of the dirt around the suffering lavender and tossed them to the floor.

"Now, take a look at this," he went on. "It's 'oneysuckle. It belongs over on that pergola, but with no one to look after it, t' little bugger 'as crept across t' conservatory, puttin' its wee roots where they don't belong." He pulled away the honeysuckle vines.

"And finally, we got a nice crop of grass which t' birds brought in with their droppin's. Grass can choke out most any delicate plant, and even t' tough ones 'ave to do a good bit o' fightin' to 'old their ground."

Ivy dipped her fingers into the damp dirt and fished out a small stone. "The lavender looks so much better now that you have tended to it. I believe you are a very good gardener, Mr. Hedgley."

"If I 'ad some strong young lads to 'elp me, I'd be a good gardener. As it is, I walk about nearly weepin' over the state of things."

"Oh, dear." Ivy could not help but put her arms around the old man and give him a gentle hug. "But you love the garden, and that is what is important."

"Nay, for a person who truly loves sommat will spend all 'is time to better it. Pluck out weeds, train vines, shear topiaries, sweep floors, let in sunshine, keep out rain and birds and insects. No matter what, 'e won't ever give up 'ope . . . as I 'ave here at Longley Park."

He stuck his hands down into his

pockets and hung his head a moment. "Each of us is gardeners in our own way, lass," he said. "We has been given things to tend. If Colin Richmond loved this place as 'e ought, ye would see such beauty 'ere, such glory. But I'm sorry to tell ye . . . very sorry indeed . . . Mr. Richmond ain't a good gardener, if ye catch my meanin'."

"Yes, I do." Ivy nodded. "I certainly do."

Even if Colin Richmond were not a pirate or a slave owner — and of those things she had no assurance — he was still completely unworthy of either admiration or respect. True, he was wealthy. But what good would all his riches do if his heart was so truly black as to abandon his family home and all the people who looked to him for sustenance? He should not go back to India! He should stay in England and do his duty. Now that she knew the truth about the man, Ivy felt she could not leave his presence too soon.

"I've always said to myself," Mr. Hedgley was telling her, "God is t' best gardener of all. T' one we should shape ourselves after. Because 'e loves us, God tends to us. Stays with us, don't abandon us when troubled times come. God tears out our weeds and feeds us with t' best sorts of nourishment."

"Indeed, Mr. Hedgley, you are right," Ivy replied, feeling her heart lighten a little. God did love her, and he had the most tenderly beautiful plans for her life. How could she doubt that her future with Nigel Creeve would be a good one? Papa had arranged it all to her benefit. Of course storms would come, and weeds, and even tangled vines. But God would be with her, caring for her and loving her. Always.

"Now, then, lass," Mr. Hedgley said, "I want to give ye this little gift, for ye've listened to me ramble on far too long. It's a wee sprig of ivy, like your name. See t' roots? She's alive. But ye must plant this ivy well, and tend it, and train it. And when yer an old lady, ye'll look at this ivy, and ye'll understand that yer a good gardener, too."

"Oh, thank you, Mr. Hedgley." Ivy took the small cutting and cupped it in her hand. "I am quite overcome with gratitude. Truly I am."

"Don't go on so. That ivy is not only a gift; she's a responsibility. When ye love sommat, ye'll do almost anythin' to protect it. And that might mean —"

"Excuse me." The voice seemed to come from a large philodendron nearby. But to Ivy's surprise, Colin Richmond himself immediately emerged from behind the plant and continued his rapid stride around the bend in the sand-strewn path toward them. He wore his riding boots — polished, she noted — and a black wool greatcoat that swept his ankles. He was a fearsome bulwark of a man, all massive shoulders, long legs, and broad chest. Noting again his deeply tanned skin and dark eyes, Ivy could easily understand why her little sister had feared the pirate rumors were true.

Stopping before them, he removed his tall-crowned, black-felt hat. "Not interrupting, I hope."

"No, sir." She glanced at Mr. Hedgley. "We were discussing the condition of the conservatory."

"Aha. Very good. And that is exactly what I should like to do just now. Talk."

"Then you must pardon me," Ivy said. "I shall return to the house while you speak with your gardener."

"Not him, *you*," Richmond said. "I wish to talk to you, Miss Bowden." And a moment later he added, "If you do not mind." And then, "Please."

She dipped her head, trying to imagine what the man could have to say to her. Perhaps he wanted to tell her he was going away to London on business. Or he intended to go riding somewhere. Well, it was no matter to her what he did. She intended to leave for Brooking as soon as possible.

"Hedgley," Richmond addressed the gardener. He glanced around at the jungle of vibrant growth. "Things are looking a bit weedy in here, do you not think so?"

"Aye, sir. But I have not t' fortitude to clean it all up myself. It would take more 'ands than these."

Richmond studied the little man a moment, his brown eyes taking in the fellow's hunched back and knotted fingers. "Yes, of course. I can see that. Well, never mind then. Good day to you, Hedgley."

"An' to you, sir." The gardener bowed. "Good day, Miss Bowden."

"Good day, Mr. Hedgley," she called after him. "And thank you!"

Richmond clasped his hands behind his back and began to walk in the opposite direction of the door. Ivy assumed she was to follow, though she had no desire to speak with the man. But as she tried to keep pace with his long stride, a sense of mission overcame her. It was a filling of purpose nearly as great as she felt when she tended to the sick and needy in the village. She must challenge Mr. Richmond with what Mr. Hedgley had told her! She must insist that he take on his proper responsibilities here at Longley. Indeed, God must have led her into this place for that very purpose.

Determined, she paused at a wrought-iron bench with its white paint peeling away and cleared her throat. "Mr. Richmond," she called as he strolled ahead, oblivious. "Perhaps we might sit a moment. I am in need of respite."

"Of course," he said. "Yes, certainly."

He returned to her as she seated herself in the center of the bench. She had no intention of leaving room for the man to sit beside her. No, indeed, he could stand at a distance to say what he had to tell her. And then he could just very well keep on standing and listen to what she had to say back. In fact, perhaps she ought to begin the conversation, for her heart burned with what must be discussed.

"Mr. Richmond," she began, "Longley Park is a vast property. God has blessed your family greatly."

He stared at her, his brown eyes unblinking. "Yes, that is true."

"Now that you are returned, I trust you plan to take up permanent residence here?"

"No, not really. My father needs me in India, you know. Business and that sort of thing. In fact, I have come to England on a single mission of some importance." He took a deep breath. "Which leads me to the matter at hand. Miss Bowden, I hope you will not be startled at my bold manner in addressing you in private. I believe the subject of my discourse is cause for discretion, and following this event, you may or may not choose to make it public."

"I see," she said, though she was not sure she did.

"You and I do not know each other well," he continued, "and yet I have cause to hope that you are a woman of sense and reason. I trust that you will see the sincere motive behind the statements I am to make, and that you will know I have only your best interests at heart." He briefly averted his eyes, then went on. "Miss Bowden, I have something very particular I must say to you. There is a question I wish to ask you."

Ivy's heart nearly stopped. *Something very particular I must say to you . . . a question I wish to ask . . .* but those words were the common opening to a marriage proposal! And how well she knew them, for her sisters spoke of little else than men and engagements and weddings.

First, a man would beg to speak to the object of his affection in private. Then he would tell her he had something very particular he wished to ask her. And next, he would profess his deepest and most ardent adoration — along with suitable references to her beauty and his sincere attachment. Finally, he would kneel before her, take her hand, and propose marriage.

Ivy's palms dampened as Mr. Richmond paced back and forth along the sandy path in front of the bench. *Oh, dear me!* He had already arrived at the second level of the proposal, and she had not seen it coming at all.

Surely, she must be mistaken. But how could she be? Just before he began speaking, Mr. Richmond had told her he had come to England on an important mission. There could be no question that he was intending to choose a wife for himself, and that she was his quarry!

But why had he chosen her? They had hardly spoken. They knew nothing of each other.

Ivy's thoughts whirled. Of course, there was some sense in all this. Mr. Richmond must be in a great hurry to get back to India. Since she was the first unmarried gentlewoman he had met since his return, he had settled at once on her. This was inconceivable! Yet it must be true. Look at him. He was clearly agitated, unable to speak — exactly the mannerisms of a man about to propose marriage.

But she could not marry Colin Richmond. She had already agreed to an attachment to Nigel Creeve. She must tell Mr. Richmond this news in the kindest way possible. Trying to calm herself, Ivy clasped her hands together and prayed for fortitude.

"Sir," she began. "I feel I ought to tell you —"

"Miss Bowden," he cut in suddenly, stopping on the path and looking directly at her. "What are your earliest recollections?"

"I beg your pardon?" Trying to breathe, she fought to make some sense of the question. "My recollections of what, sir?"

"Of your childhood. The things you remember about it."

"Oh." She looked down at her twisted fingers. What a strange question. But perhaps this was the way they made marriage proposals in India. "I have little to tell on that account, sir. I was born at Brooking House, and there I have lived all my life. I recall a loving and peaceful childhood in my home with my two parents and my brothers and sisters. We are a happy family, and all has been well."

"And you do not remember . . . further back?"

"Further back to what?"

"To your infancy, perhaps?"

"No, sir, do you?"

"Well, no, but . . ." He began to pace again. "Miss Bowden, I can think of no easy way to address this matter. I must tell you that I have been sent from India to bring you news. News of great significance."

He paused and looked into her eyes. She stared back, her mind spinning so rapidly that she felt almost worse than the day she had been hit on the head.

"Great significance?" she repeated.

"Miss Bowden, I must inform you that . . . the two people you call Father and Mother are not your parents."

"What?"

"In fact, you were not born in England, as you have been told. You were born in India to the wife of a man who was my father's closest friend and confidant. Your parents' names were Justin and Rosemary Kingston, and they were very fine people. The best, I am told."

Ivy feared that she would swoon. She held up a hand, begging him to stop. "What are you saying?" she whispered. "This cannot be true."

"It is true. Miss Bowden, I have no desire to cause you any distress." He took a step toward her and tilted his head to the side. "Are you in distress?"

"Mr. Richmond," she managed, fighting back the tears that flooded her eyes, "why have you told me such a thing?"

"Because you must understand this particular matter before I proceed further in my discourse. Miss Bowden, I beg you to hear me out. You were, indeed, born in India, and you lived there the first four years of your life."

Ivy brushed at her cheeks. How dare he say this! What could he mean by it? And what more could he possibly have to tell her? Was this his method of warming her heart toward him before making a proposal of marriage? Insufferable man!

She tried to remember the exact words of their conversation leading to his declaration. He had come into the conservatory and had asked to speak to her. Then he had begun his marriage proposal . . . and finally he had told this flagrant untruth.

Anger and hurt filled her chest. Only the most desperate scoundrel would resort to such a deceit in order to accomplish his wicked ends.

"I have this to say in response to your declaration," she said at length, rising from the bench and holding her chin high. "Mr. Richmond, I know what sort of man you are!"

"Oh?" He searched her eyes. "And . . . you are telling me, then, that . . . what exactly are you telling me, Miss Bowden?"

"That you have brought with you from India a most unsavory reputation. You are reported to be the worst sort of villain — a pirate, a slave owner, a trafficker in opium. These are rumors, I grant you, and I shall not give them credence until I know them to be true. But I have seen with my own eyes that you are no gentleman. You care nothing for England, for your family home, or for all the people who depend upon your charity for their sustenance. And now I understand that you will stop at nothing to gain what you desire. No deceit is beneath you!"

"Deceit?" He was breathing hard. "You believe this information a lie? I am not lying to you, Miss Bowden."

"Do you suppose this far-fetched tale

will somehow soften my heart toward you? That believing I was born in India will make me want to return to that country with you?"

"With me?"

"I tell you, I shall never go to India!"

"Blast it, woman, I don't care if you go to India or not." He hurled his hat onto the bench. "Why on earth do you imagine I should want to take you to India?"

"To be your wife, of course!"

"My *wife?* I have never even considered such a thing!" He began to pace more furiously. "Not that I mean to insult you, of course. Certainly, you are beautiful, and I admire a woman who can speak her mind. . . . I do respect you . . . very greatly and . . . oh, blast this whole wretched business!"

He tugged off his wool greatcoat and tossed it down beside his hat. For a moment, Ivy had the distinct fear that the man might explode. The muscles in his arms swelled, his fists knotted, and the sinews stood out on his neck. He took three strides and kicked a small clay pot right across the conservatory.

Fortunately, it landed just inside the wall, or it would have broken yet another pane of glass in the old building. Ivy wrung her hands, wishing she could run away from him. Run straight out of this place. Run to the warm and welcoming arms of her mother and father. Dearest Mama and Papa . . .

How could he have said such a thing about them? They were her parents! Of course they were. She covered her face with her hands and tried to think back to the beginning, back to the earliest moments of her life. All she could remember were Mama and Papa, standing beside her always, with love in their hearts. And her sisters and brothers, born year after year . . . with their blue eyes and golden hair . . . and curls . . . and rhyming names . . .

She looked across at the sprig of ivy Mr. Hedgley had given her. It had fallen from the bench to the marble floor. *Ivy.* She was Ivy, but her sisters were Caroline, Madeline, Clementine. She had *brown* eyes and *brown* hair and . . .

Tearing her bonnet from her head, she grasped the artful knot she had so carefully pinned up that morning after taking such pains to add the curl that came so naturally to her sisters' hair. Her hair tumbled down into her hands, rich and dark, the color of mahogany. Dark hair. So unlike the rest of the Bowden family. It could not be true! It could not, and yet . . .

Crushing the silken mass against her cheeks, Ivy wept, certain her heart would break.

Four

Colin gazed at the young woman who stood before him in such abject misery. Misery that he had caused her! But what choice had he been given? Before he could make known the purpose of his mission to England, she must be told this vital information.

The moment little Clementine Bowden had informed him the woman he had rescued was named *Ivy* — and that she was the eldest of six siblings and the beloved daughter of Mr. and Mrs. Bowden — he had known this devastating scene was inevitable. For three days he had turned the matter over in his mind, rehearsing the words he would be forced to say. He had intended to give the information to Ivy clearly and directly, with nothing that could possibly confuse her. He had meant to be forthright and wholly devoid of emotion so that she could readily comprehend the news of her parentage.

Instead, he had botched it!

How on earth had he led her to believe

his statement was the prelude to a proposal of marriage? Had he given any indication of the attraction he truly felt for the creature he had lifted from the muddy lane? Colin rubbed his brow and tried to think. He could not recall touching her inappropriately or speaking any words of endearment. Though it was the truth, he knew he had not told her he found her lovely. In no way had he intimated that her graceful form pleased him, her gold-flecked eyes enchanted him, her sweet voice bemused him. Nothing of the sort!

He had merely attempted to relay the information in the kindest possible way. And he had failed completely.

Now what was he to do? Ivy paused on the marble path, her lustrous brown hair shielding her face as her shoulders trembled with sobs. Colin took a step toward her. Then he clenched his fists and held back.

A true English gentleman would know how to proceed, which course of action to take in such a case. But Colin had spent most of his adult life on board a ship populated with the most ill-mannered ruffians known to man. A slap on the back or a night of heavy rum consumption addressed any discomfort those lads ever suffered.

"Oh dear," Ivy murmured from somewhere inside the cascade of mahogany tresses. "I want to go home. I must go home."

"Miss Bowden, I fear you are not well," he said, reaching for her elbow. "I beg you to sit down —"

"How dare you touch me!" she cried, jerking her arm from his grasp. She lifted her tear-streaked face. "Don't come near me, you insufferable rogue!"

"Madam, I should be willing to leave your presence at once, but I believe you are very ill."

"I am ill indeed! You have made me ill with your lies . . . so dreadful . . . so insupportable . . . so abominably impossible . . ."

"Though what I have said may seem false, I assure you it is the truth. You must see that I have absolutely no motivation to cause you this pain." He paused as she absorbed his words. "Madam, in my drawing room sits a locked chest containing documents verifying every word I have spoken. The record is clear. You were born in Simla in the Himalayan Mountains. I can tell you it is an area unsettled by colonists and known only for its temple to the Hindu goddess Shyamala. Your father discovered it on his travels, he built there a retreat from India's intolerable heat, and your mother spent the duration of her confinement in that place. Your birth was without complication, and it was duly recorded in the registries of the Indian state of Himachal Pradesh. I have a certified copy of this very document. You are listed as the first offspring of Justin and Rosemary Kingston, citizens of England and loyal subjects of King George III. And your full name is Ivy Elizabeth Kingston."

"No," she gasped out. "Please stop, I beg you."

As she bent over in agony, he stretched his hand toward her again. But he knew he could offer little comfort. "Madam, I have no choice but to continue until my recitation is complete. It is essential that you be given this information, and I beg you to forgive me for causing you such distress. When you were three months of age, your parents left the mountains and returned to their home in the port city of Bombay. Your father, Justin Kingston, a man of little means who was born in Manchester, had come to India several years earlier to work as a clerk in the silk and cotton trade. Before long, he rose in rank, and at length, he was able to purchase the entirety of the business from his employer. He returned to England briefly and took as his wife a young woman he had known since childhood. Rosemary and Justin Kingston spent the whole of their married life in India from that time on until . . . until you were born . . . and then . . ."

He faltered, hesitant to press forward with further information. Ivy seemed to have gone limp. Her head drooped, and her arms hung slack by her side. She made no movement, not even the slightest sound. Alarm coursed through Colin as he sensed that at any moment, she might faint dead away.

"Miss Bowden," he said. "Please may I help you to the bench?"

"Miss Bowden?" She raised her eyes, swollen from weeping. "Why do you call me that? You assure me my name is Kingston."

"Indeed, but you have never known it until now." He searched her pale face. As another tear trickled down her cheek, he fumbled in his pockets for a handkerchief. A handkerchief — of course he had nothing of the sort. Indeed, he could not recall the last time he had thought to tuck away such a scrap of nonsense. Unwilling to let her misery continue without offering some assistance, he tugged his shirt from the waist of his trousers and tore off a section of the hem.

"Here," he said, holding the white fabric out to her. "I have nothing else with which to offer you comfort. Please take it."

She shook her head. "No, I —"

"Please, madam, do take this, for I can see I have caused you great heartache. I confess I am not an elegant man, and there is in me a deficiency of decorum. Some might term me a rogue, and they would not be without justification. But I assure you I would never willingly grieve any lady so innocent . . . so wholly without flaw . . . as yourself. I beg you to accept this offering with my sincerest wishes for your recovery."

As he stood holding the scrap of tattered shirttail, it occurred to Colin how utterly helpless he felt. All his life had been spent conquering one thing or another. He had mastered foreign languages, mechanical instruments, mathematics, sailing, and every other challenge that arose in his path. He had outwitted adversaries, quelled mutinies, disrupted schemes, and made himself all but invulnerable to weakness and failure. Yet here, with this inconsolable woman, he felt as inept as a schoolboy.

As he lowered his hand in embarrassment at the foolishness of his offering, Ivy suddenly reached out and plucked away the scrap. She held it against her cheek, blotting the tears. For a moment she straightened, her nose pressed into the fabric. And then she looked up at him, her brown eyes depthless.

"It is true," she whispered. "What you have said is true. I know it because . . . because I remember this . . . because I know the scent you wear."

"My scent?" He glanced at the cloth she held cupped in her hands. Though he did not use any bottled colognes, he recalled that his garments had been packed for travel in fragrant sandalwood chests carved in Bangalore. Each morning, he washed with an Indian soap scented with cloves and spice. After shaving, he rubbed a soothing lotion of aloe and coconut oil into his skin. He had never considered these smells unique, and yet they were particular to only one place on the globe.

"India," he said. "You remember India?"

Ivy shook her head as she turned toward the bench. "Only the smell of it. But in my heart I cannot deny you speak the truth. Oh, I must sit down."

Relieved beyond imagining, Colin clasped

her shoulders and led her to the bench. He settled her gently on the seat, then took his place beside her. She spread the scrap of white fabric across her lap, staring at it in silence, her fingertips stroking the edges.

Colin tried to make himself breathe normally. So close he could see the tear droplets that fringed Ivy's dark lashes, he fought the urge to take her in his arms and hold her until her suffering had faded. Of all the things he had expected from his journey, this was the very last. How could it be that he would make any lady weep? That he would bring such agony to an innocent young creature? And that she — the object of his mission — should turn out to be a woman so beautiful, delicate, unsullied?

"There is another matter which convicts me of the truth in your statements," Ivy said. Then she swallowed hard. "I do not . . . I do not look like them."

"Like who?"

"Like my parents and my —" She broke off. "I do not look like the Bowden family. They are of Norse and Saxon descent, while I seem to be Celtic — dark and plain."

"Madam, I beg to assure you that you are far from plain. Indeed, your beauty astonishes me."

"My beauty?" Her brown eyes flashed upward in confusion, focusing on Colin's face for an instant.

"You are lovely beyond imagining. Surely you know that."

A subtle pink flush crept into her cheeks as she dipped her head. "I am not celebrated for any beauty, as my sisters are. I am known for other virtues — for my charity, I suppose, and my love of reading. I believe you flatter me, sir."

"I am many things," he said, "but I am no flatterer. I do not lie. Your captivating appearance and elegant bearing have taken me quite unprepared. Before arriving in Yorkshire, I had not perceived you as anything other than the goal of my undertaking. The object of my mission. I did not think of you as a human being, nor did I consider the effect my words would have on you . . . not until the day I rescued you and learned who you are."

"Who am I, sir?" she whispered. "I hardly know."

"You are Ivy Elizabeth Kingston, and if you wish, I shall show you the documents in my drawing room."

"I suppose I must look at them." But when he made to rise, she laid her hand on his arm. "Please tell me . . . what became of the Kingstons? And why do I live as a Bowden in Yorkshire?"

"I fear to speak of this, madam, lest you be overcome. Can I not persuade you to return to the house with me and take a cup of tea? Or something stronger? Sherry, perhaps?"

"I cannot abide strong drink, sir. To be less than clearheaded at all times goes against my conscience in every way."

"I see." Colin nodded, ruefully recalling the number of times he had found himself "less than clearheaded" for days on end. Indeed, his entire comportment had been one that would dumbfound and appall this lady. Until this most recent journey to England — on which he had transported a young missionary home from China — Colin had never considered any other way of living. The pastimes of a roving seaman were all he knew.

But the missionary had challenged him to open and actually read the old Bible kept on board ship as a good-luck charm. Colin had read . . . and read. And he had begun to see that there was a path other than the one of self-gratification and lasciviousness upon which he had been walking. One blustery day, the missionary found him alone in his cabin. They talked for many hours, and the new path became clear to Colin. It was one of selflessness, love, and forgiveness. More than that, the journey's guide could be only one person, Jesus Christ, the Son of God.

With no hesitation, Colin had made the decision to turn from his old life and step onto the new path. But making good on his promise had not been easy. The missionary departed the ship to visit relatives in Europe, and from that moment on, temptations grew rampant. Colin's friends derided him for his commitment to abstinence from the vices he formerly had enjoyed. It was with great relief that he set foot on England's shores at last.

Colin knew he would return to India and the trading business his father had established. But in the days since leaving the ship, he had decided that his life as a seaman was over. He would build a house in Bombay and remain forever "clear-headed," as Ivy put it.

Glancing at the young woman now, he saw that she seemed calmer. "When you were but four years of age," he informed her as gently as he could, "your parents made a journey inland. Your father intended to search out new sources of silk, and your mother accompanied him. While they were staying in Delhi, a terrible plague swept over the city. It was cholera."

"Oh, not that."

"I am sorry to tell you that both of your parents perished there."

Ivy lifted the scrap of his shirt to her eyes. Unable to think of any response that might comfort her, Colin took her free hand and clasped it between his palms. So slender and light, her fingers felt like nothing more than a small blossom he had captured. She was trembling, and he rubbed his thumb across the top of her hand, hoping to warm the pale skin. What was the proper thing to say? What could he do to ease her?

"Please accept my condolences," he murmured. "Truly, I feel very melancholy on your behalf."

She looked at him, and the corner of her mouth turned up just the slightest bit. "You are kind."

"I believe I am the opposite. To give you this information, to distress you so . . ."

"But you were instructed to tell me. You said it was your mission to bring me this news."

"Not *this* news exactly." Colin searched her eyes, wondering how much more she could bear. "When my father summoned me and gave me instructions to sail to England, he believed you already knew everything about your past. I had no idea that I would be required to deliver such astonishing information to you. We thought you were well apprised of every detail regarding your parentage."

"But how could I know it? I have been a member of the Bowden family for as long as I can remember."

"That was not the intention of Justin and Rosemary Kingston, I assure you." His hands tightened on her fingers. "Mr. Kingston was a most astute and careful man. For that, among many other things, my father admired him immensely. They were the greatest of friends. Mr. Kingston's affairs remained always in perfect order, and among his documents he left a detailed will — of which my father was made executor. In it, Mr. Kingston stipulated that should any mischance befall him, you were to be sent to England to live with the family of his wife's sister. That sister is the woman you call Mother."

"Mama?"

"Mrs. Bowden is your aunt. As planned, you were sent away from India to England, and you were placed in the Bowden home. At regular intervals throughout each year of your life, my father dispatched to that family a sum from your father's estate to be used for your care. You were never meant to be treated as a daughter by the Bowdens, nor was your heritage to be hidden from you. In fact, your father made a very specific plan for your future. And that . . . that is why I was sent here."

Ivy drew down a tremulous breath. "A plan for my future? What can you mean?"

"A detailed course was laid out for you, and it is to commence upon your twenty-first birthday. Miss Bowden — for I shall call you by that name until you elect to change it — I have come from India to reveal to you your future."

She gazed at him, her face devoid of emotion. "But I already have a future."

"And now you have a new one."

"Is it . . . good?"

At that, he chuckled. "I believe you will find it very good indeed."

"Then may I ask you to hold your news a little longer, sir?" She pushed back the loose hair that fell around her neck and shoulders. "I am so tired, so confused. This is my first venture out since the attack, and I am overcome with fatigue."

"Of course. Do allow me to assist you to your room and —"

"No. I want to go home. Please. I need to rest in my own bed and sit in my own . . . garden." She slid her hand from his clasp and covered her face. "Brooking is not my home! Mama and Papa are not . . . and my sisters . . . oh, what am I to do?"

"You may stay here at Longley, if you like." Determination filled his chest. "Yes, that is exactly what you *must* do. I shall go directly to Mr. Bowden and inform him of this matter. Indeed, I should have done so sooner, but I felt it was my duty to speak with you first. He will be told what great distress his actions have caused you, and he will be made to —"

"No, please." She shook her head. "Do not confront Papa. I am sure his behavior toward me had no malicious intent. He is a godly man, and I love him very much. I know there must be an explanation for what has transpired. When the time is right, I shall speak to him and Mama."

She rose, and he supported her elbow. For a moment, she stood beside him in utter silence, her focus resting in the distance on a large pot filled with lavender. Then she drew away from him and picked up her bonnet where it had fallen.

"I must go to Madeline," she said. "If you will be so good as to send for a car-

94

riage, Mr. Richmond, we shall leave for Brooking at once."

"Indeed, but may I not see you to the house? I fear you are not strong, and even the slightest —"

"No, sir, I beg you. Allow me to make my own way. It would not do for us to be seen emerging from the conservatory together."

"Ah. Well, then . . ." Such a thing had never occurred to him. "Good day, Miss Bowden."

Her eyes met his. "Good day, sir."

She turned and started down the sandy path that led to the conservatory door. As he studied her form, the simple blue gown and the dangling bonnet, he thought how very deeply he despised himself at this moment. With a few words, he had turned her life upside down. And though he hoped for the best, he could not be sure the rest of his information would repair the damage.

Ivy stepped into a shaft of morning light near the door, and the bronze hair tumbling down her back lit up like a length of the finest silk. What could he do to atone for the pain he had caused? Nothing, of course. He would go to Brooking House in a day or two, relate the rest of the information, and then leave Miss Ivy Kingston Bowden to her fate.

Sinking down onto the bench again, Colin hung his head. The missionary on the ship had assured him that no arbitrary and capricious fate controlled the destiny of man. Instead, God had plans for each of his people — good plans. God had played a part in the shaping of Ivy's life. And yet the young woman's future had been mapped out by her father. Colin knew she could do nothing but obey it.

What was God's plan for his own life? How could a man know which way to turn? Was he to follow blindly, surrendering every control he had held on his own fortunes? Colin had no doubt what the young missionary would answer to those questions. Yes, follow blindly. Follow the guide to whom you are surrendered.

Gritting his teeth, Colin offered up the same words he had prayed aboard ship. *To you, O God, I yield. To you, Jesus Christ, I submit my life. I trust in you and not in myself. Guide me, great Jehovah.*

When he opened his eyes, his attention was drawn to a small sprig of greenery lying beneath the bench. He recognized it as something Ivy had been carrying when he first came into the conservatory. At some point in her distress, she must have dropped the tendril of dark green leaves. Yet, he knew she had wanted it, for until the moment it fell, she had grasped it as though it were a lifeline.

Snatching up the sprig, Colin dashed down the path, out the door, and across the wide green lawn. Ivy was almost at the great house when he called her name. Swinging around, she laid her hand at her throat, clearly startled.

"You dropped this!" he said, jogging the last few paces toward her. "I thought you might want it. You are welcome to it, of course. Take it home and plant it. Perhaps it will grow."

Her brown eyes searched his as she took the sprig. "If it is cared for," she said softly. "If it is loved, as it should be . . . yes, perhaps the ivy will grow."

She turned to the French doors that led into a drawing room and stepped inside the house. Colin watched her fade into the shadows. "With your tender touch, madam," he murmured, "could anything fail to flourish?"

"You are very dull today, Ivy," Mama said from a settee near the open window. The gold-and-cream-patterned wallpaper in the drawing room brought the woman's clear complexion to life, and in the morning sunlight her flaxen curls gleamed beneath her white mobcap. Clearly in a lively humor, she spoke with great enthusiasm. "I am sorry the gypsies stole your bag, dearest. Indeed you are to be pitied that you must write out all the instructions again. But it cannot be such a dismal labor that you refuse to join in our conversations."

"No, Mama, I do not mind the task." Ivy dipped her pen into the inkwell, barely glancing at the woman she had called Mother for so many years.

"But, my dear, you have not been at all yourself since the attack. You have been back at home for nearly a week now, but truly, you are quite out of spirits. I have told your father that we should send to Otley for Mr. Phillips and bid him examine your poor head again."

"I think Ivy and Maddie came away from Longley too soon," Clementine said. Seated at a round cherrywood table, she was attempting to conjugate French verbs while her sisters stitched nearby. "They should have stayed longer, and then we could have gone to visit them and had a better look at the great house. Do you know Mr. Richmond has a whole room just for giving balls? It is on the third floor, and it is said to be immense, for Sarah told me so at church on Sunday. I tried to catch Mr. Richmond to ask him if it was true, but he went away in his carriage without speaking to anyone at all."

"He is a disagreeable man," Madeline said. "I am not surprised he shunned everyone at church. The whole time we were at Longley, he never spoke to us."

"Not even at dinner?"

"He kept to another wing of the house entirely. We saw him but once, at breakfast, and there he gave us nothing but the most dispassionate of greetings. Hardly even a bow!"

"Perhaps he has been pirating too long," Caroline said with a giggle. "Maybe he has forgotten his manners."

"Mr. Richmond is not a pirate," Ivy spoke up. "He works at his father's trade in India."

"Trade?" Mama exclaimed. "A family as well-off as the Richmonds can have no need to labor at a common trade. No, indeed, I should imagine Colin Richmond does nothing more than loll about all day in the shade of a palm tree, sipping coconut milk and gazing at lovely Indian princesses in their silks and jewels."

"Mama!" Maddie said. "Such a picture you paint."

"Elephants, too," Clemma put in. "Do not forget the elephants, Mama. He probably has three or four to ride on whenever he likes."

"I should adore wearing silks and jewels." Caroline held up the small bag she had been embellishing. "Instead, I must make do with these silly glass beads and this cotton fabric that is so dull as to make me want to weep."

"Oh, you will have jewels soon enough," Mama replied. "But I fear even they cannot satisfy you, Caroline. You have too great an appetite for fine things, and you distress your poor papa nearly to death with your wheedling and begging. He has given you girls everything you could possibly need, and yet you go on wanting more. It vexes him greatly."

"But, Mama, you have just said I shall soon have jewels!" Caroline exclaimed. "What can you have meant by it?"

"Did I say that?" Her cheeks flushed. "I am sure I have misspoken."

"Oh, but Mama, I must know what you meant!"

"I meant nothing, of course. Just that

your dear papa has done all he could for you."

"She meant that when Ivy marries Nigel Creeve, we are all going to be as rich as queens!" Clemma crowed. "Ivy will buy us jewels and gowns and take us bathing at Brighton and whatever we wish."

"Nonsense," Maddie said. "The Creeve family is not so wealthy as that."

"Indeed, everyone knows that old Mr. Creeve has rung up masses of debts." Caroline sorted through the beads in a small box. "Mrs. Creeve, it is said, spends money as though it were water, and their house is filled with every sort of —"

"Caroline," Ivy cut in, "you should not gossip about the Creeves."

"It is not gossip, Ivy. I have had the information from a very reliable source."

"But you do not know it to be true." Ivy carefully dipped her pen into the inkwell again. "I have come to believe . . . indeed, I have believed all my life . . . that truth is the most important of virtues."

"Quite right!" Mama said. "One should always tell the truth. An ungoverned tongue, Caroline, can lead to all sorts of mischief."

As Caroline protested the notion that her tongue was ungoverned, Ivy covertly

101

studied the woman on the settee. Every single Sunday Mrs. Bowden herded her entire family to church. She had taught her daughters to sing hymns, and she had given countless discourses on each of the Ten Commandments — though she preferred to speak very little on the seventh, because of its delicate subject matter.

Indeed, both of the Bowden adults claimed great religious piety. Each morning at breakfast and each evening after dinner, Papa subjected his progeny to lengthy readings from the Bible or some other worthy text. He had compelled his children to memorize his favorite passages of Scripture, and he liked nothing better than to engage them in a lively discussion on matters of doctrinal import.

Were the two people who had brought up Ivy truly as virtuous as they seemed? She had always believed so. But why would the elder Bowdens not have told her the story of her birth in India? How could they have concealed her true identity? Why would they want to keep hidden the truth of her parentage?

Since speaking with Mr. Richmond nearly a week ago, Ivy had turned these questions over in her mind without satisfaction. She had not been able to bring herself to announce what she had learned, and she had no idea how her family would respond. The ensuing turmoil might damage their filial bond for all time. Yet she could not keep silent forever. Morning and night, she watched them, listened to their conversations as if with new ears, and tried to decipher some understanding of the truth.

But what was true and what was a lie?

In the conservatory, she had been so certain that Colin Richmond's tale was fact. For what purpose would he deceive her? She squirmed in discomfort every time she recalled how she had misunderstood his words to be the prelude to a marriage proposal. The very idea that such a man would fix his desires on plain little Ivy — but he had said she was not plain . . . she was lovely . . . beautiful . . .

Ivy recalled clearly the sincerity written in his dark eyes as he spoke to her. *I am many things, madam, but I am not a flatterer,* he had said. *I do not lie.*

But why would Mama and Papa conceal the truth? What could it gain them to treat an orphaned niece as their own daughter? Glancing up at the woman by the window, Ivy felt suddenly awash with an awful certainty. Mr. Richmond had said his father sent regular sums of money from India — money to be used for Ivy's care. Had Papa diverted those funds to some other purpose?

She let out a small cry of dismay, but the sound went unheard as the drawing-room door opened and the housekeeper hurried across the wooden floor. "This come for ye, mum," she said, holding out a silver tray with a small white card lying on it. " 'e's waitin' in t' front room, and 'e says it's not ye nor Mr. Bowden 'e wants to talk to. It's Miss Bowden."

All eyes turned on Ivy.

"Colin Richmond wishes to talk to my daughter, does he?" Mama said. "Well, we shall see about that."

Five

When Ivy stepped into the front parlor, she observed that Papa had already engaged himself in conversation with Colin Richmond. The men's voices were contentious and growing more heated by the moment. With dismay, she paused near the door and tried to make out what they were saying.

"No, absolutely not!" Papa declared. "I cannot permit —"

"I have no choice in this matter," Colin insisted. "I was ordered by my father to —"

"My dear Mr. Richmond," Mama trilled, "how good of you to come to Brooking House." Seemingly oblivious to the tension, she strolled into the room as though she were entering a tea party. "I have brought our daughter, Miss Bowden, whom you so graciously rescued from your lane not a fortnight ago. We are most honored that you have come to ascertain the extent of her recovery."

The men fell silent as the two women curtsied in greeting. Ivy could not bring herself to look directly at their guest, though in the days since speaking with the owner of Longley Park, she had thought of little else but him. Again and again she had reviewed their conversation, trying to recall the exact intonation of his voice or the precise juxtaposition of his words. She told herself that her preoccupation with Colin Richmond had to do only with the shocking information he had given her. But she could not deny she had also entertained wayward thoughts that had nothing to do with the news of her parentage.

Though Ivy had tried to discipline herself, she was surprised at how often she had caught herself dwelling on the man's dark brown eyes, recalling the sound of his deep voice, even imagining the pressure of his hands clasped warmly around hers. More than she cared to admit, she had found herself wishing to be near him again, longing for the firm assurance of his bearing. When no one could see her, she would take the scrap of his white linen shirt from her pocket and drink deeply of the scent. She perceived that something had stirred to life inside her heart — an unexpected yearning that compelled and beckoned her . . . and at the same time filled her with alarm.

Such thoughts about Colin Richmond could not be permitted, Ivy warned herself, for her father had made an agreement with Nigel Creeve. It would be a most profitable marriage — no matter what rumors Caroline had heard of Nigel's family. More important, Mr. Richmond was a virtual stranger to the Bowden family, and Ivy knew little of his true character. Though he had shown her the greatest of courtesy, his past activities were completely unknown. He might indeed have practiced piracy, encouraged slavery, and engaged in dalliances with women in every port.

Besides, he had told her clearly that she was nothing more to him than the object of his mission. Oh, what must he have thought of her behavior in the conservatory — her ceaseless tears, her harsh accusations, her contempt for his reputation, and . . . oh dear . . . her woefully silly misconception about his purpose in wishing to speak to her in private?

Finding the nearest chair, Ivy quickly sat down and affected an intense scrutiny of a small porcelain figurine on the table beside her. Papa harrumphed several times. Mama rang for tea, all the while chattering away about the attack on her daughters. Although Ivy had tried to tell her mother that the assailants were poor Yorkshiremen, Mrs. Bowden could not stop talking about the terrible numbers of gypsies who had come into Yorkshire of late. Mr. Richmond remained mute, though Ivy sensed his presence somewhere near the fireplace.

She silently lifted up a prayer that he would give his information and then depart. In pondering the situation, she had concluded that his mission from India must have to do with the conveyance of an inheritance from her father by birth. But what did she care for wealth when she felt so betrayed by the people she had loved the most?

"Good morning, Mr. Richmond!" Clementine poked her head into the parlor. "I hope you have come to wade in our little brook at the bottom of the garden."

Ivy glanced up long enough to see Richmond's face break into a broad grin — and her worst fears about the man were confirmed. Indeed, he appeared even more dashing this morning than in the past. He wore a fine black jacket cut away in the front and falling to tails behind him, fitted trousers tucked into riding boots, a striped, gray-silk waistcoat, and small ruffles at the neck of his white shirt.

"Miss Clemma," he greeted the little girl, "how delightful to see you again. I fear I have no time for wading today, but I shall —"

"Clementine, away with you!" Mama spoke up, shooing her youngest daughter toward the door. "Be gone, child, for you are not needed now!"

"But I wanted to say hello to Mr. Richmond." Clemma gave a perky little curtsy. "You must come to Brooking House again, sir. I should very much like to hear all your stories about India, and about the sea and pirates and dragons —"

"Dragons?" Richmond laughed aloud. "I do not have much for you on that topic, Miss Clemma."

"No, of course he does not, Clementine," Mama cried. "Off with you now. At once!"

As her little sister scampered away, Ivy shifted her focus to the man across the room. At the same moment, his eyes fell on her. She looked away quickly, ruing the flush of heat that spread across her cheeks.

"Miss . . . Bowden," Richmond addressed her. "Are you better? Your injury, I mean."

She nodded. "I am quite recovered, thank you, sir."

"On the contrary, I fear my daughter is

not at all well," Mama corrected her. "Ivy's spirits are very dull, and she refuses to speak more than two words together. Since the attack, she has been quite unlike herself."

"I am sorry to hear that."

To her consternation, Ivy perceived Mr. Richmond's footsteps crossing the dark green carpet toward her. Oh dear, she did not want to be near him again! No doubt he would speak kind words to her, and then he would deliver more of his distressing news. She wanted so much to hate the man who had caused her such agony. But he was settling into a chair beside her, and she could see his strong, brown hands — firm fingers that had warmed her with comfort and support.

"Miss Kingston," he said, his voice low, "are you recovered enough that we might continue our conversation now? Or shall I return on another day?"

"What do you say there?" Papa called across the room. "Mr. Richmond, I cannot allow you to engage in a private discussion with my daughter. I must know of what you speak, sir."

"Good heavens, Mr. Bowden!" Mama exclaimed. "Why do you address our guest in such a forceful tone?"

"I address the gentleman this way, Mrs. Bowden, because I have just learned the object of his presence in our home. And it is not one of which I approve."

Richmond turned to him. "Approve or not, sir, you must accept the fact that I am determined to relate my information. My father commissioned me with this task, and I shall not be deterred from it."

"But in front of the girl?" Papa crossed the carpet. "This is a matter that I, as her father, need to know. Ivy herself has no use for such information. She is a child."

"I beg to dispute that, sir. She is a grown woman. And furthermore, she is not your daughter."

Mama gave a cry of shock. "What? What are you saying, Mr. Richmond? How do you have this knowledge? Mr. Bowden, how has he learned of this? Did you tell him? Oh, heaven! Oh, horror! I am going to faint —"

"Quiet, Mrs. Bowden!" Papa barked. "Seat yourself at once, for I am not in a humor to give heed to your hysterics."

Ivy swallowed hard as Mama collapsed onto a settee and fumbled for her fan. Papa had begun to pace back and forth across the room, his face growing redder by the moment. Glancing at Mr. Richmond, Ivy saw that he had removed his hat, and dark curls framed his intense brown eyes. His expression solemn, he was regarding Ivy as though he meant to read her every thought.

"You cannot have anything to say to the girl, Richmond," Papa sputtered. "I am her guardian, and it is my duty to prevent any distress to her composure. Sir, I must insist that you withhold your information until we can discuss the matter in private."

"Papa," Ivy said, with some effort drawing her focus from Mr. Richmond, "please allow our guest to speak. I assure you —"

"No! Upon my word, child, I am master of this house, and I forbid this conversation."

"But, Papa —"

"Leave us, girl. Take your mother upstairs to her room. She is not well, and I fear she will need her smelling salts."

"Yes, Papa." Ivy stood.

"Miss Bowden," Richmond spoke up, getting to his feet. "If you are at all able to bear the news I bring, please stay here, for I am determined to give it to you now. As you know, I have come from India for the express purpose of speaking to you, and this I must do."

"You shall tell me the information!" Papa cried. "Not her. Not the girl."

"Mr. Bowden, sit down!" Richmond turned on the older man and pointed at a chair. "Sit down now. Please."

Ivy heard her mother gasp as Papa all but fell into the indicated chair. Richmond stalked across the heavy carpet. He stood before the fireplace, fists knotted at his waist, and glared at nothing. Ivy hardly breathed, unsure whether to obey her father and take her mother away, or to stay and listen to Richmond's discourse.

Once again, the horrible truth descended upon her. Whose daughter was she? What was to become of her? She loved Mama and Papa so dearly. They had treated her well and had brought her up with love and happiness. What was she to do? What did it all mean?

"Mr. Bowden," Colin Richmond began, his glower transferring to the agitated older man on the chair. "Be assured, I shall not brook interruption again! Though it is not my intent to cause distress to you or your wife, I mean to relate my information immediately and without further ado. I have brought from India a chest of documents concerning the past and the future of the young lady standing here, whose correct name is Ivy Elizabeth Kingston."

"Oh, mercy, mercy," Mama groaned, whisking her fan to and fro in front of her face.

"Do not torment yourself so, Mama," Ivy spoke up. "Mr. Richmond informed me of my situation many days ago."

"He had no right to do that!" Papa exploded. "You are our daughter and under my regulation! Mr. Richmond had no right —"

"You had no right to keep the truth from her, sir," Richmond interjected. "Her father never intended for his daughter to have any illusion regarding the circumstances of her birth."

"Her father? *I* am her father! By all that is right, this child is my daughter. I have brought her up into the only life she has ever known. It is my home in which she makes her residence. My values have shaped her character. I have directed her education. And I claim the privilege of calling myself her father. You, sir, have no right to intrude on our bond!"

"I have told her the truth."

"Truth? From a man who would be so villainous, so reprehensible, as to approach a young lady in private? You had no right to speak to her alone. Indeed, you had no permission from me to address her at all. Had I believed you were capable of such trespass, I would never have left her in your care!"

"My own father, to whose wishes I submit with the greatest of respect, ordered me to give this information to her."

"If your father is any sort of gentleman, he could not have intended for you to breach the privacy and innocence of a young lady."

"Papa," Ivy said, "please do not admonish Mr. Richmond in such fashion. His behavior to me in the conservatory at Longley was most civil and well mannered."

"In the conservatory? There! A more imprudent place for a private conversation I cannot imagine. Were you chaperoned? Did your sister know anything of this assignation between the two of you? Did Madeline accompany you?"

"No, Papa, but I assure you —"

"Did this man touch you in any way?" Papa roared.

"Only to uphold me, sir. To be sure, Mr. Richmond guided me to a bench lest I faint away. And he held my hand to comfort me, for I was greatly distraught —"

"Held your hand!"

"Wicked man!" Mama shrieked. "Churl!"

"I beg you, please," Ivy said. "He is a kind and gentle man! Indeed, he is wholly without fault in this matter."

"He has wooed you and distorted your good mind," Papa retorted. "How can he be without fault when he has obviously distressed you? It has been my deepest desire to protect you from discomfort — to make certain that you know you are my daughter in every way that counts."

"But, Papa, I know that what he told me is true . . . because I remember . . ." She tugged the scrap of fabric from her pocket. "The scent he wears, the smell of his skin — it is India. And I remember it, Papa."

"The smell of his skin?" Papa advanced on his daughter and jerked the cloth from her hands. "What is this? You have been so near this man that you know the smell of his skin? I daresay your behavior in the conservatory is suspicious to say the least, daughter! Go to your room at once."

"Enough!" Richmond roared. "I have done nothing unworthy where Miss Bowden is concerned. Nor has she behaved imprudently in any way whatsoever! I ascertained that she did not know the truth about her parentage, and I undertook to give her this information with the least amount of distress. Now I am come here to tell her that before his death, Justin Kingston bestowed upon his daughter the entire sum of his wealth — to be awarded upon her twenty-first birthday, which is shortly to occur. This is information that I believe you knew already, Mr. Bowden. In fact, I was told you were awaiting my arrival."

"You? Not you! I was told to expect a courier. I had planned to administer this situation with the greatest delicacy, in order to protect my daughter."

"In order to prevent her from learning that she is an heiress, I should imagine! Did you suppose you could keep her inheritance to yourself, sir? I assure you, that is the only reason I can fathom for the actions you have taken against a helpless and innocent young lady."

"How dare you accuse me of such a thing!" Papa had turned so red that Ivy greatly feared for the condition of his heart. In fact, she felt as though she had been transported into some ancient pageant in which two knights did battle over the future of a maiden. Each considered himself to be her champion; each challenged the other in the most violent manner — and yet in the midst of the battle, the maiden

117

and her own desires remained completely ignored.

"I would never deprive my daughter of any good thing," Papa cried. "No, indeed, for it was out of my great affection for her that I made the decision to treat her as my own child!"

"Great affection, you say?" Richmond feigned surprise. "Then what did you propose to tell her about the estate she was due?"

"Nothing at all! Why should she know of it, when such knowledge could only taint her?" Papa shook his head. "I intended to manage all her affairs from a distance, to keep her pure and undisturbed by such painful information as you have thrust upon her. As to the legacy I knew she was due, I expected that a servant would deliver it. In fact, when I learned you had come from India, Mr. Richmond, I was most delighted, for I supposed such a servant must have accompanied you. I was awaiting this man's message, upon which I would summon him to Brooking House and receive his information. But you? Why were you sent?"

"My father is the executor of Mr. Kingston's will," Richmond replied. "Come, man, surely you did not expect a servant to be entrusted with such a considerable fortune. No, indeed, I set sail aboard my father's most heavily armed vessel in order to transport to Mr. Kingston's daughter a sum of more than two hundred thousand pounds."

Ivy grabbed for the velvet curtain nearest her and clutched it to keep herself upright. Two hundred thousand pounds? Impossible. Such a sum was unimaginable. Beyond the realm of comprehension.

"Two hundred thousand pounds?" Papa whispered. "Is that what you said, Mr. Richmond?"

"Yes, sir. And though one member or another of your family has variously referred to me as 'a villain, a churl, a pirate,' and 'a rogue,' you will find not a farthing of the sum unaccounted for. It is all there, and I intend to deliver it once the conditions of Mr. Kingston's will are fulfilled."

"Conditions?" Ivy said. She stepped away from the curtain. "When we spoke before, sir, you told me that my father had laid out my future. Mr. Richmond, please tell me what he intended for me."

"Miss Bowden . . . I beg your forgiveness for the manner in which I have been compelled to speak in your presence." He drew a deep breath. "You are to purchase property. Land and a house. Specific requirements are set down in the documents. It will be a large estate, and I am sure you will be happy living there."

"Living there? May I purchase a house in Yorkshire?"

"The location is left to your discretion."

Ivy nodded in relief. So many things were changing, and so very quickly. But she could not bear to think of leaving her beloved moorlands. "Property, then," she said. "I am to buy a house."

"And an attorney is to be engaged on your behalf to invest the remainder. Your father was interested in various projects — canals, shipping, the American fur trade — that sort of thing. He intended that the legacy should be used in a beneficial manner and that it should increase in value."

"I see." Ivy managed to find a chair. "I believe you may know of such an attorney, Papa? In Leeds? Or perhaps London?"

For the first time since the disclosure of her inheritance, Ivy looked at Papa. Pale now, breathing hard, he had sunk back into his chair and was wiping his brow with a handkerchief. He nodded.

"Yes, of course, my dear girl. I know several attorneys."

"Then we can be assured that we shall meet all these requirements." Ivy tried to make her mind work sensibly. Such a great sum — and she was to be mistress of it. Clearly Papa had known all along that some inheritance awaited her. Had he been honest about his reasons for keeping the information from her? And why — even moments before — had he tried to send her from the room? Had he meant to prevent her from knowing about the money, just as he had hidden from her the knowledge of the stipend that had been sent from India to be used for her care? Was he not the man she had always loved and trusted? Or had everything she knew about him become a lie?

And what of Mama? What had been her part in all this scheme? Ivy studied the woman who lay draped across the settee. Her fan barely stirred the air, and she appeared to be quite ill.

"Mr. Richmond," Ivy said, "I thank you for your efforts in relating this information, and I shall do my utmost to fulfill every request my father made in regard to his estate. And now, if I might ask you to allow my father . . . my other father, I mean . . . that is, we need to . . ."

"Miss Bowden." He stepped forward

and knelt beside her chair. "I know the shock of these past days has been very great. Please believe that I intended you no harm."

"Of course," she whispered. His eyes searched her face as she struggled to maintain her composure. If only he would take her hand now. If only she could feel the warmth of his comfort, the strength of his presence beside her. She bit her lip to keep it from trembling. He was so near, so close she could slip into his arms and escape for a moment the madness surrounding her. He reached out with one hand, but his fingers did not touch her.

"My dear lady," he said in a low voice, "there is one more stipulation in your father's will. I must tell you of it now before I go."

"One more?" Ivy leaned toward him. "What . . . what can you mean?"

"Mr. Kingston intended . . . I believe he was anticipating the foundation of a dynasty. In short, madam, you are not to receive any of the money until you marry."

Ivy nodded dumbly, her heart beating so loudly she felt sure he could hear it. "Marry," she said. "Yes, Papa has arranged it already."

"Arranged it?"

"My marriage." She fought back tears of denial. "I'm to be engaged to Nigel Creeve, and we are to marry in the autumn."

"Nigel Creeve?" Richmond's dark brows narrowed as he swung his head toward Mr. Bowden. "That is not the name in the document. Who is this man? Why have you made such an agreement, sir?"

"What name is written?" Ivy asked.

"Hang the name! Hang the entire document!" Papa cried, lifting his head from the back of the chair. "My daughter is to marry Nigel Creeve, and on that matter I shall not be swayed. When she was brought to me as a small child, I was given none of these details that you claim are written in my brother-in-law's will. I was made aware that she would receive something on her twenty-first birthday, but the sum of the inheritance was concealed from me."

"Of course it was concealed from you," Richmond said, "for the amount was not known until now. My father has managed the money for the past seventeen years. Though Mr. Kingston left a considerable legacy, it has grown greatly under my father's shrewd administration."

"I am glad of it," Papa said. "But that does not alter my decision to wed my daughter to Nigel Creeve. Wishing only the best for her, I have sought to arrange a comfortable future. The Creeve family is most eager to welcome her — and their commitment to the union will only be solidified when the sum of her fortune is made known."

"But this marriage cannot take place," Richmond said, "or there will be no fortune at all."

Ivy laid her fingers on his hand. "Please, sir, I can no longer bear the animosity between you and my father. Speak to me alone. Tell me what I am expected to do."

Richmond turned back to her and clasped her hand as he had done before. This time she could clearly read the agitation in his eyes. "Mr. Kingston intended security and comfort for you. You must believe that."

"But a name . . . you said he had written a name." A sudden rush of hope poured through her. Let it be this man! Let Mr. Kingston have planned for her to marry Colin Richmond!

Who better? Their fathers were dearest friends who had entrusted their legacies to one another. Why not plan to wed their children, too? Heart hammering, Ivy lifted up a prayer of supplication. *Oh, dear Lord, please let me marry this man . . . this strong, intelligent, impetuous, interesting . . . this wonderful man. . . .*

"His name is John Frith," Richmond said.

Six

Ivy stared blankly at Colin Richmond. "Who?"

"John Frith," he repeated. "Your father had formed a partnership with a young man from this region, William Frith, and together they journeyed to India and built their trade. The two intended that their association should be permanently sealed by the marriage of their offspring. In the document I have brought, the name is clearly spelled out. You are not to receive any sum from your inheritance unless you marry John Frith."

Ivy tried to make herself breathe. "But who is this man? Where does he live?"

Richmond's fingers grew tighter around her hand. "You do not know him?"

"No, sir. I have never heard the name in all my life."

"I know the blackguard," Papa spoke up. "I knew his father, too. William Frith and Justin Kingston were quite a pair. I was less than pleased to have Kingston made a member of my family, I assure you. When they sailed off to India with their wives, we all predicted they would come racing back with their tails between their legs."

"Justin was not all that bad a fellow," Mama inserted. "He was always very kind to my sister, and Rosemary thought the world of him. When he asked her to marry him and go away to India, she was over the moon. They did make a good go of it there, and might have done better had they not all been taken ill."

"Kingston and my wife's sister both died in India, as you have stated, Mr. Richmond," Papa went on. "Their daughter was placed in my care. William Frith lingered in ill health for some time, I am told. Eventually, he returned to England with his wife and son, purchased a house in Leeds, and promptly died. John Frith, the son, lives in that house to this day, and I am told there is not a more dissolute and worthless wastrel on the planet."

Richmond nodded. "I fear I must concur with this assessment. During the time you lay recovering at Longley Park, madam, I made so bold as to inquire about the character of the man whose name is listed in Mr. Kingston's will. John Frith is, by reputation, a most reprehensible fellow."

Ivy glanced at Papa and then at Mama, who continued to fan herself weakly. Finally, she turned back to Richmond. "And there is no other course open to me?"

"None whatsoever," he said in a low voice. "You must marry John Frith."

"She will do nothing of the sort," Papa interjected. "She will receive the estate that is rightfully due her, for I shall see to it in a court of law. Indeed, I shall go to town tomorrow and engage an attorney on her behalf. The matter cannot be difficult to resolve. As her legal guardian, I have made a binding agreement with the Creeve family. Moreover, Frith is an insupportable candidate, and the authorities must recognize that. My daughter will marry Nigel Creeve. And she will receive what is rightfully hers."

Ivy trembled as Colin Richmond's head bent low over her hand. His glossy curls shone in the afternoon sunlight as his lips pressed against her fingers.

"May God grant you peace," he whispered. And then he stood quickly and headed for the door. "I must go now. Mr. and Mrs. Bowden, Miss Bowden . . . I bid you farewell."

Ivy rose from the chair and clasped her

hands together, wishing she could preserve forever the warm pressure of his kiss. "Farewell, Mr. Richmond," she called. "Farewell."

"There he is!" Caroline dug her elbow into Ivy's ribs. "Ooh, doesn't he look well today? Truly, I have never seen a man better turned out than Colin Richmond."

Ivy tipped her head down, praying her bonnet would obscure the pink flush in her cheeks, and studied her hymnal. The church was very chilly this morning, and she felt glad of her warm blue jacket. Buttoned from the collar to the fitted hem that ended at the high waist of her blue-flowered frock, the jacket was snug and comforting. Ivy turned the worn pages of the volume in her lap and tried to concentrate on the coming worship service.

"He has taken the pew just behind us and a bit to the left — where the Wrens sit," Caroline whispered, elbowing Ivy again. "He is greeting Mrs. Wren. He is sitting down. Now, he is looking directly at us!"

"Then turn round!" Ivy hissed. "Good gracious, Caroline, your manners are appalling."

"Why should I not look at him? He is

looking at me, so I have every right to look at him, too." She giggled. "He is taking off his hat. Such admirable hair!"

"Caroline, please."

"He is rising again. Oh dear, now he is speaking to Eliza Wren." Her voice went flat. "But surely he cannot find anything to admire in her. She has such a poor complexion."

"Eliza Wren is very nice."

"But, Ivy, her skin!"

"Caroline, the condition of a lady's complexion has nothing at all to do with her character."

Ivy shut the hymnal and wove her gloved fingers together. How long must she endure the silly chatter of her sister? But Caroline was not her sister — not really. She was merely a cousin, and Ivy had every right to find a pew of her own in which to sit on Sundays. In fact, she had come to accept that one way or another, she would not continue living in the Bowden home much longer. If, as she feared, Papa had been dishonest in his dealings with her, then she could choose to shun that family completely. She owed her loyalty, her love, her respect to no one at all. No one except God.

As the minister rose and began to address the congregation, Ivy tried to make herself listen. But how could she concentrate when each time her attention strayed, she felt every eye in the church focused on her? Somehow — and she did not doubt its authors as the three young ladies on the pew beside her — the news of her heritage and valuable legacy had spread throughout the countryside like ripples from a stone dropped into a glassy pond.

Rumors traveled from Brooking House to Otley, from Otley to Leeds, and from there all across the Yorkshire moorlands. Ivy had begun to feel that all England must know the story by now, for not three days had passed since Mr. Richmond departed when a message arrived from the Creeve family. They were coming to Brooking House, due to arrive this very afternoon.

Realizing belatedly that everyone had stood to sing, Ivy pushed to her feet and searched for the proper hymn. She was not going to glance over her shoulder at Mr. Richmond. Absolutely not. His appearance might be fine this morning, but that meant nothing to her. In fact, she had hardly thought of the man since the day he had kissed her hand and walked away.

Well, perhaps that was not quite accurate. She had thought of him. More than that, she had wished for his presence. But each time the man's image slipped into her mind, she dismissed it. After all, she had far more consequential matters to attend to. Her time was occupied by long discussions with Mr. and Mrs. Bowden, who professed all innocence in the management of their young ward's life and affairs. They loved her, they said again and again. They had not profited from her presence in their home — except by the utter joy they had taken from raising her as their own daughter. And now they wanted nothing more than to see her happily settled with the Creeve family.

Ivy had tried to listen . . . tried to believe them. But her heart had begun to feel very small, very hard, and very cold indeed. Like a lump of black coal, it sat inside her chest completely devoid of warmth. Only when she thought of Colin Richmond did a small flame flicker to life. Why? Why did even the memory of such a man's hands burn inside her?

Why? she cried inwardly to God as she dropped back onto the pew beside those she was meant to call sisters. Why had this horrible thing befallen her? She did not care for money or land. She longed only for the loving warmth of family. Security and comfort had been replaced by betrayal — and it began to seem as though God himself had played a part in it.

Why had she been born in India? Why had her real parents died? Why had the Bowdens taken her into their home? Why must she buy a house and land? Why must she learn to manage two hundred thousand pounds? And why — oh, why — would Colin Richmond not stay out of her thoughts? *Push him away, Ivy,* she told herself. *Concentrate. Pay attention!*

" 'Thine, O Lord, is the greatness,' " the minister intoned from the front of the church, " 'and the power, and the glory, and the victory, and the majesty: for all that is in the heaven and in the earth is thine; thine is the kingdom, O Lord, and thou art exalted as head above all. Both riches and honour come of thee.' "

Ivy lifted her head, her swirling thoughts suddenly captured by the last words of the Scripture: *"Both riches and honour come of thee."* Did that mean God had chosen to give her this legacy? She had preferred to think it was all a terrible mistake — some skewing of the proper order in life — and not a heaven-ordained plan.

"From which passage is the minister reading?" Ivy whispered to Caroline.

Glassy-eyed, the younger woman turned to her. "What?"

"The Scripture. Where is it taken from in the Bible?"

Caroline scowled. "How should I know that? Honestly, Ivy."

"Maddie," Ivy whispered, nudging the girl at her other elbow. "Where is that passage in the Bible?"

"Shh!" Madeline hissed. "One must not talk in church. It is not done."

Distressed, Ivy leaned forward and looked at the third of her sisters. Clementine had taken off her gloves and was pretending they were a lady and gentleman at a ball. First one glove bowed, then the other. And then they began to dance, spinning around on Clemma's lap, weaving to and fro. She clearly was not paying the slightest attention to the sermon.

Ivy sat back and willed herself to listen to the minister. But alas, the sermon seemed to be about the glories of springtime and the majesty of the great Creator. It had nothing to do with God as a dispenser of riches or a cartographer of the map of a young woman's life, and Ivy was left alone to ponder the source of her misery.

When the last hymn was sung and the

benediction pronounced, she stood with the Bowdens, just as she always did, and started down the aisle. But how she dreaded the long afternoon that stretched ahead. The Creeves would arrive, and there would be a great hullabaloo over the mysterious and dissolute John Frith. Finally, Ivy would end in agreeing to marry one or the other of them, simply in order to claim her inheritance — an inheritance she didn't even want.

The thought of not claiming the fortune from India and not marrying anyone at all suddenly seized Ivy's heart with the power of a vise. That was it! She would simply refuse to claim the money and refuse to wed. Then she could go on living with Mama and Papa as though nothing had happened.

But why would she want to spend the rest of her life with a family not her own? Or were they her own — given to her by God as a most precious gift?

"First Chronicles," said a deep voice at her shoulder.

Startled, Ivy nearly stumbled as she stepped out into the sunlight and made her way down the church steps. Grasping the wrought-iron banister, she glanced back over her shoulder to find Colin Richmond not a breath away.

"Chapter twenty-nine," he continued, his lips so near her ear that she could feel the warmth of his whisper through the brim of her straw bonnet.

"I beg your pardon?" She found suddenly that her blue jacket was far too snug and her knees had turned to marmalade. "Are you speaking to me, sir?"

His smile set her heart ablaze as he followed her out onto the gravelled path. "Of course, dear lady. Is there any other to whom I should prefer to speak on such a fine morning — or, indeed, on any morning at all?"

"I-I see. But I should think —"

"The source of the Scripture you were seeking is the first book of Chronicles, chapter twenty-nine, verses eleven and twelve."

"Oh . . . indeed." She knew she was gaping at him, but what on earth was he talking about?

"I ascertained that you might have been curious about the reference to God as bestower of riches," he said, "for I understand the whole countryside is abuzz with the news of your inheritance. Surely you must be wondering at how this fortune came to fall upon your shoulders. You question whether God has visited this on you — or if it has some malevolent source. Or do I read too much into your urgent questioning of your sisters?"

"Oh," she repeated, thinking how stupid she must sound. "Well, I'm not quite . . ."

"Actually, I felt the following verses mentioned in this morning's sermon were far more pertinent to the situation in which we find ourselves, Miss Bowden. So important, in fact, that I put them to memory," he said, taking her arm, linking it firmly around his elbow, and leading her onto the bright green grass that surrounded the church. "King David asked of God, 'But who am I, and what is my people, that we should be able to offer so willingly after this sort? for all things come of thee, and of thine own have we given thee.' "

As Mr. Richmond strolled beside her toward the small church garden, Ivy felt quite sure she was either going to float away like a blue kite or trip and fall flat on her face. She tried to breathe, tried very hard indeed, but she did not have much success at it. She also tried to listen, but he seemed to be speaking in riddles — though his words clearly had a great deal of significance for him.

"Who are we, Miss Bowden?" he demanded. "Why have you and I been given such bounty, when others are compelled to scrabble for the few grains of rice on which they make their sustenance?"

"Well, I-I'm not completely certain —"

" 'For we are strangers before thee, and sojourners, as were all our fathers: our days on the earth are as a shadow, and there is none abiding.' Do you not agree, Miss Bowden, that we can no more claim riches of land or money than the poor Yorkshiremen who squat on my property at Longley Park? Indeed, we are all gypsies on this earth, wandering about and owning nothing that God has not given to us."

He pushed open a white wooden gate and led her down a narrow path between two beds of budding red and yellow roses. Across the expanse of lawn, Ivy could see the Bowdens assembling for the walk home to Brooking House. Caroline seemed to be delaying the party, for she was deeply engaged in a whispered conversation with one of her friends. And Maddie was scampering across the grass, pointing backward in the direction of the garden. Upon his youngest daughter's entrance into the family cluster, Papa lifted his head, caught sight of the distant couple strolling among the roses, and his face darkened.

"It seems to me," Richmond was saying as Papa began a determined march toward the garden, "that it does not matter what God has given us or how much he has bestowed upon us — or even how we actually came to have such great wealth. What matters, Miss Bowden, is what we choose to do with it."

Ivy pulled up short, removed her arm from his embrace, and swung around to face him. "Mr. Richmond," she said, "what on earth are you talking about, and where — pray tell — are you leading me?"

"We are taking a leisurely turn about the church garden while we discuss the book of Chronicles."

"We are not discussing anything! You are rambling, and I am trying to go home with my family . . . who are not my family . . . but it doesn't matter, because . . . because I have to . . . oh, never mind!"

Unable to continue, she whirled away and started back down the path toward the gate. As she reached for the latch, Richmond's hand clamped around her wrist.

"Do not leave me, Miss Bowden," he said, his voice low. "Please, I must know how you are."

"I am well, of course." She glanced at him, hoping he could not read the despair in her eyes. "My head is perfectly recovered."

"You know that is not what I mean. How has my news affected you? How goes your life with the Bowdens? Dear lady, I must know what you have decided to do."

"What I have decided to do?" She shook her head. "What choice have I been given, sir? To obey the will of the two men who have called themselves my father is my only option. Mr. Kingston could endow me with nothing but his fortune. Shall I refuse to accept that gift? Mr. Bowden has provided me with shelter and education and affection. Shall I run away from him and make my own life without family or means of financial support?"

"Is that what you wish to do?"

"Of course not!" She felt sudden tears well in her eyes. "Oh, yes, that is exactly what I wish to do. I want to run away — far away — and never see any of them again! And at the same time I long to stay here and pretend that nothing has changed. I love them and I hate them! I need the money and I reject the money! I have prayed for a husband and children, and yet I despise the very thought of marrying! Nothing is as it was or should be. Who am I, and what is to become of me? And why has God done this thing?"

"I shall tell you why he has done it," Richmond said, leaning so close she was again enveloped in the scent of spice and leather that clung to his skin. "God has given you riches in order to see what you will do in return. It is a test of your character."

"But I do not wish to be tested."

"No one does."

"Here, now!" Papa arrived at the gate, breathless, and gave Colin Richmond only the most perfunctory of bows. "Unhand my daughter, sir. What do you say to her? Surely you have no more information with which you can harm her, and yet, I see she is close to tears!"

"It is all right, Papa," Ivy said. "Truly, I am well."

"You are weeping, and this man is the cause of it!"

"Papa, surely you must see that the fault lies not with Mr. Richmond, but only with the news of my heritage that he was compelled to give me. I am in great confusion as to how to proceed in even the smallest details of my life."

"Such as?"

"Such as whether to continue calling you Papa. Whether to think of myself as

Bowden or Kingston. Whether to address Clemma, Maddie, and Caroline as my sisters. And these are the least of my distresses, for I must also attempt to answer questions of much greater consequence. Shall I believe you concealed the truth from me out of love — or from some more nefarious cause? Am I to hand this great fortune to a stranger to manage, or shall I become mistress of it myself? And what of my future? Papa, can you not see how overwhelming is the prospect of meeting with Mr. Creeve this afternoon? And then Mr. Frith must be approached at once —"

"Creeve is coming here?" Richmond cut in. "But why? Mr. Bowden, surely you have informed him of the conditions of Mr. Kingston's will. Nigel Creeve cannot imagine he still holds any claim upon this woman."

"Of course he claims her," Papa said, "and rightfully so, for we made a gentlemen's agreement. Now all that is to be done is to work out the severing of that reprobate's name from the will."

"John Frith's name cannot be removed from the will, sir. He is to marry Miss Bowden. Have you not discussed the situation with Mr. Frith?"

"Why should I discuss anything with

him? I shall not have any daughter of mine marry a Frith!" Papa took Ivy's arm. "Do not speak to this man again, daughter. I forbid —"

"Sir, I must insist that you acknowledge the reality of the situation!" Richmond stalked alongside Papa as the older man drew Ivy toward the lane. "I intend to return to India, and I shall not have my departure delayed by such nonsense."

"Nonsense, is it? I assure you, sir, I shall not delay your leaving Yorkshire at the earliest possible moment. And I also assure you that my daughter will be given her rightful inheritance, upon which time she will marry Nigel Creeve."

"You expect me to act contrary to everything my father charged me to do? No, sir. I shall not even entertain the notion. Not a farthing of that money will leave my control until Miss Bowden has purchased property, hired an attorney, and married John Frith."

"You would have me wedded to such a man?" Ivy exclaimed, pulling her arm from Papa's grasp and facing Richmond. "Is that what you believe a loving God would choose for me — life with a man who can never bring me a moment's happiness?"

"It is not what I wish!" He clasped her

shoulders. "Believe me, it is not what I would choose for you."

"Yet you insist that the will must be followed to the letter."

"Duty compels me, Miss Bowden. I gave my father my word."

"Then we are but puppets, you and I. We must follow God and our parents and all who pull upon the strings that control us. We have no choice, no free will."

She stared into his dark eyes as the impossible absurdity of the situation flooded through her. "Very well, then, Mr. Richmond," she continued. "I see I shall have to marry *both* John Frith *and* Nigel Creeve, and I shall call myself Ivy-Kingston-Bowden-Frith-Creeve and whoever else decides to lay claim to my person. It is quite clear that these riches God has chosen to bestow upon me are not a gift. They are not a test. They are shackles, and by them, my once peaceful, happy life has been utterly ruined."

Without waiting to hear any more violent arguments or windy discourses from either man, she picked up her skirts and started down the lane alone. She would not wait for the Bowden family. She did not belong to them, nor they to her. She was but a pawn in the hand of the Almighty. Men would do battle over her, not because of any beauty or generosity of spirit in her, but because she was an heiress.

"Mornin', Miss Bowden!" a cheerful voice sang out. One hand raised in greeting, a child with long, skinny legs skipped toward her from the alley between two small, thatched-roof houses. Dirty ankles showed beneath the ragged hems of his trousers as his bare feet kicked up the dust. "Guess wot! Me mum's better! She's got 'erself up and is cookin' t' rabbits Papa brought 'ome from t' forest yesterday. We'll be 'avin' rabbit-an'-bacon stew for dinner!"

Ivy could not help but smile at the glad news, and she welcomed the little boy's grimy hand as he slipped it into her own. "Jimmy, how happy I am to hear this! Is Mrs. Smith no longer coughing at all?"

"A wee bit, but not like before. Me, I think it were t' chicken soup you brought wot done 'er t' most good. But Papa says it were t' tonic."

"Probably a little of both, I should imagine."

"And now me grampa's got t' coughin', but we've just enough tonic left to last 'im a few days. Mama says t' rabbit stew will do as well as chicken soup, too."

Ivy continued on her way, so grateful for this welcome reprieve from the storms that swirled about her that she was reluctant to let the little boy return to his home. "I am very sorry to hear that Mr. Smith is ill," she said, recalling the frail, elderly gentleman. "You must keep a close watch on him, Jimmy, and mind you do not make too much noise when you play near his window."

"Oh, it's not Grampa Smith wot's ill, Miss Bowden. It's me other one, Grampa 'edgley."

"Hedgley?" Ivy was startled to hear the name. "Is your grandfather the head gardener at Longley Park?"

"Aye, and wouldn't ye know, Mr. Richmond 'as come back from India and put everybody to work as if they was slaves on one of 'is plantations. Me Papa says most of t' families wot 'ave been livin' in t' forest round Longley 'as been taken on by Mr. Richmond to clean and polish and mop and prune and plant and every sort of thing."

"Really?" She recalled the overgrown conservatory and the dusty corridors of the great house. "I am all astonishment."

"Aye, and it's a great trouble, Miss

146

Bowden, because some of t' men wot used to live and 'unt on Longley land 'as been 'ired as guards, and me Papa says it's near impossible to set foot on the place without bein' seen. 'e barely got away with them two rabbits, and then wot would we 'ave in our stew but onions and carrots and maybe a knuckle end of bacon all chopped up? And Mama says all t' work is wot brung down Grampa 'edgley. 'e's laid up in 'is cottage, and I'm t' lad must race back and forth all day with tonic and blankets and such."

"What a good boy you are to help your grandfather," Ivy said. "It must be trying to have such an important task laid upon your young shoulders, but I believe you are quite capable of it."

Jimmy beamed. "Aye, I am."

"I knew it. You must tell your parents that I shall come very soon with more tonic for your grandfather's cough. Perhaps you and I can take it round to Mr. Hedgley's cottage together."

"I'd like that!" Jimmy bent and gave the back of her hand a sticky kiss. "I better get back 'ome, Miss Bowden. I don't want to miss me mum's stew."

"No, indeed, hurry away then." She turned to watch him scamper back down the lane, and her heart ached. Jimmy's home was small, smoky, and crawling with insects, but it was his own — a place of warmth and love. How she envied him.

But she would not pity herself. The Bowdens were speeding to catch up with her, and she knew her outburst must have distressed Papa. Though she could not be certain what had motivated him, she did know that the man she called Father had taken good care of her all her life. He had treated her with the same kindnesses he showered upon his true daughters, and he seemed to have the best intentions for her future. She should be grateful. Anger, self-pity, hurt — these must have no place in her heart if she intended to find what happiness she could in life. And she did.

"Ivy!" Out of breath, Papa caught up to her and laid his hand on her arm. "My dear girl, how greatly you have dismayed me! Why have you said nothing before of these things that trouble you? I had no thought at all that you were bearing such a burden — and all alone. There is nothing for it but we must sit together and talk this very day, for as Milton so concisely stated, 'Apt words have power to suage the tumors of a troubled mind.' "

Ivy let out a breath. "Papa, please allow

me to sort through this on my own. My head is so full of discourses and speeches that I —"

" ' 'Tis not my speeches that you do mislike, but 'tis my presence that doth trouble ye.' Are not Sir William Shakespeare's words true, Ivy, my dear? I fear you find me odious. You despise your mother and me."

"No, Papa, I do not despise you." She took his hands and held them, gazing fondly at the familiar shape of his fingers and the comfortable folds that crossed his palms. "I love you . . . I love you very dearly. But I do not know what to believe, for you will say one thing and Mr. Richmond might say another, and how am I to —"

"It is that Richmond villain! All this is his doing. Well, my dearest child, you shall see it all come to rights this very afternoon."

"How is that, Papa?" Wariness filled Ivy's heart. "What do you mean?"

"I have arranged everything. The Bowden family shall entertain not only Nigel Creeve at tea, but Colin Richmond, too. Indeed, all of us shall gather in the front parlor and have it out. I have asked Richmond to bring the documents he carried from India. We shall take every matter under consideration and discuss each point of the will in great detail. And when the day is done, my dear Ivy, all your worries will be ended."

He patted her on the back and then called to the others, "Come now, everyone! 'Happy, thrice happy and more, are they whom an unbroken bond unites and whose love shall know no sundering quarrels so long as they shall live.' Who wrote that? Which of you bright young ladies can tell me? Caroline?"

"I cannot say, Papa," Caroline murmured as she brushed past Ivy and headed into the house. "Sorry."

"It must be Shakespeare!" Clemma cried.

"No, it is Milton," Madeline corrected her, following the others inside.

"Indeed, you are all wrong, and I am mightily ashamed of my progeny." Papa took his wife's hand and escorted her up the stairs of Brooking House. "Think who would have written such a marvelous message of hope, my dear daughters. 'Whose love shall know no sundering quarrels . . .' "

"Horace," Ivy said softly. "*Odes,* book one, ode thirteen. But did that great man not also write *Carpe diem, quam minimum credula postero?* Seize the day, put no trust in the morrow."

With that, she turned away from Brooking House and set off toward the vast open moorlands where neither stream nor wall nor hedge could impede her.

Seven

"Where is she?" Colin Richmond stood inside the front parlor at Brooking House. As he scanned the line of faces staring at him from the settees and chairs gathered around the tea table, he knew the answer to his question would not be a happy one. Either the young woman had been banished to an upper room. Or she had fled.

Mr. Bowden stood and cleared his throat. "Aha, Mr. Richmond! I see you have come as I asked. Thank you very much, indeed, and welcome to our humble gathering. I believe you are acquainted with Mr. Creeve, and of course you know my wife and daughters. As I always say — and I quote from the Psalms here — 'Behold, how good and how pleasant it is for brethren to dwell together in unity!' And here we are, all together in great unity of purpose and aim. Now, if I might be permitted, sir, I should like to begin by —"

"But where is Miss Bowden?" Colin repeated. "I do not find her here, and I shall not conduct any business unless she is present."

"Ivy ran away!" Clementine sang out. "We all came into the house from church, and everybody thought Ivy came in too, for she was ahead of us nearly the whole way but —"

"Clementine!" Mr. Bowden snapped. "That will do!"

"Has a party been sent in search of her?"

"Mr. Richmond, I beg you, please do sit down and join us at tea." Mrs. Bowden rose. "You need have no concern in this matter, for our eldest daughter is commonly away from the house for many hours of each day. She enjoys walking across the moorlands, and she often visits the poor and ill in the cottages around Otley. She is a very dear girl in that way. Generous to a fault."

Upon that comment, the woman gave a knowing smile to the gentleman seated nearest the fireplace. It was Nigel Creeve, of course. Colin had known the fellow during their school days together at Eton. They had not been friends, for Creeve hailed from a family of tradesmen — fishmongers, it was said — and his father had barely managed to scramble into the upper class by doing some sort of illegal favors for a member of Parliament. Of course, it was all rumor, but young Creeve had joined a circle whose families belonged to the *nouveau riche*. Colin Richmond's chums, on the other hand, hailed from lineage long and noble. Some of them even boasted of royal blood.

"At any rate," Mrs. Bowden continued, "we do not regard our daughter's absence with great concern. In fact, we expect her to return momentarily, for she does enjoy taking her afternoon tea with the family. Please, sir, do join us."

"Indeed, Mr. Richmond," her husband concurred, "for the business matters we are to discuss shall wait until after tea, when the ladies have retired in pursuit of their more leisurely occupations."

Colin could not make himself move for a moment, so uncertain did he feel. In the church garden that morning, Ivy had told him she longed to run away. What if she had done such a thing? Where would she go? And by what means would she support herself? His thoughts flew immediately to the ragged harlots who plied their trade on wharves around the globe.

"Mr. Bowden, I feel I must go in search of the young lady at once," he said. "I am deeply concerned —"

"Nonsense!" Nigel Creeve got to his feet and crossed the carpet. "You heard her father, Richmond. Miss Bowden likes to walk about. Come, man. Sit down and take tea with us, so that we might get on with this wretched business you have stirred up."

Colin regarded the pale man whose small eyes were deeply set into a skeletal face. Creeve stood nearly as tall as Colin, yet he could be hardly half the weight. It seemed clear the fellow rarely ventured out of doors — or perhaps he affected the dandy's preference for white facial powder — for his skin was nearly translucent. He possessed a noble nose, but his lips were full and soft, and his dark hair had apparently been combed through with some sort of oil. He smelled of cologne — too much cologne — and Colin found himself repulsed at the sweet reek that clung to the man. "Nigel Creeve," he said, extending his hand. "It has been many years."

Creeve shook the proffered hand and turned away quickly, addressing Colin as he returned to his seat. "Eton, of course, but I believe you eschewed a higher education in favor of sea life. I am an Oxford man, myself. Philosophy was my pursuit, though I suppose you would not be interested in that. You have devoted your life, I understand, to the shipping trade."

For the first time since leaving his iniquitous path in favor of a God-directed one, Colin found himself wishing for the cutlass he had often worn at his side. One quick swipe would part Creeve's supercilious head from his body and rid the world of one utterly unnecessary fop.

"Shipping, yes." Colin stepped to the tea table. He would have liked to add that his father's chosen profession was far more lucrative than fishmongery. But he had neither time nor interest in engaging Creeve in debate. "Mr. Bowden, I pray you will excuse me, but I fear I cannot rest until the young lady in question has been found and returned to safety. Have you any idea of her customary paths? My horse is still saddled, and I shall —"

"She likes to walk along Gallows Hill Road," Clemma said. "And when she comes to Summer Cross cottage, she turns onto Bush Lane toward Camp Field. From there, she wanders all up the fells and down the dales, always moving eastward, for she sometimes imagines she can see the ocean! Her favorite time is when the heather is in bloom, and —"

"That will do, Clementine!" Mr.

Bowden took out a handkerchief and dabbed it across his brow. "Please, sir, I sincerely urge you to abstain from this folly. My daughter is well, I assure you. She will return directly. You have no need to concern yourself over any matter but the taking of tea."

"Blast the tea!" Colin cried, realizing only vaguely that his epithet had caused every female jaw in the room to drop open. "I mean to find the young lady, and I shall do it at once. She was most distressed this morning, as you well know, Mr. Bowden. No good can come of her wandering about in this state of anguish, and I fear a storm is brewing —"

"Mr. Richmond," Creeve cut in, "may I be so bold as to inquire why you take such prodigious interest in the welfare of Miss Bowden? Is your regard based solely on the execution of your duty to your father — as you have stated to Mr. Bowden? Or have you acquired a more personal interest in the lady?"

"And may I respond by inquiring as to why you take so little interest in her welfare, Creeve? Is your eager disregard based upon the fact that you are interested solely in her fortune? Or do you hold a more personal dislike for the lady you profess to claim as your intended wife?"

Turning on his heel, Colin stalked out of the parlor and summoned his groom. In moments, he was mounted and riding east across the moors in the direction of the sea. The earth shuddered beneath the hooves of his horse as it galloped along narrow footpaths and leapt low limestone walls that crisscrossed the landscape. Curlews wheeled overhead, alternately dipping and soaring on currents of damp wind that coursed from the west. Dark clouds collected and heaped themselves into mounds across the sky, then began to roll forward like an army of Huns bent on destruction.

Colin rode heedlessly, allowing the horse to find its own path while the rider scanned the undulating landscape. How dare Creeve take such a supercilious attitude, he fumed. Philosophy? Oxford? Were those intended as hints at the man's intellectual superiority? Bah! What could a man truly know of the world, of mankind, of the interplay of culture and language and religion if the extent of his life experience was Eton and Oxford? And what sort of comment was Creeve's sneer that Colin might have a "more personal" interest in Miss Kingston?

Of course Colin cared about the young

woman. She was bright and beautiful and wholly without imperfection! Any man in his right mind could see that. How could Creeve sit there in the front parlor waiting for tea and conversation when she might be injured or weeping or falling victim to some unsavory villain?

Seeing Nigel Creeve had confirmed Colin's misgivings about that match. How dare Creeve believe he had the right to marry Ivy! As her name slipped into Colin's mind, it found its way to his lips and rose from a whisper to a cry to a shout.

"Ivy . . . Ivy!" He cupped his hand at his brow as rain began to pelt his coat. "Ivy, where are you? Miss Bowden! Miss Kingston! *Ivy!*"

Pulling his hat low, he rode on through the fog that swirled across the bracken. Thunder rumbled above him, lightning flashed its warning, rain slashed at his back and soaked his gloves. *Dear God,* he prayed, *please let her be all right. Protect her. Keep her from harm!*

"Ivy!" he shouted again and again. By now his horse had covered many miles, circling from east to north to south and back again. Several times Colin stopped and knocked at the doors of small cottages.

Standing in the pouring rain, he inquired of the poor inhabitants whether they had seen a young lady.

"Miss Bowden is missin' from Brookin' 'ouse?" came the repeated reply. "That's no good! She's a blessin', that wee lass. Brought us blankets last winter . . . brought us soup just t' other day . . . sat up with me wife two nights in a row . . . 'elped us with t' money to bury our baby boy when he passed away last autumn . . . she's a dear girl . . . she's an angel . . ."

With promises for prayers and help in searching if called upon, each cottager shut the door on the gathering night. Though the rain ceased, darkness began to encroach, and Colin finally admitted that further exploration was futile. Perhaps she had gone home. Perhaps she was taking tea with the others or sitting in a warm bath or reading a book beside the fire.

As he turned his horse and started back across the muddy dales, he spotted a lone figure in the distance. Shrouded in mist, the creature might be male or female, old or young, and yet his heart soared with hope.

"Ivy!" he cried out, goading his tired horse forward. "Ivy!"

The figure paused, turned, and a slender

arm rose into the gray sky. "Mr. Richmond? Is it you?"

"Thank God!" He reined the horse at her side and leapt down. "Are you well? You are not injured, I hope! You are not harmed?"

He folded her into his arms and held her so tightly he knew she could hardly breathe. Yet how could he release her when the thought of losing her had been so real only moments before? In his embrace she felt so small and fragile, a tiny bird without a nest. He drew back the wet woolen shawl with which she had covered her head. As her face lifted, their eyes met, and he fought everything within himself to keep from kissing her soft lips.

"Ivy," he managed, "dearest, most beautiful . . . most wonderful lady . . ."

"Shh," she whispered, setting her fingertips on his mouth. "You must not say such —"

"But it is true!" He caught her hand in his and brought it to his lips, covering her cold and trembling fingers in kisses. "I could not bear the thought of you wandering alone, so disconsolate. I feared some harm might come to you, and —"

"And you would bear the fault in it? Mr. Richmond, you blame yourself too much. I

161

do not hold you responsible for the news which you were compelled to bring me. Please, sir . . . please do not feel that you must take pity on me, or that you are in any way required to think of me beyond the execution of your duty to your father."

"Is that how you believe I see you? As a duty? As an object of pity?" He stroked her cheek with the side of his finger. "Dear lady, you mistake me entirely. How it has happened I do not know, but you have become to me among the most treasured and admired —"

"Please, Mr. Richmond!" She brushed his hand from her face. "If you feel any of these things, then you must have invented my character. You know nothing of my nature."

"That is not true, for I know a great deal about you. I know that you rose in defense of your silly, selfish cousin and took the blow meant for her head. I know you are adored by Miss Clemma — and children rarely place their admiration wrongly. You are held in highest esteem by the cottagers to whom you are so generous. Even my gardener . . ."

"Mr. Hedgley?"

"Indeed, old Hedgley cannot stop

talking of you. It seems I am surrounded by you on every side."

"I am sorry, sir."

"Do you think I rue it? Each time I hear your name mentioned, I find myself smiling. And to the knowledge of your greatness of character, I must add your uncommon beauty."

"Now you flatter me." She turned away. "I am but a wren living among peacocks. Your words ring false, Mr. Richmond, and in them I hear the practiced art of seduction — though why you would want to —"

"Seduction!" Indignation flared through him as he caught her wrist. "Is that why you think I have been riding through the rain for hours?"

"I cannot imagine why you have done such a thing!" She pulled her arm from his grasp. "What can have motivated you? I can only think you feel yourself to blame for my affliction. That . . . or for some unknown reason you pursue me because . . . because . . ."

"Because I care for you!" He shook his head. "Do you not see that?"

"Why?" Her voice was barely a whisper. "Why, sir?"

He took off his tall dark hat and knocked it against the side of his leg, sending a shower of raindrops to the grass at his feet. Raking his fingers through his hair, he stared out across the indigo night, barely able to discern the landmarks that had guided him across the moors. Why did he care for this woman? Why had he ridden through the rain in search of her? Why did thoughts of her torment him day and night?

"You and I," he said, trying out the words that seemed somehow foreign. "You and I are . . . connected."

"We are not."

"Yes, madam, we are. Many threads bind us. This land, the Yorkshire moors. Our birthplace of India. And smaller things — a love for walking the countryside, a deep admiration for the created earth, a passion for the sea."

"How do you know I care anything about the sea?"

"Clemma told me."

Ivy bowed her head. "I am not connected to you or to anyone, Mr. Richmond. I am completely alone, and without . . . without . . ."

"You are not without those who care for you. Despite their bumblings and ineptitudes, the Bowdens love you. The more I have learned of Mr. Bowden, the more I have come to think him harmless. He is well thought of and generally respected by those who know him. I believe his reasons for keeping your heritage hidden were misguided — and yet they were kindly meant. Not only do Mr. and Mrs. Bowden regard you with great affection, but their children think of you as a sister. Clemma clearly adores you —"

"As I adore her. But everything is tainted now, do you not see? Tainted by the fortune I am to inherit. How can I trust anyone's affection? The Bowden family stands to gain much by their connection to me. Clearly, the Creeves knew I was to receive a large sum, and that means Mr. Creeve —"

"Blast Nigel Creeve and his fishmongering family! He will not come near you if I have anything to say about it."

"Indeed, you would much prefer to put me in the hands of John Frith, by reputation a libertine and a sot!"

"No!" He caught her again, capturing her waist with his arm and drawing her close. "No, I would not have you marry John Frith. If I had my way —" He stopped, breathing hard. "But I have chosen to surrender my way. I have vowed to allow my life to be directed by God."

"By God?"

"You seem surprised."

"Few men I know give any thought to God. Fewer still would permit his direction of their lives. They are content to follow their own ambitions and not to submit to any divine leading."

"As was I for many years. But I am not a foolish man. I observed myself and those around me, and I recognized that the path of self-indulgence led only to destruction. I have given my life over to God's control, and I must not . . . I must not want what I cannot have."

As darkness enshrouded them, she seemed to hang suspended in his embrace, so close he could smell the scent of violets on her skin — and yet as far away as the moon rising in the night sky. She was everything he had ever wanted in a woman. And she was untouchable.

Forcing himself to release her, he stepped back. "I must take you home."

"I am home already," she said. "The moorlands are my home."

"Do not believe yourself abandoned. Brooking House awaits you, and those within it no doubt are flying into panic as the darkness grows. Your cousins will worry. Clemma will weep. You must go to them."

"You talk so easily of submission. Is this what I am to do then? Submit to the Bowden family? Bow to the Creeves and the Friths? Surrender every hope of happiness I have ever cherished?"

"Submit to God, my lady. Trust that his plan for you is a good one. Believe he will lead you to happiness — find your joy in God, if not in the earthly life you have been given."

"And this is what you will do, Mr. Richmond?"

"It is what I do already, though I can assure you that submission is never easy."

"Odd. Of all my acquaintances, you — the man who brought with him the source of all my misery — seem the only one able to speak words of sense." She nodded. "Very well then. I certainly cannot follow my own leading, for I am completely confused and dismayed at every turn. I shall, therefore, join you on this journey of blind obedience to God. I shall trust you, Mr. Richmond, to be right."

A sharp lance tore through his chest as she turned and started down the footpath toward the distant lights of Otley village. She trusted him? Colin Richmond had lived in a world where trusting someone could be fatal. Though he had not been a pirate — as Clemma had feared — his life as a sea trader was similar in character. Treachery, cutthroat dealings, slander, thievery, lies, and even murder swirled around him, enmeshing him in evil. He had cultivated fear in those who knew him. Now this fragile creature was openly choosing to place her hope for happiness in his words.

"I shall trust you," she had said.

Colin led his horse as he walked beside the woman, unable to speak, barely able to contain the emotion raging inside him. He would do everything in his power to deserve her trust. More than that, he would pray — pray with every fiber of his being — that God would bless Miss Ivy Bowden.

"Dearest girl!" Mama rushed to the door and threw her arms around Ivy. "You have never stayed out so late! We are in such a tumult! Your father has sent for the horses, and everyone in the house is gathering for a search party. What can you have been thinking? But, oh, never mind, for you have returned! You are safe! Madeline, go and tell your father to call off the search!"

"But it is muddy outside. Why should I have to go?" Madeline stared at Ivy. "Let her go. She's already wet."

"Such a thing to say to your dear sister."
Mama gasped as Mr. Richmond shouldered his way through the door. "You are here, too? But we thought surely you must have gone home to Longley the moment the rain began!"

"No, indeed, madam." He took off his hat and handed it to one of the servants. "I rode until I found the young lady. My groom is tending my horse. I trust you do not mind my use of your stables."

"But of course not! Goodness gracious, you are both soaked through. Madeline, run and fetch your father. Do as I say! And, Caroline, ring for tea at once. Clementine, hurry upstairs and lay out some dry clothes for your sister. Oh, this is such a to-do! Honestly, Ivy, I can hardly think what possessed you to wander about in such weather. And without telling anyone you were going! Well, the main thing is that you have come back to us safe and sound, and we are all in great need of calm. Clemma, hurry up!"

"Mama, just now you said Ivy is my sister," Clemma spoke up, "but Papa said she is not, not really. And now Caroline thinks she is the oldest and should have all the privileges, and Maddie is furious because she says all the order is gone out of

169

our lives, and I do not know what I am to do." At that, she burst into tears and threw her arms around Ivy. "Please say it is not true! Say you were not born in India like Papa told us. Say you are my sister, Ivy, for I want you to be my sister, and I do not want Caroline to be oldest, and I do not want the order to be gone out of our lives!"

Ivy bent and cupped her hands around the child's face. "God will order our lives, Clemma. Mr. Richmond has reminded me of that. And now you must do as Mama says, for directly I shall go to my room in search of a dry gown."

"You will not run off again, will you?"

"No, dearest. I give you my word."

"Because everyone is out of sorts when you are away, Ivy. It is horrid!" She stood on tiptoe and whispered, "Mr. Creeve has got such a bad temper! When you did not come home at dusk, he shouted at Papa and said very naughty words, much worse than anything Mr. Richmond ever said, and Mama nearly swooned."

"Oh dear." As Ivy straightened, the man himself stepped into the foyer from the parlor. Spotting the gathering near the door, he stiffened.

"I see my wandering fiancée has come to her senses." He approached Ivy and gave her a bow. "Good evening, Miss Bowden."

"Mr. Creeve." She dipped a curtsy into the puddle that had collected around her feet. "I am sorry to have troubled you, sir."

"Troubled me? It has been no trouble at all, my dear girl, for your family and I have enjoyed many happy hours together while we awaited your return." His lips parted in a smile that showed off a set of small white teeth. "And I see that Mr. Richmond has played the knight, rescuing the damsel from her distress. How very gallant of you, sir."

"Any man worth his salt would have done the same." Richmond stalked past the thinner man and headed for the stairs. "If I may be directed to a guest room, Mrs. Bowden, I should like a moment's respite before we begin our discussions."

"Of course, sir! Caroline . . ." Mama glanced about, seeming to have forgotten that she had sent her children and servants away in every direction. "Dear me, I suppose I should —"

"I shall show him to a room, Mama, for I must go upstairs myself," Ivy said. "Come, Mr. Richmond. We have a closet filled with towels, and I shall fetch you some."

She hurried past Mr. Creeve, unwilling to look at him again until she had done something with her hair. What would it be like to meet such a stern and disapproving visage morning after morning? And had he really shouted at Papa? Ivy could hardly imagine such a thing.

Mr. Richmond's heavy boots creaked on the floorboards behind her as Ivy led the way up the stairs and down the corridor to a small guest room. Pausing at a large armoire tucked into a niche, she took out an armful of towels. Then she opened the door to the room.

"There you are, sir, plenty of towels, though I'm afraid you will not find that any exotic Indian soaps have washed these cloths. They are fragranced with sunshine and our own English lavender."

He paused, looking down at her. "I shall not — I swear to you — I shall not allow that man to have you!"

At the intensity of his words, Ivy caught her breath. "If Papa has any jurisdiction over me, Mr. Richmond, there will be little choice in the matter. They have made an agreement."

"I care nothing for agreements or jurisdictions." His hand rose to her jaw, tipping her chin until her eyes were forced to meet his. "I care only for —"

"Ooh!" Clemma's gasp echoed up and

down the corridor like a tiny, shrill shriek. "Ivy! You are . . . he is . . ."

"Clementine," Ivy cried, whirling away from Richmond and racing down the hall as swiftly as her damp slippers would allow. "Have you laid out a gown for me? I hope it is not that old green one, for you know how the hem is always coming loose."

"But, Ivy!" Clemma gaped as Ivy grabbed her arm and practically flung her through the door into the bedroom. "Ivy, he was going to kiss you! Mr. Richmond was going to —"

"Nonsense. Do not be silly, Clemma. Whatever can you be thinking? Kiss me?" Ivy tried to make herself breathe as she fumbled with the hooks on her wet gown. "Honestly, you have such an imagination, Clemma. I believe Papa has been reading you far too many books. You ought to get out in the garden more, or you shall begin seeing fairies in every corner and fancying that dragons are lurking in the —"

"But I did not imagine it! He put his hand under your chin, like this, and he was leaning down toward you, and you were leaning up toward him, and it looked as if you very much wanted him to —"

"Nothing of the sort happened, Clemma. I was giving him some towels."

"But he wanted to kiss you. And you wanted him to. I saw it." Clemma gawked, her blue eyes as round as a pair of full moons. "Ivy, do you love Mr. Richmond?"

"Love him? What a thing to ask!" Ivy pulled a dry petticoat over her head. "I am going to marry Mr. Creeve. You know that. Or I might marry Mr. Frith, depending on which one of them manages to win the rights to my fortune. Mr. Richmond has nothing to do with it. He was merely the one who brought the news of my inheritance, and that is all."

"That is not all." Clemma worked the hooks up the back of Ivy's gown. "Mr. Richmond saved you from the gypsies. And he rescued you from the storm. And he was going to kiss you in the corridor!"

"Clementine Bowden!" Ivy swung around and grasped the child's shoulders. "You must never repeat a word of what you saw. You must promise me that!"

"Then it is true?"

"It is true that Mr. Richmond cares for my welfare. And it is true that I like him . . . I like him very much indeed. Perhaps I do love him, Clemma, but —"

"There! I knew it!"

"But I am going to be obedient to God and marry whichever man I am supposed to wed. Papa believes I must marry Mr. Creeve, and Mr. Kingston intended me to marry Mr. Frith, though I do not know which of them represents the will of God for my life. The only thing of which I am certain is that I am going to live out my life in the most pleasant way possible whilst caring for you and Mama and Papa and everyone else who needs my help, as long as I am able. Mr. Richmond is going to sail away back to India, and we shall never see him again. That is all there is to it."

She took a comb and tugged it through her damp hair. "You see, Clemma? That is all."

A hairpin sprang from Ivy's head, flew across the room, and hit the mirror with a loud ping. "And it is going to be quite perfectly . . . absolutely . . . wonderfully . . . all right with me!"

Eight

"Mr. Bowden, do allow me to begin." Nigel Creeve rose and moved toward the fire that crackled in the front-parlor grate.

From her seat near a small lamp, Ivy observed that her intended had somehow managed to wrinkle the tails of his frock coat by sitting on them improperly. No matter how solemnly he spoke or how severely he regarded those assembled, his gravity was impeded by the fact that he looked very much like a scrawny crow whose tail feathers had barely escaped the teeth of a fox. And the more he twittered about the room displaying his crumpled tails, the harder it was for Ivy to maintain her composure.

Perhaps it had been the soup at dinner that had warmed her and calmed her spirits. Or perhaps it was Mr. Richmond, who sat across the room glowering so fiercely that Mr. Creeve must surely be rendered powerless to accomplish any of his intentions toward Ivy.

But she knew in truth that her peace of heart had come from her long hours upon the moorlands that afternoon — hours in which she had prayed and wept and even clenched her fists in rage. As always, the sweet-smelling grass and rain-laden air had served to remind her that her troubles truly were small and that God truly was great.

Though no clear decisions had come to her, Ivy had been assured that she must face what was to come and trust God's hand to uphold her. When Mr. Richmond had appeared like a wraith in the rain and had spoken words of faith and courage, a bright light of hope was lit inside her. Nothing Nigel Creeve and his crumpled tails might do could suppress that.

"Seven months ago," Creeve intoned, "Mr. Bowden sent a letter to my home in Leeds and requested an interview concerning a matter of grave consequence. Subsequently, he and I met to discuss the future of his eldest daughter, Miss Ivy Bowden."

Here, he turned and gave Ivy a deep bow. She nodded in acknowledgment of the gesture. But as she lifted her head, her focus fell on Mr. Richmond. To her surprise, he did not appear at all attentive to

177

the discourse at hand. Rather, he was occupied with sorting through a thick ream of papers that he had removed from a leather satchel on the floor near his chair.

"Mr. Bowden is a gentleman of the highest order," Creeve continued, "and he is my peer in education and social rank. Although his financial means are substantially beneath my own, I felt it imperative to regard his conversation with seriousness. At that time he also informed me of a most delicate situation — that, unknown to herself and all in her acquaintance, Miss Bowden was, in fact, not his daughter at all. She was a niece and the child of his wife's sister, who had perished in India. Mr. Bowden is her guardian and she his legal ward. He further told me that the young woman was expected to inherit a sum of money upon her twenty-first birthday, and that this sum would serve as her dowry. Though Mr. Bowden could not provide me with the exact amount of the dowry, he did reveal the substantial provision that has arrived regularly from India to care for the girl. Upon learning of this, and after investigating the character of the lady in question and finally assessing my own future plans, I determined to enter into an agreement with Mr. Bowden whereby I would become the husband of his ward. This decision I related to him on the first day of January in this year of 1815."

He lifted from a table a roll of documents tied with a black ribbon. Pulling apart the bow, he unfurled the papers and displayed them for all in the room to observe. "I have here all of the correspondence which passed between Mr. Bowden and myself regarding the matter of his ward's future marriage. And," he paused for effect, "I have the most important document of all — a written agreement between Mr. Bowden and myself, duly signed by both of us and affixed with the seal of a barrister in Leeds who serves under the imprimatur of His Majesty, the King of England, George III."

A moment of silence accompanied the flourishing of this impressive record and its bright red wax seal. Ivy glanced at Papa, who was beaming as though he had accomplished something very grand indeed. Because Mama and the other females who resided at Brooking House had all been dismissed to a back sitting room to work on their embroidery, Ivy found herself once again turning to Mr. Richmond for support. Observing her imploring mien, he rose, set his own thick sheaf of papers on a low table, and folded his arms across his chest.

"The young lady is indeed Mr. Bowden's legal ward," he said, "but her future was never his to decide. She is Ivy Elizabeth Kingston, daughter of Justin and Rosemary Kingston, whose will bears testament to their wish that she inherit their entire estate following her twenty-first birthday and her marriage to one John Frith. The documents in my possession are also signed and sealed by the authority of His Majesty the King, and they clearly predate the agreement into which you, Mr. Bowden, entered. The matter of Creeve's claim on the woman, therefore, is closed. Tomorrow morning I shall request an audience with Mr. Frith as regards his own claim. Mr. Bowden and Miss Bowden, you are both encouraged to attend our meeting. Thank you all very much, and good evening."

With a curt nod, he gathered the papers, dropped them into the satchel, tucked it under his arm, and headed for the door. Good heavens, was he leaving already? Ivy scrambled to her feet and executed an awkward curtsy as Papa mumbled some sort of statement that made no sense whatsoever.

"Just a minute there, Richmond!" Creeve shouted. Marching across the floor, he shook his roll of papers at the man who had paused in the doorway. "Do not suppose you can end the matter as easily as that! The girl is Bowden's ward. He gave me his signature. My document will stand up in a court of law!"

"Your document is worthless," Richmond retorted, "though I suppose it might make adequate kindling."

"Now then, gentlemen!" Papa hurried to join the other two. "Mr. Richmond, I beg to remind you that I have letters in your own father's pen — written at the time of Mr. Kingston's death — certifying my position as the girl's legal guardian. Every matter of her life has been in my hands these many years. I have managed her money, seen to her schooling, provided her clothing and food, and determined everything about her to this date. It is my right and my duty to see that she is married well, and I have selected Mr. Creeve!"

"You have been her guardian, and you have performed your role admirably." Richmond glanced at Ivy. "But you are not her father, sir. That man's plans supersede your own."

"May I remind you, sir, that my position

as guardian was commissioned by her father and certified by the king himself. As our noble general Horatio Nelson said at the battle of Trafalgar, 'England expects every man will do his duty.' I shall do no less than that — for my ward, for my God, and for my country!"

"Well said, Bowden." Creeve clapped the older man on the back. "Richmond, your little satchel contains nothing but the faded remnants of a dead man's dreams. For all intents and purposes, Bowden has acted as a legal guardian and has performed the duties of father for more than sixteen years. I assure you that a British court of law will give little regard to your moth-eaten, obsolete papers stamped by some wallah in the jungles of India. We are not barbarians here."

"No?" Richmond looked back and forth between the two men. "I see very little difference."

"I beg your pardon!"

"The Indians of my acquaintance are just as eager as you to arrange marriages without the least consideration as to the wishes of the young women themselves. Should you be permitted to marry, Creeve, I would find no surprise at your keeping your wife bound beneath your total domination. Perhaps you would even wish her to be laid alive and breathing on your funeral pyre."

"Absurd!" Creeve shouted, his face bright red. "Insufferable colonial! How dare you suggest such a thing!"

"How dare you refuse to consider anyone's desires but your own. And you, Mr. Bowden, who are so duty-bound, might give some thought to the wishes of this ward you profess to care for so deeply. What does she think? What does she want?"

At that, all three men turned on Ivy, their eyes boring into her as she stood beside her chair. Swallowing hard, she took a step forward. How could she possibly tell them what she really wanted? Could she lift her chin and announce that she wanted to marry no one at all? No one, except perhaps Colin Richmond. Could she confess that she longed to melt into his arms, that she ached to hear the whisper of his voice in her ear, that she desired nothing more than to walk at his side and bear his children and live as his devoted wife to the end of her days?

"Well?" Papa walked toward her and held out his hand. She slipped her fingers into his familiar clasp. "Mr. Richmond has asked what you want, my dear. Do you wish to follow my leadership as you always have and marry Mr. Creeve, who will take care of you all your days? Or do you wish to be bound to Mr. Frith — a man your late father could not possibly have known would turn out to be a drunken libertine with a reputation that is beneath contempt? Come now, dear girl. State your wishes so that Mr. Richmond's mind may be put at ease."

Ivy looked into Richmond's warm brown eyes. "Papa," she said, "I wish . . . I wish to do the will of God. As to what that is, sir, I am quite uncertain."

"I see." Papa regarded her, his tender smile frozen on his face. "God's will. Aha."

"Quite obviously, Bowden, God's will is the same as your own," Creeve said. "God made you her guardian, and you have chosen me. It is all quite simple."

"God made Justin Kingston her father," Richmond said, "and he chose John Frith."

"God made Justin Kingston as dead as a doornail!" Creeve exploded. "By heaven, I'll not stand here and listen to this nonsense —"

"Excuse me, Mr. Creeve," Ivy spoke up. "I should ask that you refrain from referring to my late father in such crass terms. Mr.

Kingston may be deceased, but his memory is due our greatest respect and honor. He and my mother bore me, cared for me, and, in fact, planned very carefully for my future. He is not to blame for the unfortunate circumstance of his death, and I would beg you not to speak ill of him."

"Of course," Creeve said crisply. "Forgive me, please. Madam, I assure you I intended no disrespect. Indeed, it is only your future happiness of which I myself am thinking."

"Hah!" Richmond's laugh echoed up and down the corridor outside the parlor. "You agreed to take her to wife because your coffers needed a healthy infusion of funds. The marriage promised at least some income, and so you agreed to it. Now that you know the extent of Miss Bowden's fortune, you are all the more determined to have it. *You,* sir, are the person whose future happiness most concerns you."

"Lies," Creeve hissed. "This man speaks lies! I refuse to stay a moment longer in his presence. Miss Bowden, I beg you to excuse me. I shall return to Leeds, whereupon I shall submit my documents to a judge for an evaluation and a ruling on their legality. Mr. Bowden, I thank you for your invitation to the ball celebrating your

185

ward's birthday, and I shall look forward to speaking with you again at that time, if not before. Mr. Richmond, I bid you no farewell."

He minced past them out of the room, his crumpled coattails wafting behind him. Ivy let out her breath. "Papa," she said, "I confess I cannot like that man."

The elderly gentleman tucked Ivy's hand into the crook of his arm and patted it gently. "There, there, my dear. He is not so bad. Before I wrote to him the first time, I had him thoroughly investigated. Other than a somewhat severe temperament and a general attitude of indifference toward those he considers beneath him, Creeve is as fine a fellow as you can hope to obtain for a husband — or could before we knew the full extent of your inheritance." He sighed deeply. "I suppose you could do better now."

Ivy laid her head on his shoulder. "Papa, I believe we should allow Mr. Richmond to move forward with his position. I suggest it might be advisable to cut off Mr. Creeve entirely."

"Oh, dearest girl." Papa walked beside her to the nearest settee and collapsed heavily onto the cushions. "That we cannot do. I have pledged my word to the man . . . and what is worse, he has pledged his to me."

"What do you mean, sir?" Richmond asked. He followed the pair to the fire and resumed his place. "Mr. Bowden, I must ask you to be frank. Surely you can see that Creeve falls far short of Miss Bowden's aspirations in a husband. He is an ignoble man, and his family is hardly the sort from which good bloodlines are built. Why do you insist on continuing to allow his claim on your ward?"

Papa fell silent, gazing at the fire for such a long time that Ivy began to wonder if he had fallen asleep. Finally, he cleared his throat. "Very well then. I shall confess everything. My sin is great, and I can beg no mercy."

"Oh, Papa, that cannot be true," Ivy cried.

"No, no. Hear me out, and you shall understand how completely I have failed you. When my own father died and I assumed ownership of Brooking House, I learned that the estate had few funds for its support. Nevertheless, I married my dear wife and proceeded to carve out a living for us on what little remained. Then, to our great joy, a very tiny girl with very large brown eyes was sent to us from India."

"Thank you for agreeing to take me in," Ivy whispered.

"We would never have considered anything else. Of that, I can assure you. No matter what else I have done, you must know that I have always loved you as my very own daughter."

"And you are my dearest papa."

He shook his head. "But I am not proud of my subsequent behavior. The money that regularly came for you from India was more than adequate, and Mama and I spent as much on your care as we thought prudent. Still there was always a good deal remaining. For several years, I deposited this money into an account at a bank in Leeds. The sum increased, of course, as did our family here at Brooking House. First there was Caroline, a demanding child. And then Madeline, who is rarely pleased with the world. Then Hugh and James came along, strapping young boys who would need a good education —"

"And finally, to all our surprise and delight," Ivy interjected, "Clementine arrived."

"Yes, dear little Clemma." Papa laughed softly. "Despite this onrush of children, my dear Ivy, Mrs. Bowden and I had decided early on that we would not treat you as any different from the others. And though you may feel that we intentionally deceived you, nothing could be further from the truth. We began thinking of you as our own daughter so quickly that we simply neglected to mention the circumstances of your birth until they were quite nearly forgotten by both of us."

"Except for that growing bank account," Richmond reminded him.

"Yes." Papa shifted on the cushions. "I had a growing bank account and a growing family. Eventually, I am ashamed to say, I began to dip into the fund in order to support the other children."

"It is all right, Papa," Ivy said.

"No, it was quite wrong of me, but I told myself it was for your good in the long run. If your brothers and sisters should be treated worse than you — if you should be clad in silks and velvets, attended by several lady's maids, and fed on the most sumptuous foods while your siblings wore cotton and ate suet — you would grow up feeling yourself to be superior. You would know you were different, set apart, and you would acquire a very poor character, indeed."

"In other words," Richmond said, "you feared she might develop a somewhat severe temperament and a general attitude of indifference toward those she considered beneath her?"

Ivy gave Richmond a quelling look. Papa might have acted wrongly, but he did not deserve censure. It was clear the elder man regretted having withheld the truth from her all these years, and she knew now that he had acted out of love for her. He had done nothing with selfish or malicious intent. Now Ivy did not wish to increase his agony in any way.

"Truly, Papa," she said, "you were wise in this matter. I am glad you treated me no differently than the others. The intimacy I share with those I call sisters and brothers is very precious to me. I would not have it any other way."

"But I should not have spent your money." He bent forward and rested his forehead in his hands. "No, indeed, for it has come to pass that the entire Bowden family now subsists almost completely on the funds in that bank in Leeds. We are more than beholden to you, my dear girl. Our very survival depends upon you."

Ivy absorbed this information in silence. She could not bring herself to look at Mr. Richmond, for she felt Papa's shame so acutely that it seemed almost to be her own. Instead, she gazed at her intertwined fingers and turned over in her mind the ramifications of all he had told her. And what she realized was that none of it mattered. Not in the least.

"Papa, please do not chastise yourself so," she said, going to him and giving him the warmest of embraces. "I am happy that Mr. Kingston's money was able to help you. Indeed, I am very grateful, for now I know that I have in some small way repaid your kindness to me."

"But we agreed to take you without remuneration, and I should have left those funds untouched." He heaved a shuddering sigh. "I sinned against you, and in so doing, I fear I may have ruined your life altogether. Dearest Ivy . . . when I approached Nigel Creeve about the matter of marriage, I had your best interests at heart. But I also bore the welfare of the rest of my family in mind. In short, I struck an agreement with Mr. Creeve that should he marry you, he would set aside a regular amount each month to be sent to us here at Brooking House."

"Oh, Papa!"

"I cannot deny it. He agreed to the plan as a business speculation. Not knowing the full amount of your fortune, he assumed the risk that the support of our family might have to come from his own accounts. Now, of course, we all know that Creeve will have more than enough money to provide for the Bowden family, for himself and his wife, and for many generations to come."

"But, Papa, I would gladly care for all of you myself," Ivy said. "There is no need for me to marry Mr. Creeve to accomplish this."

"Yes, there is need, my dear, for I have signed a binding agreement with the man. The details are spelled out very carefully and in great detail. Should I fail to follow through with my part in the agreement, I will face far more serious consequences than the loss of income for my family."

"What have you agreed to, Mr. Bowden?" Richmond asked. "Please, sir, you must reveal it all."

"I hardly know myself. Creeve and his infernal barrister in Leeds created in their document such a conundrum of language that I could scarcely make it out — and I assure you I am not an uneducated man. But in this I was very foolish. I thought I had found a way to provide for Ivy and for the rest of my family as well. I convinced myself that everything would fall out in perfect order — that my eldest daughter, never knowing she was actually my ward, would marry a respected gentleman; that my other children would follow suit by making equally profitable unions; and that my wife and I would live out the remainder of our lives in comfort and content. I painted a vain picture of myself, not unlike one of Milton's idle philosophers when he wrote:

Others apart sat on a hill retired,
In thoughts more elevate, and reasoned high
Of Providence, foreknowledge, will, and fate,
Fixed fate, free will, foreknowledge absolute,
And found no end, in wandering mazes lost.

"You see, my dear girl, my own selfish desire to end my days in contemplation of poetry, religion, and philosophy conquered my good reason. And so I signed the agreement."

"A contrite and honest confession," Richmond said. "Despite your failings, sir, I find that you have risen in my esteem. And now I must ask that you provide me with a copy of the document you signed with Creeve in order that we may begin to determine the ins and outs of the matter."

"I do not have a copy," Papa said in a

small voice. "We signed but a single paper, and Creeve has it in his possession."

"Very shortsighted of you, if I may say so without offense. Well, then, we must find some way of detaching the document from Creeve's sticky fingers." Richmond stood. "It is very late, and I must return to Longley. Sir, you should know that I remain resolute in my determination to prevent any marriage between that man and Miss Bowden."

"I understand, of course. And I shall accept the consequences to myself. *Mea culpa, mea culpa, mea maxima culpa.*"

"This is not all your fault, Papa, and there will be no lasting harm," Ivy said. "We will be all right."

"Miss Bowden, will you be so good as to accompany me for a moment?" Richmond held out his hand to indicate the door. "Good evening, Mr. Bowden. May God grant you peace."

"Thank you, sir, thank you." Papa had leaned his head on the back of the settee and shut his eyes. "Ivy dear, please do see Mr. Richmond out," he mumbled. "There is a good girl. Yes, indeed."

Ivy accepted Richmond's arm, linking her hand around the taut muscle. At that mere touch, she instantly felt once again a great longing to be encircled by this man's warm protection. But she knew — now beyond the shadow of a doubt — that there could be no hope for any connection between them.

"I shall have to marry John Frith," she said as they crossed the marbled foyer. "If there is no other way to prevent my union with Mr. Creeve, I must wed Mr. Frith at once."

"I fear that may be true."

"It is true, for I must have the sum my father left to me." They stopped near the door, and she disengaged her arm. "I confess, in my walk upon the moor, I entertained the idea of refusing to marry either man. Though I knew I would be left destitute, I imagined throwing myself on the mercy of Papa — begging him to see to my welfare for the rest of my life. But now I understand that he would be unable to care for me at all. More important, he and the rest of the family are totally dependent upon me for their future happiness. I cannot fail them."

Richmond reached for the handle and pulled the door ajar. "I knew this would be your position," he said, leading her outside onto the great stone staircase that descended to the drive. "You are too good.

Were you a lesser woman, you would beg me to ignore the provisions in Mr. Kingston's will and give you the inheritance outright. But that I cannot do."

"No, for you are not a lesser man. You are as bound to your father's wishes and to your own moral principles as I am to mine."

They stood together on the top step and gazed out across the moonlit moors. The soft tinkle of sheep's bells drifted across from their pasture on the fells. In a moment, Richmond gave a gruff laugh.

"You find humor in this matter?" Ivy asked.

"Only in my musings. I fear you have come to think me noble in my actions and aims, my dear lady. But I assure you, could you read my thoughts, you would know I am quite the opposite."

"What can you mean?"

"Your sister called me a pirate, and she was closer to the truth than she knew. I am hardly a gentleman, and my behavior is under only the leash of my newly made commitment to God. Inside my chest there beats a rather savage heart, madam. I find myself hardly restrained from the desires that race through me — desires formed by the habit of many years of dissolute living."

"Do you speak of Papa, sir?" she asked. "I know you think him foolish and weak. But he must not come to harm at your hand. Truly, he has been very good to me —"

"It is not that old fellow I would bring to ruin." Again he laughed. "No indeed. The old Colin Richmond would make short work of this mess."

"What would you do?"

"I would begin by running Nigel Creeve through with a sword." At this, he whipped a knife from beneath his coat and thrust into his imaginary victim. "Even my little Fiji blade would do the job. That would serve him well, do you not think so?"

"Good heavens!" Ivy exclaimed, stepping away from the gleaming steel.

"Lovely, eh? I had it made by a native artisan." With a laugh, he opened his palm to display the knife and its hilt, intricately inlaid with his monogram in ivory and gold. As he slipped the weapon back into the leather sheath at his waist, he continued. "John Frith merits a less violent fate. I can see him spending the remainder of his days as a castaway on some forgotten island in the West Indies. The Bowden clan could be bought into silence, though I imagine I would keep an eye on Clemma. She might do as a good wife for one of my men.

Sailing the seas for a few years ought to keep her entertained. What do you think? Shall we avoid the courts entirely and settle the matter in my efficient if rather ungodly way?"

Ivy found herself smiling for the first time that evening. "Truly, it would not do to run Mr. Creeve through with your Fiji knife."

"No? Hmm. Well, I have considered using my cutlass to lop off his head."

"Oh dear!"

"But maybe I should just put him to work on one of my ships. Scrubbing barnacles from the keel, swabbing the decks, cleaning out the brig . . . yes, that would do."

Ivy giggled. "And what about me, sir? What would you do with the one who is the cause of all your troubles?"

"You?" He looked her up and down. "I would do with you what I have longed to do from the moment I laid eyes upon you. And it would begin with this."

So saying, he caught her roughly in his arms, dipped her backward until she was completely unbalanced, and kissed her firmly on the lips. Clutching the shoulders of his coat to keep from falling down the stairs, Ivy gave a muffled cry. Richmond lifted his head, regarded her a moment longer, and then kissed her again, only this time much more gently.

"But I see my behavior would never do," he said in a throaty voice as he lifted her upright and held her in his arms. "You are too pure. And I . . . well, I am no longer quite wicked enough to treat you ill. But I am certainly not good enough to be worthy of a woman like you."

As he clasped her close, gazing into her eyes, Ivy felt certain that she had never been so happy in all her life. Or so miserable. Her heart raced as her hands traced the solid bulwark of his shoulders. She was awake, alive, and filled with great joy. And at the same time, she knew this moment could never last . . . indeed, it should never have occurred.

"Forgive me," he said, pulling away. "I have revealed too much of myself. I beg you not to think less of me for my heedless words and boorish behavior. My past is shameful. My character is far from ideal. And yet, I wish you to understand —" At this, he caught her hands in his. "Believe that I want for you only the very best. Allow me to continue as your champion in this matter, dear lady, and I vow I shall do nothing to cause you pain."

His brown eyes searched hers, and Ivy could only nod. "I trust you, Colin Richmond."

Bringing her fingers to his lips, he kissed them — then he turned away and moved down the stairs and in the direction of the stables.

Ivy watched him until he had vanished into the darkness. Catching her breath in a sob, she held her fingers to her cheek and drank in the now familiar scent of his skin. His words echoed through her thoughts: *"I vow I shall do nothing to cause you pain."* But, *oh,* she longed to cry after him, *oh, sir, you already have!*

Nine

Clemma had forgotten to wear her bonnet
again. Ivy sighed in dismay as she hurried
down the long, sloping lawn toward the
small brook where the child was playing. A
head of golden curls bobbed up and down
among the reeds, ferns, and sedges that grew
along the bank, and a nursery song wafted
into the morning air as if on the wings of a
lark.

" 'Oranges and lemons,' " Clemma sang
out, " 'say the bells of St. Clement's. You
owe me five farthings, say the bells of St.
Martin's. When will you pay me, say the
bells of Old Bailey. When I grow rich —' "

" 'Say the bells of Shoreditch,' " Ivy
joined in.

Clemma's face appeared around the
trunk of an old alder tree. On discovering
Ivy, her blue eyes brightened. "I did not
see you there! Just look at what I have
found. Come quickly! Hurry!"

Ivy picked up her skirts and made her
way down the narrow path to the bank of

the brook. Clemma, mud six inches up the hem of her yellow cotton frock, was pointing excitedly to a small hollow near a shallow cascade at the edge of the water.

"Polliwogs!" she cried. "Have you ever seen so many in all your life?"

Ivy crouched near the pool and watched the little, black comma-shaped tadpoles darting here and there. "Goodness! You have found quite the lot of them, Clemma."

"I am going to come here every day until they turn into frogs."

"A grand idea. You will see them grow their legs and lose their tails and fatten up on all the mosquitoes they eat. And one day they will come hopping out of their little pool to bid you good morning."

"Do you think so? Will they know me, Ivy? Will they recognize me as the one who has come to visit them every day?"

"I should imagine they will. Perhaps you can hold one in your hand when they get a little bigger."

"Oh, I do hope so. I feel as though they are mine somehow, as though I am a little bit like their mama — only I am better, because I should never go off and abandon my babies as old Mrs. Frog has done. Fish and birds and those horrid diving beetles are trying very hard to eat my wee polliwogs, but I shan't allow it. Look at all of them. Hundreds of brothers and sisters. Do you suppose they have names?"

"Not yet." Ivy stretched out her finger and pointed at one of the tadpoles. "I christen you Peter Polliwog. And you will be Pamela Polliwog. You are Paul, Patricia, Preston, Patrick, Penelope, and . . . Cedric."

"Cedric!" Clemma exclaimed. "That does not start with a *P*."

"I fear I have run out of *P* names."

"What about Percival?"

"All right, then. You can be Percival Polliwog," Ivy said to a tiny black shape near the edge of the pool. "But I warn you, it is a very grand name, sir, and you had better live up to it."

Clemma giggled. "I like polliwogs."

"So do I. And even better, I like little girls who remember to wear their bonnets in the morning sunshine."

"Oh dear!"

"You shall be as brown as an acorn by the end of summer." Ivy tapped Clemma's pink nose. "Now, then, how would you like to walk with me to Longley Park? I have promised to visit Mr. Hedgley the gardener and take him some tonic for his cough."

"But I do not want to go all that way."

Clemma wrinkled up her nose. "I am sorry, Ivy, but I do not like to visit ill people as you do. They are always groaning and moaning . . . and they smell bad. And their cottages are so dark and smoky, and their children all wear rags and have sores on their feet. Please let me stay here with my polliwogs."

Ivy studied the small golden head and the muddy boots. It was tempting to leave Clemma to her play. But Ivy had more than the child's Christian duty in mind. A walk through Longley Park might include an encounter with Colin Richmond — and Ivy had made up her mind she must never be alone with him again. It was not that she distrusted the man. Rather, she knew she could no longer rely upon her own good judgment where he was concerned.

For the past four days, she had been able to think about little but that moment when he had held her in his arms. She might have taken solace in the belief that her attraction to him was based only on his physical attributes and his dashing — if somewhat roguish — affinity for kissing her. But that was not all she had come to admire about him.

No, for he was unmistakably trying to be a good man, honorable and upright. His

Christian faith, though he proclaimed it new and weak, held preeminence in his life. Not only was he handsome and admirably moral, but he was also intelligent, brave, and even amusing. And Ivy knew if she found any more things to like about him, she was in great danger of loving him. She could not allow herself to even entertain the thought, of course. Such a path would lead to heartbreak, poverty, and disgrace for the only family she had ever known.

"Clemma," she said, "I want you to come with me. I have several calls to make and lots of baskets to carry."

"Can you not make Peter carry them? He would not mind, I am sure of it."

"Peter's job is to tend the kitchen garden at Brooking House, and at the moment he is deeply mired in the stables, filling a wheelbarrow with muck to spread on the soil."

"Ooh." Clemma wrinkled her nose again. "But what about Bess? Maybe she could —"

"She is in the buttery." Ivy set her hands on her hips. "Clemma, I have asked you to accompany me. I expect you to obey."

"I do not have to obey you! You are not even my real sister, and you are not the eldest anymore, and you cannot make me do anything I do not want to do!"

"Fine then! Stay here." Ivy swung around and ran back up the path, hoping Clemma had not heard the quaver of tears in her voice. This was exactly how it had been ever since that horrid day when everyone found out the truth about her. Caroline, Maddie, and Clemma had always been her sisters, perfectly normal in every way in their various joys and snits together.

But now, Caroline fancied herself as the eldest and took great pains to walk ahead of Ivy in the family order or to insist on being the daughter served first at the table. Maddie regarded the entire situation as a plot to throw her orderly world off-kilter, and she had done little but glower and fret on an hourly basis. And Clemma seemed completely at sea — one moment weeping in fear of losing Ivy as her big sister, the next moment stamping her foot in annoyance with everyone and everything.

Mama and Papa were hardly better. It had always been Mama's character to encourage and delight in all her children. But now each time she did Ivy a kind deed or spoke tender words, she flushed a brilliant red and said she hoped it did not appear she was trying to win favors. And each time she scolded Ivy for wearing blue instead of green or failing to match her bonnet ribbons to her shoes, she again went bright with mortification — clearly fearing that Ivy would become angry with her and cast the family into dire poverty. Papa had banished himself to his study, and when he appeared at meals, he moped and recited such morose selections of poetry that everyone was quite undone.

It was a disastrous situation, and one Ivy would not have wished on her worst enemy. Filled with dismay, she entered the kitchen at the back of Brooking House, gathered up the heavy baskets she had packed for her outing, and started down the drive to the gate. But as she arrived at the lane, she heard the sound of small footsteps running on the gravel behind her.

"Ivy!" Clemma caught up to Ivy and took a basket into her arms. "I decided to come with you. And look, I have my bonnet, too!"

"Good girl. The sun is quite hot already."

They walked in silence for a minute, and then Clemma sniffled. "I am sorry for what I said to you, Ivy. It was very wrong of me."

"Indeed it was, dearest, but I forgive you. The truth of the matter is that we are

207

all a bit muddled in the matter of my position in the family. I hardly know how to feel myself."

"I know how I feel! I wish Mr. Richmond had never come from India with his satchel of papers and all his bad news. I wish you were still eldest and Caroline was second, because she is not a good big sister at all. She thinks herself far superior to us, but she is only vain and pompous because she is the prettiest, only I do not believe she really is. I think you are, and so does Mr. Richmond."

At that, Ivy paused in the lane. "Mr. Richmond? Clemma, why would you say such a silly thing as that?"

"Because he told me so."

"Impossible. You have never seen the man at any time when I was not present, and I am sure he —"

"Indeed I have seen him! Bess took me to Otley on Tuesday, because I wanted a small butterfly net from the market, and she had to go there to buy fish, and so we went together. And who do you suppose we saw but Mr. Richmond? He was walking with a gentleman who was a barrister from London and a good friend of his from their days at Eton, but even though they were deep in conversation, Mr. Richmond paused and said good morning to me and introduced his friend. And then what do you suppose he said?"

"I cannot imagine." Ivy discovered her heart was beating much too fast for the pace at which she was walking, and she feared she might lose her balance altogether.

"He said, 'How is your eldest sister?' And I said, 'I do not know who you mean, sir, for Ivy has held that position all my life, but now Caroline believes it is hers.' And what do you think he said after that?"

"Clemma, I cannot know what he said! Please tell the whole story without interrupting yourself all the time."

The little girl gave her elder a look of reproach. " 'Ivy.' That is what he said. He called you Ivy. Not Miss Bowden or Miss Kingston or anything else. Just Ivy."

"My goodness."

"So, I said you were well, though not nearly as cheerful as you used to be before he came with his satchel of papers and boxes of money from India."

"Oh, Clemma!"

"And that is when he gave the barrister a wink and took my hand and began to walk with me through the market, just the two of us. The barrister went one way and Bess went another, and Mr. Richmond and I strolled along down the rows of goods, and do you know he can tell the name of every single sort of fish for sale in the market? Even the odd ones that we never eat!"

Ivy tried to breathe in a normal fashion. Why must even the name of the man throw her into such giddiness? She found herself longing to ask Clemma a hundred questions. . . . *What was he wearing? Did he look in good health? Did he seem happy? Why was the barrister with him? Did he say when he was going back to India?* But, oh dear, these spinning thoughts were such nonsense!

"And so we just walked along talking about fish," Clemma said. "He told me some stories of the sea, and he said he thought I might like to visit India one day, because it is very lovely there, even though it is hot. He told me about maharanis, Indian princesses who wear emeralds and rubies and pearls. I asked him if he was going to marry a maharani, and he said no. I said why not? And he said because he did not love any maharanis. I told him I thought they must be very beautiful, and he said they were, but not beautiful enough to please him. That is when he said he had met only one lady who was truly beautiful both inside and out, and that was you."

"Me?"

"You, Ivy!" Clemma stamped her foot. "Goodness, why must you always doubt what I say?"

"I am sorry, but truly I —"

"Mr. Richmond told me he once saw a stone called a tiger's eye, and it is a deep chestnut color banded with glittering gold. He said real tigers have eyes just like that, and so do you, Ivy. I tried to tell him your eyes are plain brown, but he just laughed."

Ivy cradled the baskets looped around her arm. "He was teasing you, Clemma. I am quite sure of it."

"No, for then he told me you are the most admirable woman he has ever known in all his life." Clemma followed Ivy as she turned down a narrow path toward a small thatched cottage. "I said you would be more admirable if you were not always so sad about having to marry Mr. Creeve, and he said he would not allow you to marry that man for all the rupees in the world. That is what he said: 'all the rupees in the world.' Is that not romantic, Ivy?"

Ivy knocked on the roughly carved oak door. "Romance has rarely done anybody any good, Clemma," she said. "It is very upsetting and a great worry, and the best thing to do is never let it into your life for a moment."

"I cannot think you believe that. Even though you have to marry Mr. Creeve or that other fellow whose name is in the will, Mr. Richmond is very romantic toward you, and I think you like it. In fact, I think you love him. And I am completely certain that he loves you."

"Clementine!" Ivy exclaimed as the door swung open to reveal an elderly woman who was caring for three grandchildren — all of whom had hacking coughs. Trying to put Clemma's disturbing words out of her thoughts, Ivy dished up bowls of hot chicken soup for the wee ones and gave their grandmother a plaster to put on their chests.

As they made their way along the path to the next cottage, Ivy refused to let Clemma bring up the subject of Mr. Richmond again. Instead, she bade the child recite the entirety of Psalm 23, followed by enough French conjugations to keep her occupied through three more visits. By the time they finally walked down the long drive into Longley Park and located Mr. Hedgley's cottage, Ivy felt herself completely composed and in control once again.

"My name is Miss Bowden, and I have come with a tonic for Mr. Hedgley," she told the old lady who answered his door.

212

"His grandson, Jimmy Smith, told me he was suffering from a dreadful cough. And I have brought some soup as well."

"Jimmy sent ye, did 'e?" Her sharp eyes looked the two visitors up and down. "When were that?"

"Last Sunday he told me about his fears for his grandfather. I had helped the Smith family in the past, and I thought —"

"Be ye t' young miss from Brookin' 'ouse?"

"Indeed, and this is my youngest sister, Clementine Bowden. We have been making rounds this morning, and as I had promised Jimmy —"

"Ye be t' one they call Angel of t' Moors." The old woman's face broke into a wreath of wrinkles as she smiled and drew her visitors through the doorway into the small cottage. "Come in and sit down, lass. Let me make a spot o' tea to warm ye."

"Thank you, but we are truly quite warm already. I have just come to see about Mr. Hedgley. Is he in?"

The old woman sat down on a low stool and shook her head as if in awe. "Angel of t' Moors. Right 'ere in me own cottage."

"Dear lady, I am hardly an angel of any sort, and I cannot imagine why you persist

213

in calling me by such a name. Perhaps you have confused me with someone else?"

"No, indeed! Ye be t' lass wot takes food and tonics round to t' cottagers. T' one wot got knocked in t' 'ead and nearly died, but come back to life as sound and sane as ever."

"Well, I do not think I was nearly so gravely ill as —"

"Ye be t' lass wot has been sent a fortune all t' way from India. Aye, I know about ye, dearie. Angel of t' Moors."

"Please!" Exasperated, Ivy let out a deep breath. "Madam, I beg you to refrain from —"

"Everyone talks of ye, all up and down t' moorlands. Even me own 'usband said 'e met ye in t' conservatory, and 'e knew right away ye was sommat special. A livin' saint sent to us from God."

"I cannot imagine that. I spoke to him but a few words, and I assure you I am neither an angel nor a saint, nor anything of the sort."

"That is true," Clemma spoke up. "Ivy is just a regular girl like all my other sisters. She sometimes weeps and sometimes giggles, and she even shouts at us when she's angry."

"But she 'as a good soul, and all t'

people have great 'opes for wot she will do."

"What sort of hopes?" Ivy asked. "I cannot think what you mean."

"All them riches from India!" Mrs. Hedgley cackled. "Ye been so good to everyone before, now we cannot but imagine wot ye'll do with all yer wealth. There's great talk of it all up t' fells and down t' dales. Angel of t' Moors, folk says, is come to 'elp us. And now, all will be well."

"Oh dear." Ivy untied her bonnet ribbons in the heat of the small room. "This is a dreadful situation. Please, madam, where is Mr. Hedgley? I shall give him the tonic, and then I must begin at once to counter this irresponsible gossip."

"Then it ain't true? Ye'll not 'elp nobody?"

Ivy took off her bonnet and fanned herself. "I shall always try to do my Christian duty, but —"

"I knew it!" Mrs. Hedgley clapped her gnarled hands. "Go on over to t' conservatory, then, and there ye'll find me 'usband and 'alf the town of Otley cleanin' up Longley Park for Mr. Richmond."

"Mr. Hedgley is not ill? But Jimmy said he had a terrible cough."

" 'Twere naught but a fishbone caught in

'is throat," she said with a laugh. "Now then, go along to t' conservatory. Everyone will be wantin' to see ye and thank ye for what ye'll be doin' for us once yer riches come in from India. And God bless ye, lass. God bless ye and keep ye."

As Ivy and Clementine hurried out of the cottage, Mrs. Hedgley moved to the doorway and waved her apron in farewell. Letting out a groan of anguish, Ivy began to run down the path toward the long glass building where she had first met the old gardener. Clemma raced to keep up, her empty baskets swinging from side to side.

"Slow down, Ivy!" she cried. "Why must we rush so?"

"I must find Mr. Hedgley at once and make him repair all the damage he has caused with his thoughtless rumor-mongering. This is appalling — to think that everyone in Otley and all around the moors now believes me some sort of angel! They expect that I will shower them with food and clothing and every sort of gift."

"Will you not help them, Ivy?" Clemma asked, puffing out the words. "But you always help people. Does this mean you will not help us? Will you cut us off, Ivy?"

At that, Ivy came to a sudden halt, turned, and caught the child's shoulders.

"What did you say, Clemma?"

"We cannot continue as we have lest you provide for us from your Indian riches. We will have to let go all the servants, even Bess, and we will not be able to afford meat except on special occasions, and there will be no more new bonnets, and Hugh and James must stop their schooling and come home from Plymouth at once so they can go to work in the trades!"

"Clemma . . ." Ivy stared at the wide blue eyes now filling with tears. "Who on earth has told you such dreadful things?"

"Everyone says them. Papa and Mama were talking about it in the drawing room one evening, and Caroline told Maddie there will be no more beads or bonnets or new slippers for us unless you agree to marry Mr. Creeve. Even Bess said all the servants now live in fear that they might lose their positions and have to go to work at the worsted mill, for should you refuse to marry Mr. Creeve, we shall all be reduced to utter poverty!"

"Oh, my dearest Clemma, please do not say such things." Ivy put her arms around the child and drew her close. "I shall never let anything so worrisome befall you. I promise."

"Then you will marry Mr. Creeve?"

"Well, I . . . I don't know, Clemma."

"It is because you love Mr. Richmond!" she cried out. "You love him, and you will refuse to marry Mr. Creeve, and we shall have to wear wooden shoes and live in a cottage filled with smoke and bedbugs!"

"Clemma, hush, my dear . . ." Ivy took off the little girl's bonnet and kissed her hot, red cheek. "You must calm yourself, I beg you. Please try to understand that the whole matter is very complicated. Papa wishes me to marry Mr. Creeve, and they have worked out a most uncompromising agreement. But the documents from India say that I am to marry someone named Mr. Frith, a man we do not even know. I suppose I shall have to marry one of them, Clemma, if I mean to get the money Mr. Richmond holds in trust for me. And I do think I ought to get it, especially as I now realize how many people are counting on it. As for Mr. Richmond . . . Clemma, you must never tell anyone that you think I love him, for I do not love him. Not at all!"

"No?" The male voice was unmistakable. "I am sorry to hear that."

Ivy lifted her head to find Colin Richmond himself standing only paces away on the path that led to the conservatory. He smiled as he took off his hat and gave her a bow.

"Miss Bowden, Miss Clementine," he said. "This is a happy surprise. May I ask what brings you to Longley Park?"

Clemma spoke up. "We are looking for Mr. Hedgley to tell him that Ivy is not the Angel of the Moors."

"Angel of the Moors?"

"Everyone in Otley supposes she is going to dole out her riches after she marries Mr. Creeve."

"Really?" Richmond stepped forward and lifted the baskets from Ivy's arms. "Allow me to help you with these, madam. We cannot have the Angel of the Moors exhausting herself, now can we?"

"Please, Mr. Richmond," Ivy said, "I cannot bear to be teased about this matter. I have learned just now that I am expected to be the savior not only of my family but of every family living upon the moorlands."

"Surely this will not be too difficult a task for you, dear lady," he said, taking her arm and leading her toward the conservatory. "I believe you are capable of a great many things."

"But not that!" Ivy allowed him to guide her down the path, though her heart was so distraught that she felt she ought to return to Brooking House as soon as possible. "I am not an angel, and I hardly think I can make everyone rich and happy."

"Then you plan to keep the fortune for your own pleasure?"

"Oh, Mr. Richmond, of course not!" Ivy detached herself and hurried to the main door of the conservatory. If he believed her as selfish as that, he knew nothing about her. The money from her father could be used in many ways, of course. But no amount of wealth could bring happiness to every person alive. In fact, it seemed to bring just the opposite.

Pushing open the door, she stepped inside the conservatory to seek out Mr. Hedgley. But as the sweet scent of blooming flowers enveloped her, she paused in astonishment.

"What has happened?" she whispered.

"We have been doing a bit of cleaning," Richmond said, coming up behind her. "I discovered the original plans for the conservatory in a collection of maps and blueprints among my father's papers. Hedgley and I hired a few fellows from the village and set them to work. What do you think?"

"But you . . . but . . . oh, it is lovely!"

She gazed at the glorious array of misty green ferns, tumbling ivies, glowing white camellias, fragrant gardenias, and a hundred other blossoms she could hardly begin to name. Tucked into secret corners, massed in vibrant arrays, or lined up in neat rows grew orchids and lilies and strange hybrids in brilliant shades of red, pink, orange, and violet. Lemons and oranges seemed suddenly to have sprouted on trees that had emerged from the tangle of honeysuckle vines. Baskets of ripe strawberries hung like rubied lamps from chains attached to the ceiling. And far away in the heights of the conservatory, bright new glass panes gleamed in the summer sunshine. Ivy caught her breath as she turned in wonder to the tall young man who had wrought this transformation.

"Mr. Richmond," she whispered, "you have brought the conservatory back to life!"

He laughed. "I thought it a shame to let the place crumble away. A lovely lady's sharp reprimand has rung in my ears like a clanging gong. 'You are a bad man,' she said to me. 'You care nothing for England, for your family home, or for all the people who depend upon your charity for their sustenance.' "

Ivy flushed at the exact repetition of her accusations on their first meeting. "Please, sir, I had no intention of —"

"Oh yes you did. You meant to rake me over the coals of my own indifference, and you did it brilliantly. When my father handed me the title to this estate on my own coming of age, I thought it a strange gift of little value. I had hoped for a ship."

"I should have wished for a ship too," Clemma said. "Who would want a bit of old Yorkshire for a birthday present?"

"I am very glad to have this bit of old Yorkshire, dear Clemma, though it has taken me some time to admit it." He brushed past Ivy and strolled down the clean sanded path between two rows of potted boxwoods that had been pruned into clever green squares, orbs, and cones. Holding out his hands, he gestured at the lush array of growing things. "I like Yorkshire," he said. "And I adore Longley Park. May I ask you ladies to accompany me on a picnic? I have ordered a lunch to be brought into the newly arranged dining area, and it will be no trouble to set two more places."

Ivy let out a little sigh as Clemma began to skip up and down, crying out, "Yes, oh yes! I long for a picnic!"

"Really, Mr. Richmond," Ivy said, "I do think we should be getting back to Brooking House. It is most urgent that I speak with Mr. Hedgley, and then I —"

"It is more urgent that you speak with me, madam," he interrupted. "I have news that you will very much want to hear."

"News?"

"Indeed, for I have lately called upon Mr. John Frith, and I believe you will find the subject of our conversation most interesting."

"Oh dear," she said softly.

"I shall take that as an acceptance of my invitation." He gave Clemma a wink. "Come and see this chaffinch nest, Miss Clementine. You must give me a count of the eggs, for I am most particularly concerned that not a single one be disturbed until they hatch."

Ten

He did not really want to tell Ivy the news, Colin conceded as he sat opposite her during their picnic lunch. It was not good news. Not for himself, at any rate. He could not be sure how she would take it.

Delighted and surprised to find her walking in Longley Park, he had said the first thing that came to his mind to woo her into spending a few more minutes in his company. Even this.

"So, you have met with Mr. Frith," Ivy said after Clemma wandered away to watch the workers laying new water pipes. "And — in regard to the situation at hand — how did you find him?"

"Willing."

He leaned back in the wicker chair and regarded the young woman across the table. Ivy was even more lovely than he remembered, her cheeks aglow from the exercise of her journey and her brown eyes bright with intelligence. Once she had removed her straw bonnet, he was able to drink in the sight of those lustrous waves of rich bronze hair. As he observed the artful braids and curls, Colin recalled clearly the moment in this very conservatory when she had pulled the pins from her tresses and let them tumble to her waist. Even now, when any hope of a connection between them seemed impossible, he found himself longing to reach out and touch her soft hair.

But she was skittish today, and he had no doubt that any such boldness on his part would send her scampering back to the imagined safety of Brooking House. Wearing a pale muslin dress scattered with sprigs of tiny pink flowers, she appeared fragile, even a little childlike. Her large eyes were filled with innocence, dismay, and perhaps fear.

"In what manner is Mr. Frith willing?" she asked.

"He is willing to undertake the marriage. Of course, he would like to meet you first. To that end, he has added your name to the list of invited guests for a dance he will be hosting on the thirteenth of this month."

"Alone, I am to meet this man?"

"The Bowdens have been invited as well," he said. "And I shall be in attendance."

Her shoulders sagged a little as she let out a breath of relief. "Was your opinion of Mr. Frith altered in any way during this meeting? You had told me earlier that his reputation is less than spotless."

"I believe he will live up to all your expectations."

"But not my hopes?"

Colin shrugged. "If you hope for an amiable husband, one who makes it his aim to find pleasure wherever he may, one who claims hundreds of friends, and one for whom an entire night of dancing is a mountaintop experience, then your hopes may be fulfilled."

She looked down at her lap. "What of his appearance?"

"It is acceptable, I suppose, though I am hardly an expert in determining the qualities of a man's countenance. My ability to judge a woman's beauty is much more highly refined."

At this, she lifted her head, her eyes deepening in understanding. A faint pink flush spread across her cheeks, and she glanced away, as if anxious to see what had become of Clemma.

"Frith is a jolly fellow," he went on, "eager to laugh and quick to change every subject into a topic that is light and silly. I think you can hardly fail to like him, and once I told him about your character and charm, he grew very eager to meet you."

"It is the money, of course. I have no romantic illusions, Mr. Richmond." She shook her head slightly. "My own desires in a husband have little bearing on this matter. I must choose between the will of two fathers — one living and the other dead. And I must choose between two husbands — one filled with venom and bile, the other with wine and hot air."

Colin could hardly help but laugh at her description of Frith, for it was very close to truth. But as he thought of her future, he sobered. "Your husband will not hinder you from your ambitions, Miss Bowden. If you wish to continue in the good deeds that have so benefited the people of Wharfedale, Frith will certainly allow it. I believe he will permit you almost anything — so long as you return the favor."

"And allow him to continue in his licentious ways?" She regarded Colin evenly. "That is what you mean, is it not? The more I distance myself from my husband — permitting him every freedom he has enjoyed as a bachelor — the better off I shall be. But you believe that this is not a terrible fate, for I shall have my way in every other matter. I shall be able to tend the poor and ill, read long hours in the library, take walks across the moorlands, and even spend many days of each year in the company of the Bowdens. And this is all I am to wish for in a marriage."

"What more, dear lady? A man and woman can hope for mutual respect in a marriage. Fulfillment in career and leisurely occupations. Children, I suppose. Surely you do not believe in any romantic notions — love and passion and all that. You are too levelheaded, I think."

He felt anything but levelheaded as he waited for her response. Were she to say that she longed for passion and romance, he hardly knew what he might do next. Most likely, he would be unable to keep from sweeping her into his arms, carrying her away to the nearest vicar, and insisting on an immediate wedding. True love — a raging fire that nothing could quench — was the only thing that could impel him to the altar. But Ivy was not as impulsive as he. Any heedless whims she might feel were kept under close rein by duty and reason. And perhaps the intensity of emotion he felt each time he looked into her eyes was not mirrored in her own heart.

"I am indeed a levelheaded woman," she

said. "I realize the flames of passion may not burn forever between a man and his wife. But I am not so practical that I have a heart of stone. A marriage without true love cannot be happy. If a husband continues his bachelor ways and a wife goes on about her occupations as though nothing has changed, there can be no joy, no blessing in the union. And yet, you expect me to enter into such an arrangement without the least hesitation. The only pleasure I am to give my husband is a vast sum of money to spend at will. And the only happiness I may hope for from him is the freedom to live an independent life and to enjoy the possibility of children. But between the two of us — in the passing hours of our daily lives — there will be nothing. Emptiness! And with this arrangement I am supposed to be pleased?"

"Most women would be."

"I am not most women."

"No, indeed." He smiled, encouraged by the ire his news had provoked in her. Unlike ladies of Colin's past acquaintance, Ivy had strong opinions and a streak of willful determination. While she might keep her passions under strict control, she freely exercised her intelligence and singleness of mind. And this pleased him greatly.

229

"But you baffle me," he spoke up again. "Describe the sort of marriage you would choose to undertake, for I cannot imagine it."

"Again you tease me, sir, for there is no purpose in such an exercise. You know I am to marry John Frith or Nigel Creeve, and in neither of them have I any hope of finding joy. Tell me — have you managed to dissuade Mr. Creeve from his determination to have my money?"

"I fear not. He sent his barrister from Leeds to Longley Park to speak with me about the matter. It seems my former schoolmate is most avid in his intentions toward you. But you have changed the subject, and I was not finished discussing it. I beg you to tell me, Miss Bowden, of your ideal marriage."

She shifted on the chair and began to fold her napkin into an ever smaller square. "If I must spend my life with a man for whom I have no affection, I should at least hope to find him amiable. You must see to it that Mr. Creeve relents, sir. I beg you. I cannot bear the thought of living under the menace of his glowering face until I am an old woman. I shall go and meet Mr. Frith at his dance. You say he is friendly and pleasant, and despite his dissolute character, he must be my choice."

"But you have not yet answered my question, Miss Bowden." He leaned forward and took her hand in his. "Describe this marriage of 'true love' you long for. Enlighten me, please, for I am completely at sea on this subject."

"You are persistent in this line of questioning, Mr. Richmond."

"Indeed I am."

"Very well, then." She swallowed hard, and he could feel her fingers trembling ever so slightly in his palm. "I believe that an ideal marriage — a truly perfect union of two hearts — must be modeled after the pattern laid out in the Bible."

"In the Bible?" He could have fallen out of his chair at the unexpectedness of her comment. Had she spoken of pleasure-filled days and passionate nights, he would have demanded that she cast aside all her obligations to her dead and living fathers, all attachment to the fortune she had inherited, all submissive intention of marrying a man she could never love. He would have insisted that she come away with him. He could provide for her — certainly he was wealthy enough.

But in his boundless desire for this

woman, he had nearly staggered right off the path of his Christian faith! How had he managed to be so easily led astray? And how could he rectify his missteps?

"Do you read the Bible, Mr. Richmond?" she asked in her gentle voice.

Colin shifted in his chair. "Of course I do. I began at once upon my conversion. I have read the first seven books in their entirety." He paused. "But of late, I confess I have been much occupied with restorations to Longley, with my obligation to my father concerning you, and with my own restless thoughts. I have neglected my study of Scripture."

"I have found that such neglect is always to my detriment. 'Draw nigh to God,' the apostle James wrote, 'and he will draw nigh to you.' God is always seeking us, Mr. Richmond. But when we fail to seek him in return, we cannot know the joy of his presence. That is the hope I take in the prospect of my marriage to Mr. Frith — that God will be with me, leading me, and giving me strength even in the midst of a situation that might seem intolerable."

"Would a God who truly loves you allow such an intolerable situation?"

"Oh dear, I can see that you have entirely neglected the New Testament, Mr.

232

Richmond. Christians find themselves in unbearable situations all the time! The apostle Paul wrote to the Corinthians: 'Of the Jews five times received I forty stripes save one. Thrice was I beaten with rods, once was I stoned, thrice I suffered shipwreck, a night and a day I have been in the deep; in journeyings often, in perils of waters, in perils of robbers, in perils by mine own countrymen, in perils by the heathen, in perils in the city, in perils in the wilderness, in perils in the sea —' "

"Good gracious," Colin exclaimed. "All that?"

" 'In perils among false brethren; in weariness and painfulness, in watchings often, in hunger and thirst, in fastings often, in cold and nakedness' . . . well, he goes on and on. But at the end of his list of sufferings, Paul says, 'I take pleasure in infirmities, in reproaches, in necessities, in persecutions, in distresses for Christ's sake: for when I am weak, then am I strong.' "

"You believe, then, that this marriage you must undertake is to be done for Christ's sake?"

She sighed. "I undertake it for the sake of my two fathers and for all the people who so desperately need my money. I can

233

see no other way, and therefore, I cast myself upon the mercy of Christ, praying that . . . that . . ."

Her voice quavered, and she drew her hand from his in search of a handkerchief. "I am *not* going to cry over this," she announced as a tear rolled down her cheek. "If Paul suffered, think how much more Christ suffered in dying for me! He did not wish for such a cruel end to his life — and yet he cried out to God, 'Nevertheless not my will, but thine, be done.' And that is all I can do, Mr. Richmond. I can cry out to God and pray that his will is done in this issue."

Fearful that his heart would break, Colin left his chair and went to the side of the young woman. Kneeling near her, he took her hand again and pressed it to his lips. "What can I do for you?" he said. "I have brought this great suffering into your life, and I must find some way to relieve your agony."

"You can do nothing, save to spare me from the clutches of Mr. Creeve. If I must live in misery, let it not be with a cruel man. I can much better endure the infidelities and excesses of a silly one."

Her hand tightened on his fingers as her eyes searched his. "And I beg you, Mr.

Richmond," she went on, "please do not kiss me again. Please do not say kind words, solicitous phrases, admiring comments. You tease me and flatter me and in every way seek to draw me to you. I have turned this matter over and over as to the reasons for your actions. Perhaps it is some kind of game you play, some interesting pastime to entertain yourself. But I must be bold with you. I cannot bear it!"

"Forgive me, but I swear to you that nothing I have said is intended to distress you. From the moment I met you, I began to tumble headlong into a tangle of emotions from which I cannot extricate myself. I have come from India with the express intent of marrying you off to a worthless man. Yet, you are so beautiful and so good — such an admirable woman in every way — that I find my task all but impossible. I find, in fact, that the only man I can bear to think of you marrying . . . is me."

"Mr. Richmond!" Ivy caught her breath in a gasp.

"It is true." Agitated, he stood and began to pace the marbled walkway near the wrought-iron table. "I, who deserve no good reward in this life, whose behavior to this point merits only censure, I somehow have come to believe in a future for us. I love you. How it has happened, I do not know, but it is the absolute truth. Until I met you, I loved no one but myself. I thought only of my own best interests. And now that I know I love you, I am compelled to think of you first! Your own needs suddenly rank above my own — a most extraordinary situation, I assure you! *But what does she need?* I ask myself again and again. There is a vain part of me that is convinced I am all you could ever need. I should simply whisk you away to India, and we would live in great joy for the rest of our lives. But another part of me — and I greatly fear this is the side of my nature that is truly surrendered to Christ — knows you are under obligations far beyond the simple pursuit of marriage to a shallow and selfish man like myself. I think of your dedication to the Bowden family, of your commitment to the people of Otley and the moorlands, of your determination to do God's bidding. And then I know I must turn and walk away from you. That is what I must do. That is what I shall do!"

"What will you do, Mr. Richmond?" Clemma asked, skipping toward them between the rows of potted boxwoods. "You have done so many things already! Oh, Ivy, you must come and see the pipes! The water is going to come down from the Chevin to the waterworks just below Danfield Wood, and then to Longley Park, and then straight along these very pipes into the conservatory! It is a most wondrous thing!"

His chest filled with vexation and unrest, Colin stared at the little girl with her bright blue eyes and golden curls. He had just confessed his love for a woman he could never have. He had spilled out his heart to a lady who had expressed not even the slightest affection for him. He had prostrated and humbled himself before her as he had never done for any creature in his life. What a fool he was!

"Come, Miss Clemma," he said, forcing a note of jaunty detachment into his voice. He walked quickly away from Ivy without so much as a glance back to excuse himself from her presence. He didn't dare. "I must show you something at once."

"But I wanted Ivy to see the water pipes. She will find them truly wonderful."

"What I have to show you is far more wonderful than water pipes. You see, when I was a boy staying here at Longley Park one holiday from school, I discovered a small tunnel in the southeast corner of the conservatory. It should be just your size and quite mysterious enough to delight you as it did me."

"A tunnel!" Clemma took his hand and hopped along on one foot beside him. "I love tunnels!"

"So do I, dear girl. So do I." As they neared the far end of the building, Colin ventured a look through the tangle of philodendrons and ferns. Still seated at the small iron table, Ivy had thrown back her head and was gazing upward through the glass panes at a flock of jackdaws soaring freely across the blue Yorkshire sky.

"Ah, there ye be!" Mr. Hedgley tottered up to the table. "And how fares me ivy these days?"

"I am quite well, thank you," Ivy said, "though there is a matter I must discuss with you, sir."

He laughed. "But I was askin' about that wee sprig of a vine I gave ye. Did ye plant it?"

"Oh, that ivy." Flustered, she rose from the chair and gave the elderly man a brief curtsy. "Forgive me. Yes, I did plant it beside a stone wall on our property."

"Very good! And now it will be climbin' up that wall, clingin' to the rock — just as we are to cling to t' rock of our salvation!"

"Yes . . . well, but I'm sorry to say that I have not gone back to tend it. I have been busy with all sorts of —"

"Ye 'aven't tended it?" He scratched the bald patch on his head. "But that's why I give it in t' first place. I wanted ye to watch it grow."

"I am very sorry, Mr. Hedgley. You must understand that things have been difficult of late."

"But a thing untended canna grow well, miss! Did I not tell ye that? Look 'ere at what Mr. Richmond is doin' with his property. 'e's tendin' it, and see what's become of t' growin' things?" He spread out his arms and turned around in wonder at the transformation in the conservatory. "It's a miracle!"

Ivy could not help but smile at his joy. "Indeed, it is very lovely."

"As that wee sprig of ivy might be if ye tended it." He held up a gnarled finger. "Now go and 'ave a look at it, lass. Take care of it, just as ye would take care of yer own self."

"Take care of myself?" She shook her head. "That is a grand joke, sir, for I find that my life is entirely out of my own hands. I am at the whim of everyone who claims a part of me. And you, Mr.

239

Hedgley, I hold partly responsible for this turn of affairs."

"Me? What 'ave I done?"

"You knew Mr. Richmond had come from India, and I believe you must have learned the purpose of his mission. Now everyone in Wharfedale has heard that I am to inherit a fortune, and they all believe themselves entitled to some of it! Am I wrong?"

"Wrong to share yer money with t' poor and sick and starvin'? Aw, lass, ye been so kind to all of us through t' years, how can we 'elp but dream ye might continue that goodness?"

"But you had no right to spread that information!" Growing more agitated, she shook her hands at him. "I do not want to marry Mr. Frith! And I do not want all that money!"

"No?"

"No!" She grabbed her bonnet from the table. "But I shall do it because I know I must . . . because it is God's will . . . and because I have no choice . . . no hope . . ."

"Ooh, dear. Yer in a bit of a flutter now, ain't ye?"

"You would be, too, Mr. Hedgley, if you had gone about all your life thinking one thing and then learning it was all counterfeit! Nothing is right these days. Every-thing is topsy-turvy. I cannot even bring a tonic for your cough without learning it was a fishbone caught in your throat in-stead!"

"Is that why ye came 'ere? Ah, Angel of t' Moors, at her godly labors again."

"Do not call me that, I beg you! I am not an angel. I am merely a woman who . . . who cannot know which way to turn . . . who wishes for one thing but must do another . . . everything is going wrong . . . everything is a horrid mess and a terrible confusion —"

"There, there," he said, patting her on the back. "Come and see what old 'edgley will show ye now. Mr. Richmond 'ad this wee beauty brought all t' way 'ere from London. It were growed by a botanist name of William Forsyth, and ye'll not find but a few of 'em in all England."

He led Ivy to a small potted shrub with long stems on which perched bright yellow, bell-shaped flowers.

"It's a part of t' olive family," the gar-dener explained. "But it don't make olives. No, it's pure ornamental."

"It is lovely," Ivy said. "Quite magnifi-cent."

"Forsythia is t' name. And allow me to

tell ye sommat about this lovely lady. See these long limbs 'ere? They swoop down to t' ground and take root. And that's 'ow we can start wee forsythia bushes of our own. Babies, so to speak."

"Ah." Ivy found herself drawn to the old man in spite of her aggravation. "A new plant will spring up?"

"Aye, lass. But not if we don't take care of this one 'ere. Our Miss Forsythia canna do a bloomin' thing if we let 'er wither away, can she? She'll produce not a single new bush, not t' smallest of flowers. Nor will you be able to accomplish nothin', dear Miss Ivy, if ye don't take care of yerself."

"But of course, I take care of myself, Mr. Hedgley. I eat. I bathe. I dress warmly on cold days —"

"Them deeds is for t' body, not t' soul. Ye must feed yer soul, Miss Ivy. Pluck away t' weeds of worry, bitterness, jealousy." He bent and tugged out the tiny green sprigs of clover and dandelion that had sprung up around the base of the plant. Then he reached into a bucket and took out a handful of rich, black compost. As he spread it around the roots of the forsythia, he spoke softly. " 'Be of good cheer; thy sins be forgiven.' . . . 'Daughter, be of good

comfort; thy faith hath made thee whole.'
. . . 'Freely ye have received, freely give.'
. . . 'Fear ye not therefore, ye are of more
value than many sparrows.' . . . 'Come
unto me, all ye that labour and are heavy
laden, and I will give you rest.' "

Ivy watched the old man's gnarled fingers massage the compost into the com-
pacted soil around the little bush. Then he
took up a ladle and dipped it into a nearby
pail. Slowly he poured the water into the
dirt, soaking the roots through to their
tips.

"See what I mean, Miss Ivy?" he asked.
"Ye must cling to t' rock of yer salvation,
aye, indeed. But ye must also take care of
yerself as God intended. Be cheerful, be
comforted, fear not . . . and most of all,
dear lady . . . rest."

"Thank you, Mr. Hedgley. I shall remember what you have said."

"Now then —" he patted her on the arm
— " 'asn't God given ye this Mr. Frith to
marry? And 'asn't God given ye all that
grand fortune from India? Well, then, ye
must obey t' Lord and do what is right. Ye
must wed Mr. Frith and take that money
and do good with it. And do not worry
about nothin', for all will be well."

Ivy stared at the little forsythia, trying to

make the old gardener's words ring true. She could see now that in his words to believers, Jesus had given many admonitions to care for the soul. Despite all Ivy's rushing about the dales and fells to do good for others, she acknowledged that she had not done well in tending to her own needs.

But was Mr. Hedgley right about everything? Had Christ truly sent Mr. Frith for her to marry? Was God the source of all the great fortune from India? And if she must marry Mr. Frith, then why — oh why — had God allowed Colin Richmond to so possess her heart? Or was the great desire she felt for that man something that had come from Satan? Was it evil that she found him so kind and clever and witty and romantic and handsome . . . and every wonderful thing she had always longed for in a husband? Was it a sin that his confession of love had filled her heart with utter joy, that even now the very memory of his hand in hers brought tears to her eyes?

Oh, God, she lifted up, *where are you? What is right and what is wrong? And what am I to do?*

"Grow, Miss Ivy," Hedgley said, clapping her on the back. "Grow good and strong, ye 'ear me?"

As she nodded, a whoop echoed through the conservatory, sending all the nesting birds into the air with a screech. And then around a gigantic fern came Mr. Richmond himself, racing at top speed as he spun an iron hoop along the marble floor with a stick. Behind him, Clemma scampered as fast as her legs would take her, laughing as she tried to catch up.

"We found his hoop!" she cried as they barreled past Ivy and Mr. Hedgley. "We found it in the tunnel! But he will not give me a turn unless I can catch him. Come, Ivy, please help me catch Mr. Richmond!"

As the girl vanished down the row of boxwoods, Ivy glanced at Mr. Hedgley. He gave her a wink.

" 'Rejoice ye in that day,' " he said, " 'and leap for joy: for, behold, your reward is great in heaven.' "

Ivy took a deep breath. Then she picked up her skirts and ran like the wind. Her bonnet tumbled to the ground, and her pins fell from her hair, but she hardly cared. In no time, she had ascertained the direction of Mr. Richmond's course, and she swept quickly through a grove of potted palms straight into his path.

"Got you!" she cried, grabbing the stick from his hand and neatly whisking the hoop away down a row of blooming tropical orchids. "Clemma! Clemma, where are you?"

"Blast!" Richmond shouted as he stormed after Ivy. "That was a nasty trick!"

"Merely an ambush," she cried. Spotting Clemma's bouncing golden curls, Ivy wheeled the hoop to the little girl and set the stick in her hand just as Mr. Richmond bore down on them through an opening in a collection of bamboos. "Go, Clemma! Go! Run!"

Clapping her hands, Ivy squealed with delight as Clemma bounded away toward the opposite end of the conservatory. Richmond came to a stop at Ivy's side and drank down a deep breath.

"You have quite undone me, madam," he said with a laugh. He sobered as he took in her long flowing hair and rumpled gown. His eyes met hers and he took a step closer. "Indeed, I am most assuredly undone."

"The sentiment is quite mutual, sir," she said with a small curtsy. Then she forced herself to look away. "You must hurry, Mr. Richmond. Clemma will have your hoop halfway to Brooking House by now."

He hesitated only a moment before breaking away and vanishing back through the bamboos in the direction of the little girl.

Eleven

The town of Leeds lay but ten miles south of Otley, yet the journey proved arduous for the Bowden family. Ivy knew that the family's light carriage was unsuitable for traveling any great distance. The entire party, therefore, had to go into the village and wait at the White Horse Inn for the passenger coach. For all concerned, it proved a most lamentable situation indeed.

As they hurried along the lane into Otley, Mr. Bowden voiced much dread about the upcoming meeting with John Frith. Not only did Frith hail from a wretched family, but he was unlikely to be pleased to learn of Ivy's legal attachment to Nigel Creeves. With many lengthy quotes from John Milton, William Shakespeare, and the Bible to bolster his opinions, Papa expressed his deep fears about the Bowden family's prospects. Though Ivy tried to lighten his mood, he could not be encouraged. The coming events, he predicted, would be most dire.

As the family waited for the coach, Mrs. Bowden found her own reasons to lament. She complained of the fare of two shillings and sixpence that each member of her family had to pay for the excursion. Not only had they to spend such a great sum for the journey to Leeds, but they must pay the exact same amount all over again to return home to Otley. The turnpikes charged an outrageous amount, she opined, and for all they took in, they only managed to repair the roads by lining them with sandstone. When ground beneath wheels and hooves, it turned straight into sand and washed down the slopes of the Chevin at the first rainfall.

As the family entered the coach to begin the climb up the fells, Caroline and Madeline bemoaned the walk that awaited them. The steep parts of the road were impossible to navigate, even for the strongest horses. And so the able-bodied passengers were forced to get out and walk — which meant, unfortunately, that the young ladies must wear their boots rather than their slippers. A grave disappointment.

To Ivy's chagrin, even young Clementine managed to find something to rue. As the coach finally pulled into the outskirts of Leeds, she expressed her great misery in being required to give up three days for a party where she was not permitted to dance and a meeting she was not allowed to attend. How, she wondered aloud, would she fill her time when Leeds had nothing to boast of save the hundreds of cloth markets that lined its crowded and filthy streets?

Only Ivy endured the miles with anticipation, for she had made up her mind to love her new husband. If Mr. Frith was amiable and amusing, she would find what joy she could in his company. She would learn to delight in his parties and welcome his many friends. And eventually, they would have children in whom she could take the greatest pleasure. And most important, she would be fulfilling the terms of her late father's will and inheriting a fortune that could be used for good. Surely that must be what God wanted her to do.

Not only would she learn to love her husband, Ivy had decided, but she would use her money to become a patroness of all things worthy. There must be a hospital built for the care of the sick. An almshouse would feed the hungry. But she would not stop there. No, indeed, for conditions must be altered to benefit the common people of Yorkshire. The flocks of sheep must be built up and kept healthy. The worsted mills should be cleaned and better lit. And people had to find new forms of employment so they would not be forced to resort to poaching.

Ivy gazed out the window as the coach rattled along the cobbled street, and she felt her heart swell with gratitude. In the days since she had met with Mr. Richmond at Longley Park, she had managed to put him out of her mind almost entirely. Even his declaration of love she had relegated to the furthest recesses of her heart. She could not — would not! — allow herself to dwell on the man. Though she believed he had spoken the truth when he told her of his ardor, she knew she had no choice but to proceed on the path God had laid out for her. It was beginning to seem abundantly clear that Mr. Kingston's legacy must indeed be God's will. And Mr. Richmond must continue on his own path, a journey that soon would take him back to India.

In place of confusion, distress, and longing, Ivy filled her head with Scriptures and plans for the future. As Mr. Hedgley had instructed, she spent time resting, laughing at Clemma's antics, and stitching a lovely gown to wear to Mr. Frith's party.

Furthermore, she had walked into Otley on two occasions to meet with some of the village leaders. They were eager to speak with her even though she was a woman, because of what her wealth might do for the community. In all, she had decided, her situation could not be more advantageous, and God had blessed her greatly.

"Is that Mr. Frith's house?" Clemma cried suddenly into the silence of the coach. "But it is falling down!"

Ivy stiffened as everyone leaned toward the windows on the opposite side of the coach. No matter what the Frith house looked like, she told herself, she was not going to be disappointed. Rather, she would view anything negative as an opportunity to make pleasant changes. But as her sisters exclaimed in horror and Mama let out a groan of anguish, Ivy found herself drawn to the scene outside the window.

The drive into which the coach had pulled was lined with unkempt hedges whose stray limbs shot out in every direction like a bad haircut. The house itself, built of dark gray stone, seemed to stare at the approaching carriage through half-lidded eyes, its stone steps stretching into a bored frown, and its chimney leaning at a rakish angle. Chunks of mortar had fallen out from between the stones, and several glass panes were broken. Ivy tried not to gasp in dismay as she clutched her small handbag. Were there no draperies in the windows? no topiaries at the steps? no roses in the garden?

"Gracious!" Mama cried. "I cannot believe this man employs a gardener at all, for his pond is quite black with muck, and the shrubberies are altogether dead!"

"It is a horrid house," Clemma cried. "The stones in the walls are going to fall out, and the roof will come down! Oh, Ivy, you cannot live here!"

"I knew this would be a dreadful situation," Papa intoned. "The Friths were never known for any good thing. Wastrels, all of them."

"This is insupportable," Madeline muttered as she stepped out of the coach into a mud puddle. "I am utterly appalled."

Ivy breathed up her hundredth prayer for strength and courage. She left the coach and tried her best not to smell the overwhelming odor from the open sewer that ran down the nearby lane. Lifting her skirts, she climbed the stairs and pulled on the doorbell. In a moment, a young woman opened the door and peered out at the family gathered on the stoop.

"Eh? What ye want now?" she asked, her pale blue eyes blinking in the sunlight. "Me master ain't of a mind to talk to no creditors this mornin', so off with ye!"

Ivy stepped back in surprise as Papa took his place beside her. Was this young girl a maid? But where was her uniform? With frowzy hair and a poorly fitted gown that revealed a shocking display of décolletage, she looked more like a lady of the evening. And could it be possible that Mr. Frith employed no butler?

"We are the Bowden family," Papa said, enunciating clearly as though the girl might be deaf. "We have come from Otley to speak with Mr. Frith about the possibility of a forthcoming marriage to my daughter."

"Marriage?" The girl's eyes widened. "Can ye be serious?"

"Indeed, madam, and I am most earnest in my plea that we be allowed to escape the wretched stench of these streets and step inside the house!"

"All right then, laddie, follow me."

As the Bowden women trailed after their father down a long dark corridor, Ivy felt Clemma's hand slip into her own. "That woman called Papa 'laddie'! Is she the maid, Ivy? Why is her gown so low in front? Where is her uniform? I do not like this place. I want to go home!"

The girl, who introduced herself as Miss Smith, led the family into a front parlor, where they took seats on a set of faded red settees. As she lit the array of lamps, Miss Smith eyed the guests until her focus fell on Caroline.

"Be ye t' new bride?" she asked. "Mr. Frith will like ye well enough. 'e's fond of blondes." So saying, she gave her own pale tresses a tug. "I'll go and see if 'e's awake yet."

She managed a small curtsy before hurrying out into the corridor. Fearing suddenly that she might faint, Ivy let out a breath and searched through her bag for her fan. The room smelled of cigar smoke and stale perfume. Empty glasses littered the tables, a large purple stain covered the far end of the carpet, and the draperies that remained in the room hung from their rods by threads.

"I knew Nigel Creeve would be a better choice for Ivy," Papa muttered to Mama. "His home is very well kept. Very tidy, indeed, for Mrs. Creeve rules the household with an iron hand."

"How can Mr. Frith be hosting a party

tonight?" Mama whispered back. "It will take more than the whole afternoon to clean this one room! And did you hear the maid say she would see if he had arisen yet? What can he be doing still abed at this late hour of the day?"

"The Friths were known for their sloth. It is a wonder his father ever made a go of that business in India."

"This room smells bad," Clemma said.

"There are no fresh flowers," Madeline observed. "And no family portraits."

"No, but it is obvious they were all having a lovely time here," Caroline said. "I believe I should welcome a great company of friends, even if they left my home in a bit of a state."

"This parlor is fit for nothing but pigs," Maddie said.

"Madeline!" Ivy admonished the younger girl. "Such a thing to say about Mr. Frith's home!"

"I speak the truth. How can we be expected to stay here three days? I shall be bitten all over by bedbugs, and I fear we may be exposed to every sort of —"

"Welcome, welcome, one and all!" A slight young man with thinning brown hair and a broad grin walked into the room and spread his arms wide. "How marvelous to see you! The Bowden family, is it? What a fabulous surprise to have you drop in early! Allow me to introduce myself. I am John Frith, the owner of this lovely —" He paused and regarded the array of empty glasses strewn about the room. "Blast it all, Veronica has shown you into the gentlemen's parlor! My friends and I were up a bit late last night — discussing business and other matters, of course — and I'm afraid the maids have not had time to . . . well, never mind, for you are here, and I am very glad indeed to welcome you to Leeds and to my home!"

With a loud harrumph Papa rose, prompting the ladies to rise as well. "We are the Bowden family, sir, my wife and four daughters — Ivy, Caroline, Madeline, and Clementine. My sons, Hugh and James, are away at school."

Everyone bowed and curtsied as if they stood in a grand hall of the royal palace. Frith strode to the barren fireplace and propped his elbow beside a figurine of a lady whose head had been knocked off and now lay — Ivy noted — beneath the brown fronds of a very dead fern.

"Well, well, this is grand!" he said, his focus darting from one female Bowden to the next. "All of you at once. How fortunate! Richmond told me the whole story, of course, about the provisions of Mr. Kingston's will and all that. Odd that my father never mentioned such an agreement with his partner. On the other hand, I hardly knew my father — I was barely ten years old when he died, and he had been ill most of my life. He fell sick with something or other while living in India, you know. Ah, yes, well, of course you know, for I understand that Mr. Kingston died of the same sort of malicious fever. Dreadful place, India! I am glad I left it at a young age. Hot, they tell me. Very hot indeed!"

"I knew your father," Papa said. "He came to Otley now and again. A good friend of Justin Kingston, my wife's brother-in-law."

"You knew him! Magnificent! How grand!"

Ivy gazed at her intended husband, wondering if he always spoke in exclamations. Though she could find no fault in his appearance, she discovered that she was having a difficult time making herself fall in love with him at first sight, as she had planned to do. He did have nice teeth, very white and straight. Thin hair had never been a bother to her, though she usually liked it arranged a bit more tidily. And when he smiled, his eyes crinkled at the corners. A charming effect, she told herself. A very nice-looking man. And clearly an amiable personality. Perhaps she was managing to feel a little weakkneed over him, after all.

"Tea, then!" he said, rubbing his hands together. "We shall have tea and get to know one another better! Excuse me while I ring for the maid. Veronica? Where are you?"

As he hurried out of the room, Ivy felt every eye turn on her. She smiled. "He is quite . . . friendly. And . . . affable."

"I find him repugnant," Maddie said. "He had not even bothered to comb his hair."

"I do not like his house at all," Clemma added.

"I think him charming." Caroline rose and strolled to the window. "He smiles often and speaks in an elegant manner. His behavior is very gentlemanlike —"

"Gentlemanlike?" Maddie laughed in derision. "He lives in squalor. Papa is right. Ivy must not be forced to marry such a man. Mr. Creeve will do her better."

"Nigel Creeve is far too fastidious for my taste," Caroline said. "I like a man who enjoys life. I hope Ivy will marry Mr. Frith straightaway and then bring other such carefree men into our path."

"No, thank you!" Maddie crossed her arms. "I would not care to wed any such slovenly specimen of the male species. My advice to Ivy is this: do not marry him!"

"No, please!" Clemma cried. "I would not marry him for all the world."

"I must marry him to get my two hundred thousand pounds," Ivy said in a low voice. "And that matter is settled."

"Now then, dear girl," Papa said. "You make it sound as though you are being sold into bond slavery. Surely it cannot be so bad as that."

"No indeed, Ivy, for think what you can do with such a grand sum." Mama reached over and patted her on the arm. "This house might become a real beauty, if you engaged a good gardener and several reliable maids. I should dismiss Miss Smith straightaway, I assure you, but certainly there are many good girls in Leeds who would welcome the opportunity for reputable employment."

"And do not forget," Caroline said, "Mr. Richmond instructed you to purchase property of your own, Ivy. If I were you, I should buy a grand country house and invite all my friends out for shooting parties and dances. Can you imagine owning a town house and a country house? Ooh, I must say I envy you."

Ivy tried to look happy. "I am quite certain a few coats of paint and some new carpets will set this place to rights. Caroline, perhaps you will help me select fabric for the draperies — you are so clever with colors. And Madeline, we shall need to have a fine library here. Will you assist me in building a good collection of books?"

"Only after the walls are painted and the beds rid of bugs."

"What can I do to help?" Clemma asked. "I want to do something for you, Ivy!"

"You must see to the pond, Clemma. I want it well cleaned and stocked with all sorts of lovely fish. And as you are such an expert on polliwogs, perhaps you might reward us with a nice array of frogs to serenade us in the evenings. I am ever so fond of a good chorus of croaks."

"Oh, I beg your pardon." Colin Richmond suddenly appeared in the doorway and stopped in surprise. "Good afternoon, Mr. Bowden . . . ladies. I had not been told you were to come to town early."

"Dear me," Papa said, rising to greet the newcomer. "What are you doing in Leeds,

Mr. Richmond? We had not thought to see you until tonight."

"I came to speak to John Frith, sir. I bring news." Richmond glanced at Ivy, who realized to her dismay that she had been gawking at the man like a silly schoolgirl. He nodded to her, then returned his attention to Mr. Bowden. "Sir, may I ask what has brought you to town at this hour?"

"I thought . . ." Papa cleared his throat. "I thought it might be a good idea to meet this Frith fellow before the party. A private setting, you know. Ivy should not be introduced to her future husband at a public event. And . . . well, I hoped we might find him open to discussion regarding the future of our daughter."

"You were hoping to dissuade him from the marriage," Richmond said. "But I fear you are out of luck there. Frith will not be dissuaded. One look at what he has to lose should tell you why."

Ivy shivered suddenly, wondering if Mr. Richmond might say publicly such things as he had said before about her — might mention her eyes, her figure, her skin. Might he actually speak such flatteries in front of Papa? Might he let his own feelings about her be known?

261

"Indeed," Richmond went on. "Frith is wholly committed to the idea of marriage, and the reason is obvious. He needs the money."

Ivy squared her shoulders, annoyed at the bluntness of his statement. Long ago, she had recognized Mr. Richmond's lack of elegant manners and his tendency to speak his mind. She had chalked up his behavior to years spent at sea and away from good society. But she had never thought him rude.

"Money or not, Mr. Richmond," she said, "it is clear that Mr. Frith and I shall make an acceptable match. You were correct in your assessment of him. He is amiable and will make me a suitable husband."

"Did I tell you he would make a suitable husband?" His brown eyes gazed into hers. "I do not recall that."

"Perhaps not," she conceded. "But I am determined to do the will of my late father and make a success of this arrangement. It is to the benefit of all concerned."

"I am glad to see that your character has not altered since our last encounter. You will need that stiff spine, dear lady, for Mr. Creeve has just sent me a ruling that was handed down from a local judge." He displayed a rolled sheet of parchment. "It seems that Creeve's agreement with Mr. Bowden stands, and he wishes to marry you on the day before your twenty-first birthday."

"Tea, then!" To the consternation and surprise of all in the room, Mr. Frith appeared carrying the tray of tea things *himself*. "The maid seems to have gone out, and I don't mind puttering about in the kitchen. Ah, Richmond, I see you have arrived for our meeting! And what do you suppose, but that the Bowdens are here as well. Fortuitous, eh? We shall just get on with the matter today and be done with it!"

Ivy gazed in horror at the badly stained teacups her future husband set about on the table. The tip of the teapot's spout had been knocked cleanly away, leaving a ridge of exposed pottery over which the tea must be poured. There was a plate of small cakes, three to be exact, and they appeared to be at least a week old. Mr. Frith hastily meted out the tea, spilling much of it into the saucers. Then he dropped in lumps of sugar left and right, and used a single spoon to stir every cup. There was not a pitcher of milk in sight.

Flipping back his coattails, he dropped onto a settee and regarded his guests with an enormous grin. "So, which of you lovely ladies is to be my lucky bride?"

A moment of utter silence followed, after which Mr. Richmond rose. "I am pleased to present to you Miss Ivy Bowden," he said. "She is the daughter of Justin Kingston and his wife, Rosemary, though as you know, she was brought up mainly here in Yorkshire as the daughter of Mr. and Mrs. Bowden."

Mr. Frith's face sobered only slightly as he took in the appearance of his intended wife. "Capital!" he cried. "So pleased to make your acquaintance, Miss Bowden. I do look forward to the many happy years we shall spend together as husband and wife."

Ivy tried to make herself smile. "Thank you, Mr. Frith. I am honored."

"Nonsense, for I am the glad recipient not only of a lovely young wife but also of a vast fortune! It seems the gods smile upon me, eh?" Laughing, he glanced around him. "And of course your family is welcome here at any time! I am an eager host, you will find — especially when the guests are such pretty girls!"

Caroline giggled, while Madeline let out an audible groan. Ivy forced down a sip of the tepid tea, and for fortitude, she silently began repeating every verse of Scripture she had memorized: *"The Lord is my shepherd; I shall not want."* . . . *"Study to shew thyself approved unto God, a workman that needeth not be ashamed."* . . . *"Honour thy father and thy mother: that thy days may be . . ."* may be what? Why couldn't she remember the rest of the verse?

Mr. Richmond was unrolling the judgment and showing it to Mr. Frith and Mr. Bowden. Ivy searched through her mind. *"That thy days may be . . ."* happy? blessed? fulfilling? And now Mr. Frith was expressing his deep unhappiness that Mr. Bowden had entered into such an agreement with Mr. Creeve. *"Honour thy father and thy mother"* . . . but who were her father and mother? Ivy wondered. And what good would it do her to honor them? *"That thy days may be . . . that thy days may be long!"*

"Oh no," she muttered, just loudly enough that everyone turned to look at her. She grabbed the spoon and gave her tea another good stirring. She did not want long days upon the earth — not if those days must be spent with Mr. Creeve or Mr. Frith!

Any man who could not serve a decent cup of tea was not fit to be a husband. And that was all there was to it!

Ivy clasped her hands together and fought the urge to race out of the dilapidated house, leap over the open sewers, and run all the way back up the Chevin where she might at least have clean air to breathe. She looked across the room at Mr. Richmond, who apparently was intent upon the heated conversation between the other two men.

He did not love her — not truly — or he would never continue to insist upon a marriage that could only make her miserable. He was not her admirer, not even her friend. He was, in fact, the source of all her troubles.

"Then I shall take the entire set of documents to London," Richmond said finally. "The dispute must go before a higher court. The ruling will doubtless fall in your favor, Frith, and I trust you will make yourself worthy of the responsibility of this undertaking."

"Oh, of course! Certainly!" He glanced at Ivy again, smiling broadly. "I am thinking of engaging an advisor . . . someone who can help me manage this money in a prudent way. Responsibility is quite the thing! Yes, indeed!"

"That has been seen to already," Richmond said. "You will receive a generous allowance. The remainder of the funds, as Mr. Kingston requested, will be invested in various enterprises."

"An allowance?" Frith frowned, for once unable to summon a joyful exclamation. "But you say it is generous?"

"Quite. You will be pleased."

Frith sat back in his chair and beamed at Mr. Richmond. Papa ran his finger around the inside of his stiff collar, clearly agitated at this turn of events. It appeared his hopes to unite Ivy with Mr. Creeve were dimming. Feeling very much like a pawn in a game of chess, Ivy realized she was suddenly very close to tears. In all of this great discussion, she did not matter at all. Money mattered. Men mattered. The law mattered. But the single female upon whom the entire event turned did not occasion even a brief mention or glance.

Why did she care so much about herself? Ivy wondered. She knew she must tend to her own needs, as Mr. Hedgley had cautioned. But God had never intended for any human to be elevated. In fact, Christians were instructed to act as servants. So why was it difficult to be obedient? Why could she not simply bow to the will of all these men? Why did she want to scream and shake her fists in their faces?

Fearing she might lose control, Ivy swallowed as Papa turned the conversation in a new direction. "I wonder, Mr. Frith," he said, "if provision might be made for the care of my family. You see, we have exhausted all our resources in the . . ."

Ivy could not listen to this. Losing faith in his future with Mr. Creeve, Papa was now working hard to secure a promise of financial assistance from Mr. Frith. Had he not heard her when she told him she would care for the Bowden family? Or did he believe her so inconsequential as to have no influence on the spending of her own fortune?

"Excuse me," Ivy said softly. She stood, garnering a hasty round of bows from the gentlemen in the room. "I believe I shall walk about the gardens."

With a tip of her head, she hurried out of the room and down the corridor to the foyer. But the moment she stepped outside, she realized a walk in the gardens was no pleasure in Leeds. A nauseating stench slammed into her face, and she recoiled in horror. Shutting the front door again, she made her way down another corridor of the house, in hope of finding an empty drawing room in which to rest.

Never had she witnessed such an appalling lack of care as this poor house had suffered under its owner. Beds were unmade, carpets rumpled, draperies torn, candles burned to the bottom of their wicks, tables overturned, and upholstery gnawed by mice. She slipped into a small room that might once have been a library. Books lay scattered on the floor, dust covered every shelf, and paintings of a most audacious nature lined the walls.

Sinking to her knees, Ivy laid her hands on a chair and began to pray. How could her once carefree and happy life have come to this? What could God be intending for her? Was she to submit to every creature who tugged on her arm and asked for a bit of her money? *Oh, dear Lord, why have you given me this future? I cannot bear it! I cannot endure!*

Unable to express her anguish further, she leaned her head upon her hands and began to weep. The Holy Spirit, who dwelled inside her, knew her torment and would cry out on her behalf to God the Father. She must trust that, for she had no one left on whom to rely.

Twelve

Feeling as if she were climbing to the platform of a guillotine, Ivy ascended the stairs that evening to the third-floor ballroom of the Frith house. Her new blue gown and favorite garnet necklace did nothing to give her confidence. Her determination to make the best of everything wavered with every step. Not even her short time of praying and weeping had done much to assuage her dread, for she knew that in these coming hours, she would learn the pattern of her future life. She would become acquainted with her future friends. And she would dance in the arms of her future husband.

"There she is!" Mr. Frith's loud cry and sudden lunge toward her nearly sent Ivy backward down the staircase. But before she could topple over, he grasped her hands and pulled her out into the middle of the crowded ballroom.

Surrounded instantly by unfamiliar faces, Ivy did her best to acknowledge the introductions to her fiancé's numerous friends. But where had manners gone? For these were neither Mr. and Mrs. So-and-So nor Lord and Lady Such-and-Such, but Tom, Mary, Will, Rupert, and Janet. Even more appalling were "good old Jack" and "naughty Nancy." And some of the assemblage had no proper names at all, but were introduced as Ruggles, Crackers, Jocko, and Colonel Curlytop. These people, it quickly became apparent, gathered at the Frith home two or three evenings a week for dances and parties. Invitations were not checked at the door, for none had been sent out. Miss Smith — or Veronica, as she was known — seemed the only female to fulfill the role of maid, and there were no butlers, footmen, or grooms.

As the introductions dwindled, Ivy managed to work herself away from Mr. Frith and his intimates and find a place along the wall of the large room. There she observed the gathering of musicians who were attempting to follow various editions of sheet music that did not seem to quite match. But no one cared, for as the dancing began in earnest, so did the flow of alcohol.

"Did you see the great quantities of wine and gin at the other end of the room?" Madeline whispered, a look of horror on her face as she joined Ivy. "They even have ale! I assure you, I have never seen so much liquor in all my life. It is a disgrace. And nothing is served on a tray, but each guest pours his own glass straight from the bottle. I declare, this is worse than a roadside tavern!"

"Maddie, lower your voice, I beg you." Ivy drew her fan from her bag and held it before her mouth to hide her words. "You must not speak ill of this gathering. This is to be my home, and these people are to be my society."

Madeline made a face. "I should never marry Mr. Frith. Have you not seen the bedrooms in this house? It looks like a brothel!"

Ivy whisked her fan shut and smacked Maddie on the arm. "Enough, Madeline! Would you have me estranged from these people and forced to live as an outcast among my husband's friends? Or would you prefer that I not marry him — and leave you and your family destitute?"

"*My* family?" Maddie's eyes went wide. "The Bowdens are *your* family too, Ivy!"

"Are you? I feel as if I belong nowhere and to no one. I serve no purpose in your life but to make you miserable with the company of my future husband. That, and by this marriage to provide for the Bowdens."

"That is not true. Though Caroline makes much of your change in relation to the Bowden family, Clemma and I view you as we always have — as our sister. And what is more, we wish only the best for you. As to the fact that we are now reliant on you for the provision of our needs, we trust that you will act as you always have, Ivy. You will do what is right."

"Thank you, Maddie. Your words are a comfort."

"But, Ivy, you must not marry Mr. Frith!" Madeline cried, clutching her sister's arm. "You must marry Mr. Creeve, for certainly he is far more tolerable."

"It is not my choice! Whichever man wins me in the courts of law is the one I must wed."

"But will you have no voice at all in your future? Surely God is not so harsh as to deprive you of the very brain he gave you! You must use your wisdom and judgment to make careful decisions. I cannot believe God would expect you to have no will of your own . . . to be a puppet or a . . . a . . ."

"A pawn? Indeed, I am a pawn in the game these men play with my life. I must confess, dear Maddie, that I have wondered on occasion whether I am but a pawn in God's hands as well!"

"Oh, Ivy, please —"

But her words were cut off as Mr. Frith suddenly caught Ivy by the hand and whirled her into the midst of the crowd again. Before she could think or act, she found herself thrown into a line of dancers and compelled to take her place opposite the man who would be her husband. As she attempted to work out her proper position in the configuration, she tried to concentrate, but all about her seemed utter confusion.

How different from this melee were the country dances at the assembly hall in Otley! Her society in that small village was made up of well-to-do burghers, a few members of the landed gentry, several mill and factory owners, and a smattering of others — the vicar, a barrister, and one actual lord. Though Ivy's friends were unsophisticated and simple people, they behaved with grace and decorum. They observed every small regulation of propriety. Dance cards were filled out, ladies were greeted with a bow, foul language was banished, and the smoking of cigars was restricted to a far drawing room.

Here in the home of John Frith, every

last shred of decency vanished beneath an assault of raucous laughter, a torrent of alcohol, and a wildness of behavior that shocked Ivy to her very core. The dancers hardly followed the proper steps, but reeled and frolicked about the room as though among a gathering of Greek nymphs and satyrs. Ivy tried to keep to the carefully memorized movements of the dance, but Mr. Frith spun her and whirled her and slung her about the room so violently that she thought she might become ill.

When the song finally ended, she clutched her stomach and hurried to her former place beside the wall. But solitude was not to be.

"Having a good time?" Frith cried above the roar in the room as he joined her. He leaned one shoulder against the wall, effectively trapping her. "You will find we are a jolly society here! A great deal of fun to be had in the evenings!"

Ivy did her best to focus on the man despite the spinning of her head. This was an opportunity to know him better, and she must take every advantage. "You have . . . you have dances often?"

"Nightly!" he shouted in her ear. He drew a large cigar from the pocket of his coat and proceeded to light it. "If we're not at my house, we all go over to Puggy's or Rupert's or someone else's. Colonel Curlytop puts on a grand show!"

"How fortunate for you."

"And for you! I cannot imagine how bored you must have been living in such a backward place as wee old Otley. Your sister, Caroline, has proclaimed it deadly dull! I say, she is a delightful girl, isn't she? I've had two dances with her already, and I wager she will not sit down a moment the entire evening! Quite popular already!"

"Ah," Ivy said, trying to spot Caroline among the revelers. She sincerely hoped the younger girl was behaving herself properly — though experience had taught her to fear the worst.

"We are very modern here, you'll find," Mr. Frith continued. "We give no thought to stiff regulation or piety. No, indeed! We are all of the philosophy that life is meant to be enjoyed! Would you not agree with that, Miss Bowden?"

Pleased that he had asked her a question, she drew out her fan in an attempt to keep his cigar smoke at bay. Perhaps now they might engage in an erudite discussion.

"I believe," she began, "that enjoyment

in life may have a different meaning to each of us."

"Really?" He scratched at the back of his neck. "And how is that? What do you take pleasure in?"

"I like to read."

"Books!" he exclaimed with a laugh. "I suspected you might be bookish! You have that look about you. Ah, well, you'll be welcome to bring a load of books here once we're married, though I doubt you'll find them of much use. Amid all our parties and gatherings, we have little time for dull activities. Not that I find reading boring, mind you! No, for I have read a book or two in my time. School, you know!"

"A book or two?" Ivy stared at the man in disbelief. Surely he was jesting. "But what do you do in the mornings?"

"Sleep, of course! We never go to bed until well after midnight. Often it is nearly dawn!"

"And in the afternoons? What do you do then?"

"Eat, I suppose. Got to pack it in sometime, eh? What about you?"

"In my free time I enjoy walking on the moorlands. I believe I have seen some of the most beautiful dawns from the top of the Chevin. There is nothing quite like the glorious array of gold and pink that fans out across the sky when —"

"I say, do you like this song? It's rather a new one — a bit of a jig, I think! The musicians learned it in London last month. Shall we have another trot round the dance floor?"

Ivy grasped at freedom. "Thank you, sir, but I fear I am rather tired this evening. The journey from Otley this morning was —"

"I should think it's all your gallivanting about on the Chevin at ungodly hours! Exhausting for anybody! Hey? Am I right?" He elbowed her and gave a hearty laugh. Then he doused his cigar in a half-full glass nearby and threw himself again into the fray.

Ivy stepped back and pressed her palms against the wall to hold herself upright. A glimpse of golden curls amid the dancers might have been Caroline. But where was Maddie? And what had become of Mama and Papa? Surely they would not abandon her here. The thought of it was too awful, and yet Ivy knew she must be abandoned altogether very soon. Once she was married, she would have no opportunity to run to the arms of Mama or listen to one of Papa's lengthy recitations, which now seemed so welcome, so sensible, so gentlemanlike and sober.

Quite certain she was becoming ill, Ivy clapped her hand over her mouth and turned toward the door. Her first step took her face forward, straight into the solid wall of a large man's chest. As her knees buckled, warm hands cupped her elbows and held her upright. Somehow a glass door swung open and a balcony appeared beneath her feet. And then, miracle of miracles, a draught of clean fresh air filled her lungs.

"Are you better now?"

She looked up to find Colin Richmond leaning against the iron railing of the balcony and regarding her with deepest concern. Nodding, she clasped the rail and drank down another breath.

"I feared I should be ill in there," she said. "And I could not imagine this to be any better. But the air outside . . . the smell is gone."

"A stiff breeze blows down from the fells on occasion and sends the odors east toward the ocean." He laughed. "I recall certain times aboard ship when I would have sworn I had caught a whiff of poor old Leeds."

Ivy studied him, the moonlight silvering

his dark hair and outlining the breadth of his shoulders. "I thought you went away to London today, Mr. Richmond," she whispered. "The documents. You were taking them to a judge in the city."

"I go tomorrow at sunrise. In the past weeks I have developed a great passion for riding across the Yorkshire moorlands at dawn. It has done much to quench my thirst for the sea. But tonight I thought it prudent to stop in at the dance and see how you were faring."

"I am well, of course." She gazed down at the darkened alley below and knew she could never be less than forthright with this man. "No, I am not, as you have seen for yourself."

"May I ask what has caused you such distress?" He paused only a moment. "But I need hear no answer, for I know you too well. The activities beyond that door repulse you to the very core of your being. You reject such a setting. You revile its participants. Your pure soul cannot bear the stench of such carnality."

Now it was her turn to chuckle. "Oh, dear, I fear you are ready to title me the Angel of the Moorlands once more. I assure you, sir, I am not so pure and perfect as I would wish. Or as I ought to be. But

280

you are correct in your estimation of my response to Mr. Frith's party. I have been in attendance for little more than an hour, and already I am at the end of my reserves. If one hour is too much, how am I to endure a lifetime of such excesses?"

"I confess, I cannot imagine it."

"But I sense that you feel no revulsion for such an event, and so perhaps I, too, shall become hardened eventually. Perhaps I shall even learn to enjoy my husband's friends and their pursuits of pleasure."

"I pray not." He folded his arms across his chest. "I feel little revulsion here, dear lady, only because I have seen much worse. Indeed, I have spent much of my own life in such pursuits — and have found them utterly futile. But I cannot revile the participants here tonight. I can only pity them. Mr. Frith and his friends live in emptiness, always seeking true joy and never finding it."

"You say you have found joy in your Christian faith. Perhaps Mr. Frith will, too."

"Perhaps. It is to be hoped." He regarded her. "I have wondered if God has placed you in Frith's path for the purpose of leading him to salvation."

Ivy shrugged. "You begin to sound very

much like your friend, the missionary. Mr. Richmond, I confess I do not begin to understand what God has planned for me. I know only that the father of my birth believed John Frith would make a good husband. He wished for the relationship of our families to continue many generations beyond his death. But he did not know the man inside that room."

"Nor did he know the woman you would become."

"What sort of woman am I, sir? I hardly know myself these days."

"You are perfect and pure and altogether without blemish —"

"Please, Mr. Richmond! At such false flattery, I am sorely tempted to topple you straight off this balcony."

"It is not flattery. And it is certainly not false."

"Then you think too highly of me, which does not speak well for the stability of your mental condition."

He laughed. "Well, you are the most perfect woman I have ever met. But it is not your perfection that delights me most. It is your stubbornness."

"Am I stubborn? I have always thought myself very compliant."

"Hardly! Dear lady, you have a will of

iron. You are, in fact, the most willful woman of my acquaintance."

"How can you say such a thing? I am not willful!"

"No? If you encounter a band of thieves on the lane, you rise to your sister's defense, never mind the consequences to yourself. If you make up your mind to walk the dales in the midst of a rainstorm — never mind that your entire family awaits you with great anxiety — you set off at once. And if you decide to submit yourself to the judgment of the English courts, it seems nothing can persuade you to change your mind. You will marry Mr. Creeve and live with his sour temperament until you have withered into nothing but a shaft of dry straw. Or you will marry Mr. Frith and suffer the indignities of his excesses until you fall into such revelries yourself or manage somehow to reform your husband entirely."

"You think it is my willful nature that compels me to marry one of these men?" She could hardly believe his intimation. "You are wrong indeed! I am neither stubborn nor filled with selfish willfulness. I am humble and meek, submitting my own desires to the will of God."

"The will of God? Miss Bowden, has

God truly willed you to marry one of those two devils?"

Taken aback, Ivy stiffened. "*You* are the one who brought the decree from India!"

"But I do not recall God's signature at the bottom of the document, madam. In fact, it seems to have been signed merely by a man named Justin Kingston and sealed by an Indian wallah."

"What are you saying, sir? Do you not believe I should obey my father's will?"

"Are you speaking of your heavenly Father or of Mr. Kingston?"

"Oh!" She wanted to screech at him. How dare he be so infuriating and obtuse? "I must do what Mr. Kingston wished, and you know it! You pressure me toward it yourself. If I do not marry, I shall never inherit the fortune — and then what is to become of everyone who relies upon it?"

"Do what you feel you must, dear lady. Only do not confuse the will of Justin Kingston with the will of God. I am beginning to believe they may be two very different things."

"But how am I to know God's will? I have always believed he uses the people around me to shape and guide my life. It was through Mr. Kingston's foresight that I spent my childhood in Mr. Bowden's home. And it is Mr. Bowden's guidance that has made me who I am. God has used these two men. Where should I look if not to them?"

He reached out and brushed a fallen curl from her shoulder. "A very wise — and I might add, very stubborn — young lady once informed me that I ought to look to the Bible for answers. 'Draw nigh to God,' she said, reminding me of the apostle James's words, 'and he will draw nigh to you.' "

"You believe God's will may be found in the Bible," she said. "But, oh dear, I fear I am far too weak in my understanding and far too confused and troubled to know where to begin my search. Certainly in the Scriptures there is no mention of a Mr. Creeve or a Mr. Frith —"

"But there is a great deal about marriage." As if on cue, he reached for the door and opened it to Mr. Frith himself, who came barreling out onto the balcony. "You challenged me to learn the nature of God's plan for marriage," Richmond continued as Frith slammed against the rails, "and I challenge you to learn the nature of God's will. Good evening, Frith. Come to take some air?"

"Oh, Richmond — you are here as well!

How glad I am to see you, for we've had a most wretched turn of events!"

"Is it Papa?" Ivy cried. "I knew he would never be able to endure —"

"It's that rotter Creeve!" Frith said. "He is press-trassing . . . trass-pessing . . . he's on my property! Inside there! Making a great muck of my pratty . . . prity —"

"Invaded your party, has he?" Richmond said. "I am hardly surprised, Frith. Did you not expect him to give you a run for your money?"

"For *my* money," Ivy corrected him. "Should I speak to him, Mr. Richmond?"

"I believe we must all have a bit of a tête-à-tête, or we shall never be rid of the fellow."

"I don't want to talk to him," Frith grumbled. "I think I should rather toss him out on his ear than have a vonger . . . sonk . . . songervation with him! And there you have it!"

"There, indeed," Richmond said. "But I am afraid we have no choice in the matter, for here he comes now." He opened the glass door to the second intruder. "Nigel Creeve, what a surprise."

"Nothing surprising about it," Creeve snarled as he stepped out onto the balcony. "Did you expect me to stand aside while a judge's orders are violated?"

"I beg your pardon, Mr. Creeve," Ivy said, "but no judge has forbidden me to attend parties."

"Ah, Miss Bowden." He gave her a stiff bow. "Good evening to you."

"And to you, sir." She curtsied.

"You are quite correct in what you say. Yet the judge has upheld my right to take you as my wife, and I find it reprehensible that you should fraternize with such a libertine as John Frith."

"Is it his character to which you object, sir?" Ivy asked. "Or is it his claim to my hand in marriage?"

"I am not a liberline . . . bilerteen . . ." Frith stammered. "Take it back, Creeve, or I shall be forced to challenge you to a duel."

"That would be quite a challenge." Creeve laughed derisively. "In your present state, I believe you would have great difficulty holding steady enough to spit off the Leeds Bridge."

"Blackguard!" Frith cried, lunging for his rival. "Out of my house! How dare you —"

"Stand back!" Creeve held up his hand to block the blow. "Vile worm!"

At the insult, Frith stepped up the assault as Creeve attempted to fend off the flailing fists. Ivy moved back against the railing of the small balcony, but to her horror, she saw Richmond insert himself into the fracas. With one hand he tried to keep Frith at bay, and with the other he pushed Creeve backward.

Unwilling to stand aside as the men wrestled, Ivy grabbed Creeve's coattails and tried to pull him back. As she struggled to hold the man, she saw a flash of metal. A pistol? Or a knife?

"Stop! Stop it at once," she cried in disbelief. "You go too far!"

"The woman is mine by rights!" Creeve shouted at Frith. "I have a judge's orders to prove —"

"Dash the judge and his orders!" Frith snarled. A swift punch landed on Creeve's jaw. "That's for your judge, and this is for your arrogance!"

Frith swung again, this time missing and spinning around on his heel in a dizzy circle. Ivy gasped as he tilted toward her. She reached out to steady him, but he crashed into her, forcing her back against the railing. Their combined weight caused the rusty iron to give way with a loud pop.

"Look out!" Richmond shouted, as the railing bent outward and Ivy and Frith began to sway backward, completely off balance. "Miss Bowden, take my hand!"

As the loose iron bars cut into her back, she stretched out her arms toward him. But Frith's weight pushed against her, and she could feel her body slipping into the gap where the railing had broken. Her shoulders squeezed through, and then her head snapped back.

Frith screamed, flailing for a grip to stop himself from falling. "Help!" he gasped. "Save me!"

"Ivy!" Richmond threw himself across her feet, wrapping his arm around her ankles as she dropped off the balcony. Her whole body swung free, swaying back and forth in the night air. Far beneath her, the cobblestones that lined the alley dipped and twirled in nauseating circles. Her mouth opened in a scream, but no sound emerged.

"Ivy, Ivy!"

Richmond's voice cut through her terror, and she finally understood that somehow, she was not falling. Somehow he was holding her. Somehow she was alive.

"Help me! Help!" Frith wailed. "I'm slipping! I can't stop myself!"

And then there was a silence. A choking silence as Ivy and Frith dangled in midair. They hung, helpless, for the space of a heartbeat before Frith was finally lifted away from her. Colin Richmond's hands drew Ivy up through the emptiness, raised her into the light, and carried her to safety.

As he cradled her tightly against his chest, the sound of screams and cries reached her ears. The ballroom doors were flung open, a blast of heated and perfumed air billowed out onto the balcony, and the crowd surged forward.

"Stand back!" Richmond bellowed as Ivy clung to him. Head forward and breathing hard, he stalked off the balcony and shouldered his way back into the ballroom. The gawking crowd parted on either side as he carried her across the room to the stairs and started down.

"Ivy!" Mama's voice was filled with terror as she hurried to join them. "Ivy, are you injured? They say you tried to throw yourself from the balcony! Oh, dearest child!"

"Ivy, who pushed you?" Maddie cried, rushing along at Mr. Richmond's side. "Did Mr. Creeve try to kill you?"

"Darling girl!" Papa's face appeared at her side as Mr. Richmond strode down a corridor. "I shall see to the arrest of that blackguard Frith at once! How dare he try to harm you!"

"No, Papa, please!" She attempted to speak, to calm the hysteria around her, but all she could see was a vision of the cobblestone alley that had awaited her fall. Shivering, she closed her eyes, but there it was again . . . the dark night . . . the snap of the railing . . . the slowly bending bars . . . and then the stony lane far beneath her head. With a shudder, she buried her face against Mr. Richmond's neck. Oh, take it away, this horrible vision of death!

"Where will you take her?" Papa cried as the whole group left the house and started down the street. "Our things are here."

"I have secured rooms at an inn within walking distance." Richmond's words reverberated against Ivy's cheek. "You may stay there in my place. I shall instruct my groom to have your baggage brought to the inn."

"But what about Clemma?" Mama cried. "She is still in that vile house, upstairs asleep."

"I shall fetch her at once, Mrs. Bowden," Papa assured her.

"Come then, Caroline, Madeline," Mamma said. Then, looking about, she exclaimed, "Mr. Bowden! Where is your second daughter?"

Madeline glanced at the others. "Caroline must have stayed behind."

"Wretched girl!" Papa exploded. "I shall fetch her away at once. How dare she stay in such a house, and when her own dear sister has so nearly come to harm! Oh, but she is a bad and selfish girl, always seeking pleasure and never using her head! Believe me, I shall teach her about family loyalty on this night!" He stormed back toward Frith's house.

Mama turned to Mr. Richmond. "You are too good, sir! Oh, this is a dire turn of events. How dreadful! And yet I can well believe such villainy of John Frith. He is a wicked man, and I knew he would not take well the news of Creeve's victory in the courts. But to strike at my daughter!"

"Frith did not strike her," Mr. Richmond said.

"I would wager it was Mr. Creeve who hit Ivy," Maddie cried. "I cannot bear that man."

"No one struck her, Miss Madeline. The railing broke."

"She was trying to throw herself over!" Mama wailed as the party turned a corner. "I knew it would come to this! I sensed how hopeless she felt! Oh, we have failed as parents, failed indeed. Everything we have done is wrong, vile, villainous. And now my dearest child is driven to this desperate act —"

"Calm yourself, Mrs. Bowden," Richmond said. "Truly, it was an accident."

"It is criminal that any man should keep his house in such poor condition!" Mama continued. "John Frith has proven his unworthiness in every way! His gardens and drawing rooms are a disgrace. His friends are all drunkards. And even his railings have rusted!"

"Mama, please, it is all right," Ivy said softly. She reached out and laid her hand upon her mother's arm as Mr. Richmond carried her up a short flight of stone steps into the inn. "I am well enough. Truly, Mr. Frith keeps his house ill, but he has neither wife nor children to urge him in the direction of domesticity. You must forgive him, I beg you. And Mama, be assured I had no intention of throwing myself from the balcony. The broken railing was indeed an accident. Perhaps one day we shall be much diverted in the retelling of my evening's adventure."

"I shall never laugh about it," Maddie said. "There is no humor in it at all."

Mr. Richmond laid Ivy on a settee near the inn's fireplace, and she took her sister's hand. "No, Maddie," she murmured, "it is not amusing. But it is behind us now, and we must go on."

"Come then, Madeline," Mama said. Let us repair to the rooms that Mr. Richmond has so graciously extended to us and prepare a bed for poor Ivy.

Ivy let out a breath.

"Your gown is torn in the back," Mr. Richmond said, kneeling beside her. "I did not wish to alarm the others by mentioning it. I fear the railing may have injured you."

Ivy shifted a little on the settee. "I am unharmed. I believe we have whalebone to thank for more than my fine figure."

Lowering his head, Richmond chuckled. "You continue to astonish me. First you calm your family — though you were the one who had every right to a fit of hysterics. Now you make a joke about the incident."

She laid her hand on his. "The debt I owe you is no laughing matter, sir. Twice now, you have carried me to safety. I thank you for saving my life tonight."

"I believe you would have done the same for me. Indeed, I saw you leap to my defense. It was a very dangerous action, for the two men were bent on destruction."

"But I am willful and stubborn, as you

have told me yourself. I confess that I now see the truth in your statement, for I would not have permitted either of those men to . . ." She paused, focusing on his hands. "Mr. Richmond, you are injured!"

He glanced down, staring in surprise at the red stain on his palms. "I am in no way harmed. But it must be your back where the railings cut you! Let me look at you."

She leaned forward, and he quickly ran his fingertips over the tattered fabric of her silk gown. No, she knew the truth before he even spoke the words. She, too, was unscathed.

But someone . . . someone on that balcony . . . had been gravely wounded.

Thirteen

"Such a to-do!" Mr. Bowden burst through the inn's front door, a sleepy Clemma in his arms and his daughter Caroline following close behind. "Look sharp, Richmond, for the constable is close on my heels! Ivy, get yourself up to your mama at once! Caroline, see your sister to the stairs!" He set Clemma on her feet and waited while Caroline meekly led her up the staircase.

Colin rose from the floor where he had been kneeling beside Ivy. "Mr. Bowden, what has happened?"

"It is Frith! He lies mortally wounded! Stabbed with a knife — your knife, Richmond, for a police inspector found it in the alley below the balcony. It is set in gold with your monogram and covered in blood!"

"Oh no!" Ivy cried.

Colin checked the sheath beneath his coat. Empty. "Blast! Creeve must have taken it during the scuffle."

"I saw a flash of steel," Ivy said. "I

thought it might be a pistol. Oh, Papa, will Mr. Frith die?"

"It seems likely, God rest his soul. But in my mind far worse is the implication that either you or Mr. Richmond was his assailant."

"Preposterous!" Colin snorted. "It was Frith who went for Creeve, and I who stepped between them. Obviously, at some point in the scuffle, Creeve took my knife and stabbed Frith. Both Miss Bowden and I did our best to part the two men and quell the quarrel."

"You must tell that to the constables, for they come now!"

Mr. Bowden grabbed Ivy's arm to rush her away, but he was too late. Three men from the Leeds constabulary stomped into the inn, followed closely by a throng of Frith's friends. As they surrounded the settee, the constables put a halt to any hope that Ivy might escape to the upper rooms.

"Mr. Colin Richmond!" A sergeant thrust out his chest. "Is this your knife, sir?"

He held up the familiar short blade. On the island of Fiji many years before, Colin had ordered the knife to be crafted by a highly skilled native artisan. He kept it honed to a fine edge.

"The weapon is mine," he acknowledged.

"Then I must hereby arrest you on suspicion of murder."

"That is insupportable," Ivy said, coming to her feet. "Sergeant, I beg you to hear me out. This man was in no way responsible for any injury that occurred tonight. I witnessed the event —"

"Indeed, you were a participant in the fracas, I believe? The subject of the quarrel among the three men?"

"Yes, but only two of them —"

"Madam, I would advise you to speak no further on this matter until you have consulted a solicitor."

"I shall speak as I must, sir. I assure you, the two combatants were John Frith and Nigel Creeve. Mr. Richmond was merely an onlooker who sought to dissuade them from fighting."

"Then how is it that his knife was used to wound John Frith? And whose blood stains his hands? Is he injured, Miss Bowden, or are you?"

"No, sir, neither of us was harmed. Yet I have complete confidence that this man is innocent of any wrongdoing."

"The judgment shall be left to a judge and jury," the constable replied. "Mr. Richmond, you are to accompany me to the constabulary. Mr. Bowden, I should engage a solicitor to defend your daughter as soon as possible."

Not for the first time since arriving in England, Colin wished mightily for the cutlass and pistols he normally wore while at sea. With such weapons at his side, he would make short work of this nonsense and be gone from this filthy, stinking city before sunrise. To think that he had come from India under the assumption that he would deliver a fortune to a very happy woman and then sail away back to his former life.

Instead, he stood in the midst of a furious mob of people he could hardly tolerate, and now he must face the ridiculous accusation of attempted murder. And yet the constables were clearing a path to the door, and he was walking among them toward incarceration in a country both foreign and utterly repugnant to him.

The moment he was set free on bond, Colin decided, he would leave. He would go to London and board the first ship to India. Or America. Or perhaps he would take himself off to Africa. A steaming jungle and a few marauding lions could be nothing to this wretched place.

"Mr. Richmond!" The voice that carried over the mutterings of the crowd stopped him in his tracks. He turned and focused on the young woman who was pushing her way toward him. Ivy should not speak to him, Colin realized at once. Any contact between the two of them might be seen as evidence of an unseemly attachment.

"Mr. Richmond, 'draw nigh to God,' " she said softly, her brown eyes depthless, " 'and he will draw nigh to you.' "

He regarded her for a moment. Of course he knew what she meant, for they had been discussing this on the balcony. She was telling him that each of them must seek God's will by first seeking God himself. But could God have any will in such a catastrophe as this? Did God care about what had happened? Did he even bother with such trivialities? What sort of heavenly Father would allow his children to experience such misfortune?

"Why?" he said through clenched teeth. "What is the point?"

"You gave him your life. He holds you in the palm of his hand."

Colin looked down at his own bloody, condemning palms. Then he pivoted and walked out the door.

"They have got their legs!" Clemma cried as she knelt at the small pool beside the brook. "Look, Ivy! My polliwogs have legs!"

Ivy lifted her head from the book she was reading and regarded the golden-haired figure beside the water. "Legs, yes, indeed."

"You cannot see them from over there. Do come, Ivy, please! I want you to see!"

Heaving a sigh, Ivy pushed herself out of the wicker chair she had brought to the end of the garden and laid her book on the cushion. Looking at frogs was the last thing she wanted to do. Yet how could she refuse? For Clemma — indeed for all the Bowdens — life had resumed its calm, contented heartbeat in quiet little Otley. The morning after the incident at Mr. Frith's home, Papa had whisked his family back over the Chevin and ensconced them safely at Brooking House. For the past two weeks, breakfast had appeared at seven each morning, tea had arrived promptly at ten and four, embroidery and French lessons filled the silent hours, and the notes of the pianoforte graced the evening air. As always.

Ivy knelt beside the pool and studied the dark frogs. "They still have their tails, but you are quite right about the legs. Those definitely are legs."

"The tails are smaller." Clemma dipped a stick into the water. "I thought the tails would fall off, but they have not."

"I believe they somehow shrink. You must see if Papa has a book on amphibians."

"I wish we could ask Mr. Richmond. He would know what happens to polliwogs' tails. He knows everything."

"Not everything." Unbidden, the memory of the man's face flooded Ivy's thoughts. Daily, she had fallen on her knees before the Lord to beg for divine protection and sustenance on behalf of Mr. Richmond. But she had heard nothing of his fate at the hands of the authorities. Nothing of the welfare of Mr. Frith. Nothing of the vile Mr. Creeve. Oh, that she was forced to behave as a proper young lady . . . that she was compelled to sit about and wait for news . . . that she must do nothing at all — or risk public censure for her behavior . . . it was too much to bear!

"I cannot believe Mr. Richmond stabbed Mr. Frith," Clemma said, bringing up the subject that until this moment had been taboo in the family's discussions. "He would not do such a thing as that."

Ivy shook her head. "No . . . no, indeed."

But even as she asserted his innocence, she recalled his laughing words to her one evening: *"I'd begin by running Nigel Creeve through with a sword. That would serve him well, don't you think?"* he had told her, and later he added, *"Even my little Fiji blade would do the job. That would serve him well, don't you think?"* Then he had gone on to imagine dispatching all other obstacles in his path. John Frith had been relegated to life as a castaway on a forgotten island in the West Indies. The Bowden clan were to be bought into silence. Finally, Mr. Richmond had asked Ivy a question that now struck horror in her heart: *"Shall we avoid the courts entirely,"* he had asked, *"and settle the matter in my efficient if rather ungodly way?"*

"Oh, dear me!" Ivy murmured, crumpling down onto the grass beside the stream and searching for her handkerchief. What if Mr. Richmond had resorted to his former methods of dealing with trouble? What if he had indeed unsheathed his knife in the heat of the struggle on the balcony? What if he had actually used that knife to stab Mr. Frith?

"What is the matter, Ivy?" Clemma said, crouching beside her and slipping a warm arm around her neck. "Why are you crying?"

"I am not crying." Ivy dabbed at a stray tear that had trickled down her cheek. "All right, I confess I am crying. It is the whole infuriating tangle of my life. And here I sit beside a brook staring at frogs!"

"It is all my fault!" Clemma wailed suddenly, and she burst into tears herself. "Oh, Ivy, you made me promise not to tell anyone what I saw in the corridor that evening when Mr. Richmond wanted to kiss you. But when I went into the bedroom, Caroline was there. She said it was obvious you had no heart, for if you did, how could you even consider marrying that horrid Mr. Creeve? And she said that you never had a romantic bone in your body, and that you did not love anyone or anything but your silly charities and all the poor people of the moorlands! And I said that is not true, for Ivy loves Mr. Richmond and he loves her! So you see, it is all my fault! Caroline told the constable Mr. Richmond killed Mr. Frith out of love for you!"

"Oh, Clemma!" Ivy held the sobbing child. "Do not weep so, I beg you, dearest. Surely Caroline would not have believed what you said about Mr. Richmond and me."

"Indeed she did, because that night when Mr. Richmond was leaving, we all peered out of the window and saw him sweep you into his arms and kiss you! It was so romantic and wonderful and beautiful! And Maddie was astounded, and Caroline said she had never seen anything so marvelous in all her life, but I think she was jealous because nothing romantic ever happens to her. Then when you did not tell Mama and Papa that you loved Mr. Richmond, and when he did not ask for your hand in marriage, and when you kept on saying that you meant to marry Mr. Frith or Mr. Creeve, Caroline was furious! She said you were wicked to form a secret attachment to Mr. Richmond. She said you did not deserve to have a fortune of two hundred thousand pounds all the way from India. And she said she was glad you were not really our sister, and she did not care what happened to you-hoo-hoo . . ." Her words formed into hysterical sobs as her small shoulders heaved in anguish.

Ivy held the child tightly, wishing that every horrible thing in their lives might melt away like polliwog tails. *Oh, dear Lord in heaven, what is the sense in all this? What am I meant to do? Which way should I turn?*

"Clemma," Ivy said, trying to calm the child, "we must trust that God is with us now. Mr. Richmond reminded me that in all times of trouble . . . indeed, no matter whether joys or sorrows confront us . . . we must draw near to God, and he will draw near to us. We must seek his will and follow him. That is the only way out of the tangles in which we find ourselves."

"But I did a wrong thing! I created the tangle that has tripped you and Mr. Richmond."

"I, too, have done many wrong things, dearest Clemma. I have not trusted God as I should have. I have worried when I should have placed my faith in him. I have said things, and wanted things, and wished for things . . . many things . . . that were not right. But Clemma, you and I both know what we are to do when we behave in a sinful manner."

"Beg forgiveness. And I am so sorry, truly I am! I shall never tell secrets again, Ivy. I promise!"

"Very good," she said, pressing the golden curls to her bosom and closing her eyes. "And dear God, I, too, am sorry for the many wrong desires I have felt and for things I have said. In Jesus' name we pray. Amen." Letting out a breath, she lifted her head. "And so, dear Clemma, you and I are forgiven."

The child sighed. "That was not very hard."

"No, indeed, it is quite a simple thing, and I cannot imagine why I so often fail to ask forgiveness for my sins. I wish to follow God's will in everything, Clemma, but I find I do not know what he wants from me."

"From you? Does God have a different will for you than he does for me?"

"I have always believed he has each of our lives ideally ordered and planned, and somehow — if we wish to obey him — we are to find that path and walk upon it. But truly, I am so confused at this moment that I cannot find any path at all."

Clemma pondered for a moment. "I think you are wrong about all the different paths, Ivy. I think God's will is the same for both of us. Indeed, for everyone in the whole world."

"For everyone? My goodness. Well, Miss Clementine, tell me then. What is the will of God?"

"He wants us to love him."

"Ahh . . . yes, he does. You are quite right about that." Ivy tugged off her slippers and stretched out her legs until her toes touched the cool, clear water that flowed down from the Chevin. "But what am I to do about poor Mr. Frith? And stern Mr. Creeve? And . . . yes, Clemma, I shall confess to you that I do love Mr. Richmond. No formal attachment — no secret engagement — has been made between us, nor must it ever be. But how can I deny the truth? I love him dearly. He is all I have ever hoped for in a husband, more than I have ever dreamed of in a man. I know how I feel, and yet I do not know how God feels! Why do I have such strong passion for Mr. Richmond? Why can I not care for Mr. Frith or Mr. Creeve? And what does God want of me?"

"Just to love him," Clemma repeated with confidence. "God loves us tenderly, the way I love my polliwogs. And he wants us to love him back, and to do as he says in the Bible, and to help him at his work. He would be very happy with us if we would do that, but we are always making things much more complicated by adding Creeves and Friths and Richmonds into it. And Caroline!"

Ivy laughed. "I believe you are right, Clemma. To love God . . . to obey him . . . and to help him at his work . . . my goodness, Clemma, I think you are quite a theologian."

"Am I?" Her blue eyes shone. "I love you, Ivy."

"I love you too, dearest Clemma." She kissed the soft forehead. "And now I must return to my reading, for Papa expects a review of this book at dinnertime."

As Ivy wandered back to the wicker chair beneath the old beech tree, she could hear Clemma whispering to her polliwogs. What a precious child she was. And perhaps she was correct in her understanding of the character of God. Ivy sank down into the cushions and closed her eyes. Could she go wrong if she followed the will of God as Clemma had stated it?

To love God . . . that was never difficult. Ivy adored her heavenly Father and was filled with gratitude each day for his saving presence in her life.

To do what God says in the Bible . . . well, such obedience certainly called for a diligent study of that text. Though Ivy had memorized large portions of Scripture, she sometimes neglected daily reading and prayer. Worse, she often failed to act according to biblical principles. Feeling contrite, she resolved to do better.

To see where God is working, to go there, and to help him . . . but where was God at work? And how could Ivy possibly make any difference?

As she turned those questions over and over in her mind, the sweet scents of cinnamon, cloves, fragrant sandalwood drifted across her. A soft cloud of silk . . . blue silk and pale yellow silk . . . wafted over her face, dancing on her skin . . . and words whispered across the hills and valleys . . . familiar words . . . words she had heard so many times . . .

So, jao . . . so, jao . . .

A tinkling laugh, like Christmas bells, played into Ivy's thoughts and stirred her eyelids to lift just a little. But through dark lashes she could see it was not winter, for the sun beat down on her cheeks, and a grasshopper was sitting on her lap. She pushed back a strand of hair that had fallen across her forehead and gazed at the tiny creature. Mmm, she must have fallen asleep while reading.

"Ribbons of crowfoot," someone said.

Ivy turned her head in the direction of the voice. A tall man stood ankle deep in the brook, his trousers rolled to his knees and his white shirt unbuttoned at the neck.

Good gracious, it was Colin Richmond!

Sitting up straight, Ivy gaped in shock as

he reached into the water and lifted a green streamer into the air. Suddenly, Clementine emerged from behind a bush that jutted out over the water and tilted her head to examine the plant.

"The white flowers bloom in early summer," Mr. Richmond said. "They open as soon as the buds break the surface."

"But why is it called crowfoot?" Clemma asked. "That is a very unlovely name for such a beautiful plant."

"Why, indeed? I have no idea!"

Both of them laughed, and now Ivy knew where the tinkling sound had come from. What on earth was Mr. Richmond doing in the stream at the bottom of the garden? He was in jail . . . or in London . . . or sailing away on his ship to India. He could not possibly be here.

"Look, a kingfisher!" Colin grabbed Clemma around the waist and lifted her onto his shoulder. "Just there, on that stump. Look quickly before he flies away."

"I see him!" she crowed. "Oh, what a marvelous color!"

"He looks as if he ought to live in Tahiti or along the shores of the Amazon. Certainly not here in gray old Yorkshire."

"Gray old Yorkshire? We are not gray here. We are green moss and purple heather and blue kingfishers and white crowfoot and pink butterbur flowers and every other wonderful color of the rainbow. Mr. Richmond, how dare you call us gray?"

"My mistake, Miss Clemma, for you are quite right."

"And golden daffodils . . . and red strawberries . . ."

"Yes, indeed."

"Do you want to go back to the Amazon or to India where the colors are brighter? Please say no, for I like you better than any of the other adults of my acquaintance, and I cannot bear for you to go away. Who will tell me about polliwog tails and show me kingfishers, Mr. Richmond? I do want you to stay here very much!"

"That is a kind sentiment," he said, swinging Clemma down from her perch on his shoulder and setting her into the stream. "But I regret I must tell you I have already booked my passage back to India."

"No!" Ivy gasped, then clapped her hand over her mouth. It was too late, for both Mr. Richmond and Clemma turned in her direction. She attempted to sit up straighter, and the grasshopper jumped away. Feeling the need to say something, she asked, "If you go, sir, what will become of Longley? The tenants are in great need of a landlord."

He smiled and gave her a bow. "Good afternoon, my sleeping beauty. I see you have awakened from your repose."

"It is a warm day, and I grew drowsy at my reading." Her cheeks flushing at his endearment, Ivy rose from the chair and stepped toward the stream. "Mr. Richmond, what brings you to Brooking House? And what news have you of Mr. Frith?"

"He is not dead!" Clemma cried. "He was put back together and stitched up, and there he lies in his horrid house the same as ever!"

"My goodness." Ivy tiptoed into the water. "Then you are free of any charges in the incident, Mr. Richmond?"

"Not quite. Miss Clemma paints too rosy a picture, I fear. Frith has not yet regained consciousness. His wound was severe, and he has suffered greatly from loss of blood. The doctor warns that putrefaction is common in such lacerations. There is concern that he may never fully recover."

"Oh, how dreadful." Ivy looked down at the clear water swirling about her ankles. "I feel I should go and tend to him."

"Because you care so deeply for him?"

She glanced up. "Because it is the right thing to do."

"I see."

"And what of Mr. Creeve? Does he escape all blame?"

"Not entirely. A police inspector has come down from London. He interviewed the witnesses and inspected the scene of the crime. In time, he will relay his findings to the courts."

"But you will be gone away to India by then?"

His brown eyes lingered on her lips a moment, then lifted. "I am free on bond, but I am not permitted to leave England. Yet I have certain connections. As India is under the dominion of His Majesty, I believe I shall be permitted to travel there."

"Ah, yes, of course." Ivy felt suddenly that she might begin to cry again, and that would never do. She bent down and began to examine the crowfoot blossoms that floated atop the water. How could she bring herself to look at him again? to know that he would go miles and miles away and never return to England? to admit that she might grow into an old woman and never set eyes on him again? It was too much to bear.

"I realize that Longley Park is of great

concern to you," Colin said. "I wish you to know I am taking pains to ensure stability for my tenants and a productive future for the estate. Mr. Hedgley tends the gardens well, and I have established a fund by which he may continue the employment of a full staff. As for the house itself, I have ordered repairs to the roof and drains, and I have laid plans for new plasterwork, fresh paint, and a thorough cleaning and inventory of all the furnishings. I have also —"

"You are very good, Mr. Richmond," Ivy cut in. "My criticisms of you were entirely unfounded. And now, if you will excuse me, I believe it is time for tea."

Before he could reply, she waded out of the stream and started up the bank. No doubt he would sail away to India at once, for a man in his situation could not afford to stay long in a country where his freedom was in jeopardy. And why should he not go? There was nothing here in England to hold him, she realized as she hurried across the expanse of grass toward the house.

Nothing had changed between them. She must marry Mr. Frith — if his health permitted — or Mr. Creeve at the last resort in order to get the inheritance, as the judge's ruling would surely decree. For she knew she must put the money to work for the people of Yorkshire. Clemma had told Ivy to help God at his work, and who could need divine assistance more than the ill and the poor of the moorlands? God had given Ivy that money, and she must do good with it.

"Miss Bowden!" Catching her arm at the corner of the small hedge maze, Mr. Richmond swung her around to face him. "Do you run from me?"

"Oh . . . no, indeed, sir . . ." She brushed at her cheek, praying he could not see the telltale trace of her tears. "It is teatime, I am quite certain, and . . ."

"I came here to Brooking House to speak with you, and I have not completed my conversation."

"A conversation requires two people. And I cannot . . . truly, I must not —"

"You are angry with me." He caught her arms. "That night in the inn, you tried to reach out to me. You spoke to me, telling me words of comfort, of God's presence in my life, and I turned from you and walked away. I have been haunted by that moment! I was angry and full of myself, and I confess, my pride was shattered that you should see me led off like a common criminal. Please forgive me, I beg you. My behavior was unconscionable, and I cannot —"

"Do not trouble yourself so, sir," Ivy said. "Your behavior deserves no censure. Indeed, you were far more gentlemanlike that evening than any of the men attending Mr. Frith's party."

"Then why do you run from me? I know my behavior is often boorish and uncultured. I was inadequately educated, and I . . . Miss Bowden, have I offended you in any manner?"

"No, sir. Your actions toward me have been in every way admirable."

"You cannot even bring yourself to look at me." He paused, breathing hard. "Do you believe I stabbed Mr. Frith? Is that the —"

"No, Mr. Richmond!" she cried, taking his hands and squeezing them hard. "Please believe me when I say there is nothing about you that displeases me. You are altogether . . ." She shook her head, fighting the emotion that welled inside her. "You are a good man in every way, sir," she whispered. "And that is why . . . that is why I must go to tea now."

Again she drew away from him and started for the house. His hand on her arm stopped her. "Wait, Miss Bowden, please hear me out. I know I shall express this poorly, and yet I wish to say that during my stay in England you have been the one bright and shining . . . angel —"

"Mr. Richmond, please."

"But it is true. You are a light sent from God himself, and your friendship has guided and encouraged me each time we have met. While I have little to offer you, I wish to make you a parting gift before I go. Though I shall not be in attendance, Miss Bowden, it would be my greatest pleasure to see you host your birthday ball in the conservatory at Longley Park."

Ivy lifted her head and forced herself to meet his eyes. To her surprise, she realized they were red-rimmed and filled with deep feeling. She reached up and stroked her fingers down his cheek.

"Thank you, Mr. Richmond," she said softly. "I shall be delighted."

Fourteen

"Time for tea!" Clemma sang out as the sound of a bell drifted down the hillside from the Brooking House kitchen. "Mr. Richmond, you must come and sit with us. Papa will welcome any news of Mr. Frith — though he may not be pleased at the outcome, for he favors Mr. Creeve — and Mama always loves visitors."

Colin tugged on a leather boot and unrolled his trouser leg over it. "Thank you, Miss Clemma, but I believe I shall return to Longley instead. I have been away in London a fortnight, and I must look over my affairs before I return to India."

"Oh, but please take tea with us today! Cook is very good at baking scones, and she bought the most delicious strawberry jam in the market at Otley yesterday. You have never tasted anything like it!"

He studied the little girl, her rosy cheeks and bright eyes a testimony to perfect health. Clementine Bowden was a delight, and a surprise as well. Colin had not been aware of the pleasure to be found in children. On board ship, only gruff seamen and a scrawny cat or two offered company. Ashore, he had spent his time exploring the exotic ports or passing the hours with unsavory characters. But children? He had hardly given them any thought until little Clemma burst into his house — and into his heart.

As he pulled on his other boot, Colin recognized a sharp pang in his chest. It was a familiar ache that seemed to be ever present with him these days. When he looked at Clemma's golden hair and thought of sailing away, something sharp twisted inside him. When he found himself wishing for children of his own — soft, round babies, bouncing boys and giggly girls — that pang settled in as though at home in his heart.

But it was when his thoughts turned to Ivy Bowden that he began to wonder if he would ever be free of pain. How could he sail away and never see her again? Colin stood and lifted his coat from the crook of a branch where he had laid it. He could not! And yet, what could be done? She would never go with him to India. She was devoted to her home and her family. Her deep commitment to the people of Yorkshire was one of the things about her that he loved the most.

But could he leave her here? Could he actually abandon her to the arms of John Frith? or Nigel Creeve? The very idea of either of those men touching Ivy made him nauseous. They did not deserve her!

Did he? No, of course not. He had no right to her, no claim on her heart. Yet the thought of leaving her was impossible.

Colin tossed his coat over his shoulder, made another excuse for not staying to tea, and gave Clemma a farewell hug. As she skipped away, he considered the only option that made sense: he must stay in England. Somehow, he must be near Ivy. Even if she were married, he could see her now and again — love her from afar, just as the old troubadours had adored their fair and untouchable princesses.

But Colin knew he could not stay in England. Not only was his freedom in peril here, he had no ties to this land. It was true he had come to care for Longley Park, care far more than he had expected. But his father had planned a future for him in the shipping business. Colin had spent his life in preparation for that destiny. How could he abandon it just to be near a woman who could never truly be his?

As he started for the lane, he saw Ivy herself emerge suddenly from a side door of the house. Carrying a small milk jug, she hurried across the grass toward an old stone wall. Kneeling beside the wall, she poured something into the long green grass that grew beside it. Then she lifted her skirts and clambered onto the wall.

Surprised at her action, Colin stood at a distance behind her. He did not know whether to catch her attention or to hide himself and continue to observe her odd behavior. Pausing, he watched her stand on tiptoe atop the wall and hold her hand over her brow to shade her eyes as she scanned the countryside. What was she seeking? What had she poured into the grass?

Colin had hardly begun to ponder these things when a horse and rider broke out of the shadows on the lane and pounded toward Brooking House at a gallop. At the sight of them, Ivy stiffened and clutched her stomach. Then she leapt down and dashed toward the house, leaving the small white jug on the wall.

As the horse approached, Colin recognized the rider. It was Nigel Creeve. Gravel flew beneath the steed's hooves as it cantered up to the entrance of Brooking House and came to a skittering halt.

Creeve dismounted, detached a satchel from the saddle, and climbed the steps to the door.

Colin frowned in confusion as Creeve was admitted by a maid. Had Ivy been expecting this man? Did she stand on the wall to watch for and eagerly await him? Had her strange action with the milk pitcher been an excuse to permit herself outside to await his arrival?

Hardly able to believe what his eyes told him, Colin strode to the wall, grasped the little jug, and walked to the front door himself. Dispensing with niceties, he gave the maid a quick nod and walked past her to the drawing room from whence various sounds of greeting emerged.

As he paused in the doorway, the maid brushed by him and cleared her throat loudly enough to draw the attention of everyone in the room. "Beg pardon, Mr. Bowden," she said. "Mr. Richmond has come."

Colin stepped toward the gathering and held up the pitcher. "I noticed this on the wall just now as I was leaving. Thought I ought to bring it inside. Might be valuable to the family."

"You were *leaving?*" Mr. Bowden said. "We had no idea you were here to begin with."

"He was here, indeed, and I knew it all along," Clemma piped up. "Mr. Richmond has been wading in the brook with me and Ivy."

"Ivy and me," Mrs. Bowden corrected. "Well, sir, this is a great surprise and very welcome. Do come and join us for tea. You can see we have a guest already."

"Nigel Creeve." Colin approached the other visitor. "I did not know you were expected in Otley today."

"Richmond." Creeve bowed. His sallow skin looked positively yellow in the afternoon sunlight. "I have come in regard to my betrothal. What has brought you to Brooking House, besides dallying with the Bowden ladies in the stream?"

"Mr. Richmond came to Brooking House to inform us of the welfare of Mr. Frith," Ivy spoke up, addressing the entire assemblage. "Thanks be to God, he has survived his injury, though his condition remains grave."

"Survived?" Mr. Bowden exclaimed. "I am surprised."

"Papa, I believe I must go to Leeds to visit Mr. Frith. He is seriously ill, and it is only right that I call on him."

"You shall do nothing of the sort!" Creeve declared. "John Frith has no claim

324

on your affections, Miss Bowden, and he has no right to your attentions."

"I beg your pardon, sir, but I believe every human in need or in suffering has a right to Christian charity. Mr. Frith was wounded because of me, and I have tarried in Otley far too long."

"I forbid you to go to him, madam, for such behavior would be unseemly. The rumors in Leeds are rampant as it is, and I would not have my wife made the subject of idle gossip."

"Miss Bowden is hardly your wife, Creeve," Colin said. "Frith lives, and his claim to her is the stronger one. I have taken the documents to London, and I have spoken with several experts who confirmed this."

"This is an outrage!" Creeve exploded. "My own documents are legal and binding. I vow I shall not stand by and listen to the presumptive arguments of a common seaman. You have nothing to recommend yourself, Richmond. Your family deserted England, your property lies in ruins, and your reputation is of the worst sort. You were sent from India merely to transport the rightful inheritance of Miss Bowden. You have done that, and now I strongly advise that you be gone from this place!"

"Not until I am informed of the reason for your sudden appearance here."

"You will know nothing of my affairs! I am not beholden to you. You have inserted yourself into a matter that is not your concern, and you are no longer wanted or needed. The outcome will be decided in the courts!"

"Indeed, and you will lose your suit, for Frith lives. So long as that is the case, he has the right to wed Miss Bowden."

"Insufferable lout! Be gone at once," Creeve cried, "or I shall be forced to —"

"To what, Creeve? To stab me, as you stabbed John Frith?"

"That was *your* knife —"

"And *your* hand that wounded Mr. Frith," Ivy cut in. "Gentlemen, please, may we leave off threats and accusations for the duration of teatime?"

"Miss Bowden, do you accuse me of assaulting Frith?" Creeve asked Ivy. "Surely you know the knife belonged to that blackguard who stands beside you there."

"It was his knife, sir, but not his hand that wielded it. At the time of Mr. Frith's injury, Mr. Richmond was attempting to prevent me from falling from the balcony to the alley below."

"You cannot mean this, madam!"

"Indeed I do, and I shall testify to such if I am given opportunity."

Nigel Creeve stared at Ivy as though stunned by her words. A pair of bright pink points appeared on his bony yellow cheeks, and his small eyes narrowed further.

"Miss Bowden." He addressed her in a clipped voice. "I am unaccustomed to such insubordinate behavior from a woman. And yet I cannot hold you to blame. Clearly, you have come under the influence of Colin Richmond. Ladies are delicate of sensibility and easily swayed in their thinking. You have been forced to spend much time in the company of a man whose behavior is crass and whose aims are of the lowest order. It is clear, dear Miss Bowden, that he has made you an unwitting party in his deceit. He has compelled you to confirm his falsehoods despite your clear knowledge of the truth."

"On the contrary, sir —"

"Speak no further, madam, for I — who care so deeply for your reputation — would not have you subjected to the censure of those who know what actually occurred that evening." He smiled warmly at her. "Indeed, I beg you to sit and take your ease. And you, poor Mrs. Bowden, have been kept standing while our tea grows cold. Please . . . everyone . . . let us behave in a civil manner, keeping ourselves above the rough company of those not of our level of society."

So saying, Creeve sat down on his tail-coat and spread his arms in a welcoming gesture that took in everyone except Colin, who tried to hold his tongue but found it impossible.

"You insult me, Creeve," he snarled, "and you diminish Miss Bowden with your patronizing airs. Why have you come to Brooking House? I demand to know the answer at once!"

Before Creeve could reply, Ivy stepped to Colin's side and laid her hand softly on his arm. "Good sir, I thank you for your kindness in bringing us news of Mr. Frith, and for your most excellent assistance to my family throughout these difficult weeks, and especially for your devoted attention to my own welfare. Might I beg you now to stay to tea? You are most welcome to join us."

Colin searched Ivy's eyes, trying to read the message in them. Did she need his presence now? Or was she trying to dismiss him without insult? Why did people not say what they meant these days? And how dare Creeve be so nearly right in his assessment of Colin's presence — *rough company of those not of our level of society.*

"Thank you, dear lady," he began, wishing he could recite florid compliments or intricate flattery to please her. But he hadn't any hope of it. Finally he seized on what he knew must be his only course of action — the blunt statement of fact. "I must return to Longley Park. I have matters to attend."

"Sir," she said, her fingers tightening on the fabric of his sleeve, "I would not have you leave us until Mr. Creeve has shared the reason for his visit to Brooking House. Though he states that the problem at hand is no longer your affair, I know that you hold the keys to the chests containing my father's legacy — a fortune which is so eagerly anticipated by one and all."

Before continuing, she bestowed a condescending smile upon Creeve and then turned her attention again to Colin. "Lest I — with my delicate feminine sensibility which is so easily swayed in any direction — be persuaded to act in a way that might subject me to further ridicule from the honorable citizens of Leeds, I beg you to stay and bear witness while Mr. Creeve reveals the objective of his journey here."

Colin gazed at Ivy in amazement as she

329

seated herself and quietly began to pour the tea. In the space of a few breaths, she had managed to inform Creeve that she found his posturing insufferable and to pave the way for Colin to stay and hear what the man was up to.

Taking a chair nearby, Colin noticed that Creeve had begun to perspire visibly. While the man was clearly at a loss for words, how could he refuse to speak? The woman he already considered his wife had bidden him to announce his mission to everyone in the room.

"My good man," Colin said to Creeve, "you have indicated you believe Miss Bowden incapable of clear discernment in matters of right and wrong. She cannot be permitted to hear your reason for coming and make a judgment about it on her own, for what if she should respond wrongly? What if your words should lead her into some action that might cost her the opportunity to collect her father's legacy? Therefore, it is imperative that I, who hold the fortune, and Mr. Bowden, who guides her thoughts, should hear what you have come to say."

Creeve shifted on the settee, his coattails tangling beneath him. He took out a handkerchief and blotted his brow. Then he blew his nose, a loud honking sound that fairly shook the windowpanes. Finally, he cleared his throat.

"Aha," he said. "I see the reason in these words you speak, Richmond. I have nothing to hide, and all may know the purpose of my journey to Brooking House." Here he produced a document from his satchel and unfurled it before them. "This letter states unequivocally that Miss Bowden abhors any connection between herself and John Frith, that she honors the agreement made between her guardian and myself, and that she vows to become my wife. The barrister I have employed on my behalf in this matter assures me that once Miss Bowden affixes her signature to this letter, everything at issue will be resolved and she can indeed lay claim to her late father's inheritance."

From the satchel he now produced a quill and inkwell. Setting the ink before Ivy, he removed the lid and dipped the tip of the pen into it. Then he held out the quill to Ivy.

"You expect me to sign this?" she asked.

"Certainly. How can you object?"

"How indeed?" Mr. Bowden cried. "We object because we do not know the truth about your character. Though you profess innocence in the stabbing of Mr. Frith, I trust my daughter's opinion in the matter. And yet I see some sense in this plan." He paused. "Certainly this document, together with the contract made between the two of us, would seal your claim on my daughter's hand. As you say, she could surely receive her inheritance. Ivy's future would be secure. No matter the health of John Frith, no matter his poor character, no matter his appalling house and wicked friends, for she would be forever rid of him."

"And it would fulfill the terms of your contract with Mr. Creeve," Ivy said softly.

Mr. Bowden lowered his head for a moment. "I confess this solution intrigues me for more than one reason, my dear girl. I have been duplicitous with you in the past, but no more. You know what wrongs I have committed. Were you to sign this contract, all may be resolved for the best. You would be provided for, and we — your family — would have sustenance to the end of our days."

Ivy turned the pen over in her hand. It was all Colin could do to keep from taking it and flinging it across the room. Surely she would not sign such a document! Surely she could not even consider anything so detrimental to herself! She smoothed out the paper and carefully read it from start to finish. Then she looked up at Mr. Bowden.

"Papa," she said, "you know I do not love Mr. Creeve, and I am entirely certain of his guilt in stabbing Mr. Frith. Our union cannot be a happy one."

"I say!" Creeve spluttered. "Your happiness is entirely beside the point! I am a decent man of an upstanding family. Once upon a time you did not object to me, Miss Bowden. You agreed to the marriage, or your father would never have arranged it in the first place. Until Mr. Richmond arrived, you were fully prepared to wed me. Has the news of your inheritance changed you so greatly?"

Ivy did not speak for a moment, and Colin held his breath in anticipation of what she might say. If she confessed any affection for him — even the smallest indication of love — he would tear the contract into shreds. *Let her speak from her heart!* he begged God. *Let her tell the truth! Oh, dear Lord, please let her love me.*

"It is not the news of my fortune that makes my will waver," she said softly. Her brown-and-gold eyes flashed in Colin's direction. "You believe God's path for you leads you back to India, Mr. Richmond?"

"I have received legal clearance, and I have booked passage, but I —"

"Speak no more, sir. That is all I need to know." She dipped the pen into the ink and signed her name to the bottom of the letter. As she handed it to Creeve, she looked at Colin once again.

"Thank you, Mr. Richmond," she said. "You have been good to stay the course of this meeting. Unless you wish to remain for tea, you have our leave to return to Longley now, for I am certain there are many things that call upon your attention."

Breathing hard, Colin stared at her. "You leave me no choice."

"You have made your choice." She smiled sadly. "I am certain you have chosen well, sir. May God go with you."

Fighting the eruption of emotion that swelled in his chest, Colin stood and nodded a curt farewell to the assemblage. As he left the room, he could hear the clink of teacups and the polite laughter that followed someone's comment. *Leave them to their society*, he thought. He had no place in such company. Nor could he lay claim on the heart of such a pure and delicate woman as Ivy Bowden. He had no right to mourn her loss, for she had never been his.

Before too many days had passed, he would again drink in the salty sea air and know the rise and fall of a deck beneath his feet. It would be good to leave all this behind him and return to the place he belonged.

Unwilling to look back, Colin set off down the drive toward the shady oak tree where he had tied his horse. He must think to the future. His plans for Longley Park were unfolding well. A sizable account he had set up in London would see to the salaries of his staff, and the house itself would be put to good use. He could go away to India with the knowledge that he had not abandoned his responsibilities in Yorkshire. Indeed, he could take comfort in the assurance that he had done well. Ivy would have nothing but pleasure in the certainty that Longley . . .

Catching himself, Colin tried to purge all thoughts of the woman to the furthest recesses of his mind. He would not dwell on her. In time, perhaps he would not even remember her. He would bury himself in business. He might even choose a wife from among the daughters of the colonists who made their homes in India. A wife and children would take his thoughts from Yorkshire and the brown-haired slip of a girl who had captured his heart.

As he passed the low stone wall on which Ivy had stood to survey the lane, Colin paused. What had she poured into the grass? And why had she come out so eagerly to clamber onto the wall?

Colin turned the questions over and over, trying to will himself not to care. Before he could stop himself, he was crossing the grass to the wall. Stepping up onto it, he stood where Ivy had been and gazed out across the countryside. What had drawn her to this place? At first he saw nothing out of the ordinary. A brook trickled near the road, and a lone cart rolled toward the village of Otley, nestled in the dales. But before the village, a forest rose up. He recognized it at once as the estate of Longley Park. The massive house in which he lived stood like a gray sentinel in the midst of the verdant grove.

And then he understood. From this place Ivy could see his home. From here she could perhaps feel a connection with him. His heart warming at the thought that she might indeed love him, he stepped down from the wall.

What had she been doing as she knelt here? Crouching, he noted a few acorns, a thick growth of summer grass, and there

. . . surrounded by a cleared patch of damp earth . . . a little sprig of English ivy. Its tendrils were frail and green, very pale, as though the slightest brush with a strong wind might uproot them. Yet it clung to the recently watered ground and spread its vines up the warm stone, tenacious in its hold on life.

Ivy! Oh, this was his dearest, most beloved lady! This fragile yet strong and determined bit of greenery could not be more like that beautiful creature. What would he do without her? he wondered as he ran his fingers over the small vine. How could he go on?

Thinking of her words to him — her command that he must draw near to God — Colin knew the answer. He had no right to lay claim to Ivy's heart. He had no place in her life. And so he must keep his focus where it ought to be. He must cling to God and trust that God would draw near to him . . . comfort him . . . heal him . . . renew him.

Standing, he covered the small ivy plant with grass to protect it from the elements. And then he made his way toward the old oak tree and the horse that would carry him far from this place.

Fifteen

As Ivy climbed the stairs inside the crumbling house in Leeds, she recalled the evening of the dance . . . that dreadful moment when she had felt as though she were ascending to her doom. She had not been far wrong, she realized as she stood before the closed oak door and thought of the man who lay beyond it. Her future had been determined that night. Mr. Frith, it appeared certain, would never return to a normal life. Mr. Creeve would become Ivy's husband. And Mr. Richmond would flee to India to avoid being tried in an English court.

She removed one hand from the bowl of warm soup she had brought up from the kitchen and knocked on the door. Of course there would be no answer. Despite his many so-called friends and acquaintances in Leeds, Mr. Frith could not count a single soul who had stood beside him during his darkest days. Though Colin Richmond had visited several times, Ivy was told, his stays had been of short duration. Even the strange little maid, Veronica, came and went with furtive speed, pausing only to throw together a porridge or cook a pudding for her employer. The doctor had given up all hope of the man's recovery, for John Frith lingered in a stupor that nothing could affect. Indeed, Ivy had begun to believe that if she had not convinced Mama and Caroline to accompany her to the inn, if Papa had not agreed to their week of shopping for gowns and trimmings to wear at Ivy's birthday ball, and if Ivy herself had not called at Frith House several days earlier, its owner might have perished altogether.

Pushing open the door, she carried the bowl of soup to the bed and set it on a low table. "Good afternoon, Mr. Frith," she said softly. "I hope you are feeling better. It is a lovely day outside with a fine wind blowing from the west. Indeed, you will be delighted to know that there is hardly any odor at all in town. Mama and Caroline will surely return from their visit to the cloth merchants' shops in better spirits today. At least I hope they will, for our room seems very small indeed when the day is hot, the smell is intense, and they are out of sorts."

He stared with a dull, glazed expression

as she tucked a cloth beneath his chin and began to spoon soup into his mouth. Though he dribbled most of it, the poor man swallowed now and again, and a little of the liquid went down. Grateful, she went on telling him about her own activity of the morning — a bold journey to several of the fine homes that lined the streets of Briggate, Kirkgate, and Boar Lane.

The Leeds cloth merchants who had made a fortune in Yorkshire's woolen industry were hardly enthusiastic about Ivy's plans to improve the area. They felt that a woman should marry and settle into a routine of female pastimes such as rearing children and calling upon friends. But Ivy's large legacy soon drew their attention, and a few listened to her ideas with interest.

"A hospital is a primary concern, do you not agree?" she asked her patient, in hopes there might be some response. "Had you been given better medical care, Mr. Frith, it is likely you would not be in this dreadful condition. I should also think that the state of the water here keeps you plagued with ill health, and having that in mind, I have spoken about improving the waterworks and the sewage system in Leeds. In Otley, we are blessed with the flow from the Chevin, and our water is very sweet and good."

Here, Mr. Frith gave a low groan, and Ivy set the bowl aside. Gazing down at him, she shook her head. What on earth could be the matter with this pitiable man? While his wound had festered, treatment seemed to be clearing the infection. Yet he remained in this daze, and nothing could draw him out.

Ivy knew he had lost a great deal of blood the night of the incident, and she wondered if that were contributing to his lethargy. But the doctor gave such an idea no credit. Indeed, twice a day, he came to the house and drained great bowls of blood from Mr. Frith's veins in order to balance his humors. All to no avail, for it seemed that the patient grew weaker and less responsive by the day.

"I believe it is the condition of the sewers," Ivy said, taking up the bowl again, "which keeps the king from granting Leeds the status of a city. How can one elevate a town with such dreadful conditions? The council should be ashamed! The slums must be cleared, Mr. Frith. Schools must be built. Churches must be erected. And above all, the water must be cleaned. Then, perhaps the king will grant Leeds a royal charter."

As she ladled the last of the soup down his throat, Ivy wiped the corners of his mouth with the cloth bib. "Mr. Frith, you would want Leeds to become a city, would you not? Of course you would. Had you not been so caught up in dancing and frivolities, you would have seen the deplorable condition in which you and your neighbors live. Yet it is not you who have suffered so greatly, as have the poor and hungry of Yorkshire. Can you see what I mean?"

Letting out a sigh, she drew away the cloth and wetted it in a nearby basin. Of course he could not understand what she meant, she realized as she carefully washed the man's forehead and cheeks. He was oblivious now — but Ivy knew in her heart that he would have been equally unconcerned in the past.

John Frith was a nice-looking sort of fellow, Ivy thought as she contemplated the sallow visage of the man in whom her birth father had placed such hopes. But she had the gravest doubts about his character. Though he had been filled with humor and goodwill, his morality appeared sadly compromised.

In many ways, Ivy was grateful. Not for this dreadful calamity, of course. But she was glad the poor man was in no condition to become a husband. Reforming him would be beyond her. And how could such a marriage ever have been pleasing to God? or to her? or to their children?

But, oh dear, the thought of marrying Nigel Creeve was hardly better. Ivy let out another deep breath. What a dismal prospect faced her. The very idea of spending hours in the company of Mr. Creeve gave Ivy a chill she could not shake off. And to tolerate the touch of his thin, cold fingers was beyond her. How would she ever endure it? Especially after . . . but no, there she had been wrong indeed. To have so greatly enjoyed the company of Mr. Richmond had been a serious mistake, for now any other man must suffer by comparison.

She allowed herself one small moment of reflection on the one who had captured her heart. His handsome face and gentle voice filled her, and yet she knew she must banish all vestiges of him from her thoughts. He would go away to India soon. Perhaps he already had. And she must step into her own future.

Mr. Creeve would not be such a terrible husband. Ivy knew he could not prevent her determination to do good with her money. Though his demeanor was somber and his words could be fierce, he was really nothing but a crumple-tailed old rooster. She was not afraid.

"I am to visit the Marchioness of Hertford tomorrow," Ivy told the dozing man. "I shall take a carriage out to her estate, which is called Temple Newsam, and ask for an audience. She stays there this month, I am told, though she spends a great deal of time in London, and her presence in that city is of great import. Though I am not one to gossip, I have heard accounts of her influence over the prince regent. Indeed, some call her the queen of the regency, though I consider that to be a somewhat malicious title. She will, nevertheless, hear me out, and I am most hopeful that two ladies of wealth and influence cannot fail to —"

"Oh, excuse me, miss!" Veronica exclaimed as she burst into the room and caught sight of Ivy sitting beside the bed. "I thought ye must be away back to t' inn by this hour."

"I should have been, but I dallied overlong in making morning calls and was late for my afternoon visit." Ivy rose and faced the girl. "I made Mr. Frith a good strong oxtail soup, and he has taken a good deal of it. Please convey this information to the doctor when he arrives. Perhaps our patient makes a turn for the better."

Out of breath, Veronica pushed a mass of blonde curls away from her eyes and made an awkward curtsy. "Of course, Miss Bowden. I thank ye."

"Good day, then." Ivy started for the door, but thought of something and turned. "Oh yes. Veronica, might you suggest to the doctor that he leave off the bleeding for a day? I wonder if the lack of blood is keeping Mr. Frith in this weakened state."

White-faced, Veronica nodded quickly. "Aye, miss. I'll tell 'im what ye said."

"Thank you." As Ivy turned away again a strange sensation crept over her. A quiet prickling of foreboding. A shadow of doubt. She made herself walk to the door without looking over her shoulder. But as she slipped out into the corridor, she glanced back into the room.

Veronica was removing something from her pocket.

Ivy pulled the door to, but left it slightly ajar. Her heart hammering, she moistened her dry lips. It was wrong to observe others in a covert manner. She should hurry down the stairs and return to the inn for the evening.

Yet something in the character of

Veronica had troubled Ivy from the beginning. And now . . . with her pale face and
breathless racing in and out of the room
. . . she seemed all the more suspicious.
Quelling the moral rectitude that bade her
leave at once, Ivy leaned one shoulder
against the door frame and peered through
the narrow slit. For a moment, she could
not find the location of the bed. And then
she saw a flash of blonde hair.

As Ivy focused on Veronica, the girl held
up a glass of water, stirring it with the tip
of her finger. Round and round, round and
round. Then she lifted it to the light of the
candle and gazed at it. Satisfied with what
she observed, she slipped her arm under
Mr. Frith's neck and began to drip the
water into his mouth.

Ivy swallowed, uncertain how to proceed. Had anything untoward occurred?
Or was Veronica merely tending to her
master as any good maid should do?
Peering through the slit again, Ivy now saw
that the young woman had begun to weep.
Tears trickled down her cheeks, and she
leaned her head against that of Mr. Frith,
as though she loved him dearly and her
heart were breaking.

Enough. Ivy fled down the stairs on
tiptoe, embarrassed that she had witnessed

such a tender and private moment. Gathering her skirts, she hurried out into the street and all but ran toward the inn. Oh dear! What had she witnessed? Had anything been amiss? Had Veronica put something into Mr. Frith's drink? If so, it must have been a powder the doctor had ordered — though Ivy felt certain the complete course of Mr. Frith's treatment lay on the table beside his bed and not in Veronica's pocket. And what of the loving tears that had flowed down the girl's cheeks? Oh, the passion was clear to any woman who had ever loved a man . . . and Ivy knew she herself fell among that assemblage.

Mr. Richmond. The image of his strength, courage, and wisdom rose up before her as she entered the inn and climbed the stairs to her room. Mama and Caroline hardly looked up from their intent discussion over an array of fabric swatches they were evaluating. Ivy brushed past them on her way to the window. As she pushed open the leaded glass pane, she lifted up a prayer for wisdom.

What troubled her was not the expression of love she had seen on Veronica's face. It was not even the strange stirring of the water. It was the utter stupor into which Mr. Frith had lapsed.

Ivy had spent many years carrying food and medicines from cottage to cottage on the moorlands that surrounded Otley. She had observed coughs and gout and fever and croup. Even typhus and diphtheria had made occasional appearances in the darkened cottages nestled in the dales. Many times Ivy had tended to severe wounds — deep gashes from swinging scythes, limbs torn away in mill accidents, even the horrid injury caused by a pistol's ball. But never in all her experience had she seen a man fall into such a senseless, dull state of existence as had overcome Mr. Frith.

It was not right.

More than that, it was not *natural*.

Certain now that she must attempt to inform the one man who seemed to give any heed to Mr. Frith's welfare, Ivy left the window and took out her writing desk. In moments, she had penned a short note, folded it, and set her wax seal upon it.

"I shall return directly," she told Mama as she left the room.

"Indeed, you must, my dear," the woman commented, barely giving her a glance, "for Caroline and I are in violent disagreement about this pink silk. I say it is wretched, and she maintains it is divine.

You must hurry back and settle the matter for us."

"Momentarily, Mama, I assure you." With a rueful sigh, Ivy hurried down the stairs and found a man who could carry her message upon the hour.

"Take this to Otley," she said, handing him the note and a coin. "If he has not gone away to India yet, place it in the hand of the owner of Longley Park, Mr. Colin Richmond."

Colin stamped the dust from his boots before the doors of the inn at Leeds. Though it was only an hour past dawn, he had been unable to wait a moment longer before leaving Longley Park and riding the ten miles over the Chevin toward town. The short and cryptic message from Ivy Bowden carried to him the previous night had so alarmed and consumed him that he had paced the long corridors of Longley Park for many hours.

Her note had begged him — if he were not yet gone away to India — to come to Leeds to discuss with her a matter of great import. A life, she felt, was in danger. But whose?

Colin hammered on the innkeeper's door and was greeted by a sleepy woman in a dingy mobcap. Upon hearing Mr. Richmond's errand, she informed him that the hour was too early and that the Bowden ladies would not be at breakfast until seven.

"Then I shall arouse her myself," he said, starting for the second floor. This propelled the little woman into action, though not without an exaggerated sigh, and she puffed her way up the rickety staircase and vanished down the corridor. Before long, she returned to inform the gentleman that Miss Bowden would greet him within the hour.

"Though I shouldn't be in too great a rush for it, meself," the innkeeper's wife informed him. "Ye know 'ow long it takes these grand ladies to do up their 'air, don't ye? Could be afternoon before yer ladylove makes an appearance."

Colin was taken aback at the label the woman had placed upon his relationship with Miss Bowden. Did he appear as an eager young suitor impatient for the presence of his beloved? Chagrined, he shrugged and sauntered to a bench near the fireplace. He was not some fool-headed young swain. He had come to Leeds at Miss Bowden's request for assistance. This had nothing to do with any misguided romantic feelings he might have for her.

As the minutes on the face of his pocket watch ticked by, Colin reminded himself for the thousandth time that he had no claim whatsoever on Ivy Bowden. He had come to England to see her wed to John Frith. Indeed, he should be pleased at the concern she had taken over the man's welfare following his injury. That Ivy had made the journey to Leeds to tend Frith was a good thing, an indication of her concern for a man her father had intended her to marry. It was also a clear sign that she would brook no romantic nonsense from her own heart — or from the heart of a man she could never be allowed to love.

She did not love him, Colin told himself. And his own love for her was ill founded. He would return to India where he belonged and take over his father's business as planned. He must keep his focus on God and on the path he had chosen that day on board ship when he had become a Christian. He must be single-minded and stouthearted. He must —

"Good morning, Mr. Richmond."

Her voice snapped him straight up off the bench like a soldier coming to attention. "Miss Bowden," he managed, suddenly out of breath. "It is a fine day."

As she approached, he made a bow, but he could not bring himself to take his eyes from the vision descending the staircase. How could one woman be so beautiful? Clad in a pale blue gown caught above the waist with a ribbon of indigo silk, Ivy might have been an angel drifting down to earth to visit a most humble and imperfect man. A crown of bronze braids and a cascade of ringlets at her temples drew his attention to the brown depths of her eyes. Black lashes fanned her cheeks as she curtsied.

"Mr. Richmond, I am so glad you are not gone away from Yorkshire just yet," she said softly. "I thank you for your prompt attention to my message, and I hope I have not detained you from your preparations for departure."

"No, indeed. I would have come last night, but the hour was quite late."

"You are very good. I fear my mission may be misguided, and you have many responsibilities to undertake before your ship leaves for India, yet I feared —"

"Speak no more of my departure, madam."

"Do you stay in Yorkshire then?" she asked, a light filling her eyes. "Will you make Longley Park your home?"

Colin would have given anything to be certain that light was a ray of hope. Did she want him to stay? Did she long for his presence in her life?

"I am scheduled to sail for India within the week," he told her. "Miss Bowden, you wrote of a dire foreboding that has possessed you. Come, you must tell me of this at once."

She lowered her gaze and nodded. "But we should not speak in such a public place. May I be so bold as to ask if you might accompany me on my journey to Temple Newsam, sir? I go there to speak with Lady Hertford, who, I hope, may be willing to lend her support — and perhaps her fortunes — to my efforts in assisting the people of this region."

"Assisting the people?" Colin studied Ivy for a moment. "What is your aim in this endeavor?"

"Mr. Richmond, do you recall your words to me in the churchyard not long after our first meeting? I asked you why God had visited upon me the curse . . . or the blessing, as some may see it . . . of my father's large fortune. 'I shall tell you why he has done it,' you answered me. 'God has given you riches in order to see what you will do in return. It is a test of your character.'"

"And you have decided to use the money for the good of the people of Yorkshire?"

"I have." She held out her arm and he stepped forward to take it. "Shall we walk, sir?"

Filled with wonder at the fortitude of the young woman at his side, Colin escorted her out of the inn and down the street in the direction of the large estate that had belonged to the descendants of Sir Arthur Ingram for nearly two hundred years. That Ivy Bowden would boldly and without proper invitation approach the formidable Marchioness of Hertford revealed the extent of the changes that had occurred within her since the moment of their first meeting. Once upon a time, Ivy had been a quiet, dutiful girl who spent her hours tending the needy and planning birthday balls. Once she had been too quick to equate her earthly father's directives with the will of her heavenly Father. Now she seemed to realize that her own God-given mind and the study of Scripture must also play a part in discerning that path.

"May I ask the nature of your plans, Miss Bowden?" Colin said. "I am most curious as to their bent."

"I appreciate your curiosity, sir, but I fear I cannot answer you. I intend to remain anonymous in all my activities, and therefore, I speak of them only to those who may wish to join me."

"Perhaps I shall join you."

"You go to India, sir." She flashed her brown eyes in his direction. "You can be of no service to me, and I would not wish to accept your money."

"Why not? What makes Lady Hertford a more acceptable donor than I? Is my money somehow tainted?"

She laughed. "No, not at all, but I have made it my aim that those who assist financially must also observe the effects of their donations. I would have them see what good they do — not only for the betterment of their own characters, but that they might find it in their hearts to give again . . . and perhaps a greater amount!"

"I appreciate your intent, but I certainly do believe that I could —"

"Mr. Richmond, please, may we leave this discussion and turn to the issue at hand?" She released his arm as they stepped onto the crowded and filthy Leeds Bridge. Though the cloth merchants who once sold their wares here had long ago moved into Briggate Street, this span across the river Aire was the busiest bridge in all Yorkshire. Ragged children clustered to beg for crumbs; tattered women hawked breads, cheeses, eggs, and fish from their market baskets; and weary men of all ages crossed on their way to and from the fulling mill.

Colin could hardly bear to see the delicate Miss Bowden in her floating blue dress enter this tide of scruffy humanity, but she seemed oblivious. She was completely comfortable among these bedraggled souls. Pausing at one particularly ill-kept old dame, she bought a loaf of dark bread for which she paid far too great a price. Breaking the bread, she gave a portion to Colin, kept a small bit for herself, and handed the remainder to the crowd of urchins who swarmed her.

"I believe you would be perfectly at home in India," he told her as they finally made their way out onto a country road. "Indeed, you are the only Englishwoman about whom I could say such a thing — including the ones who already live in that country."

"Is that so?" She beamed. "Oh, I do wish I could see India again! I sense that I have stored its beauties away in my heart somehow. All the sights and smells and sounds. There are times when I think I remember something. And then it vanishes before I can capture it."

"You would remember everything in an instant the moment you set foot on India's shores."

"Really? Do you believe it would all come back to me?"

"Without a doubt. And you would be charmed by the people and amazed at the elephants and delighted by the monkeys and —"

"Say no more!" She held up her hand. "I cannot think of such things. Already I have been forced to admit the terrible damage I have caused by permitting my thoughts to wander where they should not go. I must speak to you now of Mr. John Frith and the disturbing scene I witnessed yesterday evening."

"Is he the one of whom you wrote? Do you feel his life may be threatened?"

"I cannot say for certain, sir, yet I greatly fear something is amiss." She again slipped her arm through his and leaned close, lest her words be heard by any passerby. "Upon departing Mr. Frith's room to return to the inn, I turned my head in time to witness Miss Veronica Smith engaged in a peculiar activity. She drew an object from her pocket, but I could not discern its shape or substance. I turned away, yet I confess my curiosity would not permit me to leave without looking at her again. By then, she was stirring the water with her finger, examining the glass in the candlelight, and then carefully pouring the liquid into Mr. Frith's open mouth."

"A drug!" Colin's fists tightened. "I should have guessed it at once! No wonder Frith cannot recover from his wounds. The young lady keeps her master in a drugged state for some nefarious purpose. But what can be her aim? Does she plan to kill him eventually, in the hope of collecting something from his estate?"

"I cannot believe this, sir, for hear what next I witnessed. As she gave Mr. Frith the drink, Miss Smith gathered him close in her arms and began to weep! Her sobs were genuine. She loves him."

"Loves him? How can you say such a thing of that wretched creature? She clearly means him harm!"

"No, for I saw the look in her eyes. I saw the agony behind her tears. She was in great pain over the loss of her love, of that I have no doubt whatsoever."

"But her duplicity against him seems so obvious now. I cannot think how I missed the signs. She drugs him daily, and no doubt her aim is wicked. That she loves him is impossible."

"She does love him. I saw her face, Mr. Richmond." A sigh left her lips. "Miss Smith mourns the loss of her love, sir, for I know this feeling all too well. I have endured such tears and such grief. I am not mistaken."

Colin fell silent, turning her words over and over in his heart. Could it be possible that Ivy spoke of him? Had his coming departure for India caused her great mourning? Was he the love whose loss was unbearable? Or was there some other man? Had there been a great romance in Ivy's life — a man of whom she had never spoken?

"You must understand," she said softly, "that I did not truly observe anything untoward. I did not see what she took from her pocket. I did not see her pour anything into his glass of water. Though she made him drink the water and though he does appear to be drugged, I have no proof of such a thing. Miss Smith's tears belie any evil in her behavior."

"You defend her . . . and yet you summoned me. Why did you call upon me, Miss Bowden?"

"Because I needed your wisdom. I do believe Miss Smith loves Mr. Frith. And yet I fear for his well-being." Ivy shook her head. "Mr. Richmond, I called you because I could not reach a satisfying conclusion. You are the only man I know who cares for Mr. Frith and who might help me arrive at some acceptable explanation for what I observed."

He strolled along for a time, enjoying the bright morning and the beautiful lady at his side. How odd to find that this pastime filled him with greater pleasure than any he had ever known. No exotic jungles or stormy seas or gleaming jewels could thrill his heart more completely than did this simple woman with her pure heart and gentle smile. What would he do without her in his life? he wondered, as he had so many times before. How would he ever find joy again?

"Have I called you away from your duties in vain?" Ivy inquired at length. "I fear you think my observations silly."

"Not at all. I believe there are mice at work, gnawing away at the health and life of John Frith."

"And what is to be done about these mice?"

"What is always to be done about mice, Miss Bowden?" He laid his hand over hers, enclosing her slender fingers in his warm grasp. "This very evening, at least one wee mouse will have her cunning gambit observed by a pair of clever cats."

Sixteen

Ivy tucked the last spoonful of chicken soup into Mr. Frith's mouth and wiped the dribble from his chin. She had greatly enjoyed her morning's sojourn with Colin Richmond. And her visit with Lady Hertford had not been in vain. But these next hours, she knew, would be difficult. Perhaps even disastrous.

As she straightened from the bedside table where she had set the empty soup bowl, she heard a tapping on the window-pane. Though it was nearly dark outside, she knew at once who had scaled the back wall of Frith House and had come here to meet her. Her heart hammering as distress filled her breast, she hurried across the room and drew back the tattered velvet curtain.

"Mr. Richmond, I fear our plan may be ill advised," she whispered as she opened the window to admit him into the chamber. "If anyone saw you in the alley or climbing the wall, what must they think?

Surely they will call a constable! And if we are discovered here together, you will never go free from the charges already drawn up against you. My own reputation will be ruined completely. I am dreadfully uneasy, and I believe our best course may —"

"Shh." He placed his fingers over her lips. "All is arranged. A constable waits in readiness below, and Miss Smith was arriving at the kitchen door just as I started up the wall. There is no time to waste. We must hide ourselves at once."

Without allowing another word of protest, he drew her to the window and settled the curtain around them. Flattening herself against the wall, Ivy prayed that Veronica would not suspect anything amiss. Yet how could the girl fail to note the empty bowl, for Ivy always returned Mr. Frith's dishes to the kitchen and left the bedchamber tidy and clean? Worse, what if Veronica dawdled and Mama grew worried over the long absence of her daughter? What if Mama and Caroline suddenly appeared at Frith House? And what if . . .

"It will be all right," Mr. Richmond whispered, his breath warm against her ear. "I am here with you."

Though she knew her fingers trembled,

Ivy drank down a deep breath. This *was* the right thing. Mr. Frith could not be abandoned to the evil machinations of the mice. The cats must do their duty.

"Evenin' to ye, Johnny," a voice said suddenly near the curtain.

Ivy stiffened and slipped her hand into Mr. Richmond's. Veronica Smith had entered the room. Through a ragged moth hole in the curtain, Ivy observed the girl as she crossed toward the bed.

"Miss Clingin' Ivy left t' window open, did she? I'll warrant she thought t' night air would do ye good."

Ivy held her breath in dismay as Veronica moved to the window beside her hiding place. How could she have forgotten to close it? Oh, what else had been left amiss? She squeezed her eyes shut, wishing she could become invisible, as the girl's hand brushed back the curtain and drew the window shut.

"I cannot know why that woman stays on and on," Veronica said, turning back toward the bed. "Perhaps she still thinks ye'll marry 'er, eh, Johnny? Well, I've seen to that, 'aven't I?"

Ivy let out a sigh of relief as the girl settled down beside Mr. Frith, propped her legs up on the bed, and drew his head and shoulders against her. "Oh, Johnny, Johnny, what am I to do?" she murmured as she held him. "Whatever is to become of us?"

Feeling as though she was intruding on a very private moment, Ivy flushed as Veronica cradled the groggy man, kissed his forehead, and brushed back his hair. Something in the ease with which she touched him revealed an intimacy that could not be mistaken. It was as if Veronica knew everything about the man in her arms, as if there were no secrets between them.

Aware of the stark emptiness in her own life, Ivy could not help but feel a twinge of envy. Though she had a strong faith in God, and she enjoyed the company of many companionable friends, such a comforting openness with another human being was missing. Aware that she must focus on the matter at hand, Ivy tried her best to keep from sensing the warmth of Mr. Richmond's hand around her fingers. She tried not to notice the subtle scent of spice and leather that clung always to his skin. Most of all, she tried to make herself oblivious to the sweet tug of desire that danced in her heart.

But oh! how wonderful to run her fingers through a man's soft curls, as Veronica now caressed Mr. Frith's hair. And how blessed to kiss his cheek without a hint of shame. Yet surely there must be shame in the intimacy between the two who reclined in the room. Indeed, there must be even greater shame in the wayward thoughts that constantly filled Ivy's head. She must not long for Mr. Richmond . . . must not wish for things that could not be . . . but how could she deny the depth of love that filled her?

"Well, Johnny," Veronica said, drawing Ivy out of her reverie, " 'tis time for yer potion, me lad. Come now, bide a wee bit whilst I stir t' drink."

She drew a small packet from her pocket and untied the string that bound it. In full view of the two observers behind the curtain, she took a pinch of powder from the packet and dropped it into a glass of water beside Mr. Frith's bed. Just as Ivy had witnessed before, she stirred the liquid with her finger and then began to pour it down the poor man's throat.

"That is all the evidence I need," Colin whispered in Ivy's ear. "Have you seen enough to satisfy you?"

"It must be a drug," Ivy returned, "and yet I do not know the type nor the motive."

"It is clearly a sleeping potion. She means to keep him insensible until you are wedded to Mr. Creeve."

"But if she loves this man, why would she do such a dreadful thing to him?"

"It is a misguided, selfish love." He reflected for a moment, observing the scene through a tear in the old curtain. "I am in the midst of reading the Scriptures about marriage, as you recommended. I begin to understand —"

"Now, then, Johnny," Veronica said, settling beside him again. "How do ye feel? Does t' potion ease yer pain?"

"There . . . she wants to free him from pain," Ivy whispered. "That is her motive."

He shook his head. "It cannot matter the motive. The action is wrong, and the cats must catch that wee mousie by her tail. What say you, Miss Bowden?"

Through the moth hole, Ivy studied the petite woman as she began to weep again, and at length she nodded. "Yes, we must stop this."

Keeping her hand in his, Richmond threw back the curtain and stepped into the room. Veronica let out a shriek that surely must have been heard all up and down the street. Leaping to her feet, she grabbed for the packet of powder on the table. But not quickly enough.

"I shall take that, madam!" Richmond cried, whisking it away. "An apothecary will soon identify for me the potion with which you keep Mr. Frith in such a stupor."

As he folded the packet and placed it into his own pocket, her shrieks transformed into tears of remorse. "It ain't my fault, sir! I didn't mean 'im no 'arm. I swear, I never meant to do nothin' wrong!"

"No harm?" Richmond snapped. "You have kept the poor man senseless for weeks. I daresay you mean to kill him in time."

"No! No, I don't mean nothin' of the sort! I would never 'urt Johnny, no sir, not at all."

"Then why do you do this?"

"To keep 'im from pain is all. I saw 'ow bad 'e were sufferin', and I thought to meself that such agony could not go on!"

"He is no longer suffering, for his wound is all but healed. You have done this in order to lead him slowly toward death. You mean to steal his household belongings. Perhaps you know where he keeps his money."

"No, that ain't it, sir!" She fell to her knees, sobbing. "I don't want nothin' from 'im. I never took a thing from this 'ouse that weren't rightfully mine. I swear to ye —"

"Swear it to the judge," Richmond said, "for a constable awaits you on the street below."

"Owwww!" This wail of agony was more than Ivy could bear, and she crouched down beside the miserable woman and took her by the shoulders.

"Miss Smith, you must be truthful or you will be taken straightaway to gaol," she said in the most gentle tone she could muster. "If you have not taken money from Mr. Frith, how did you afford to purchase the sleeping powder?"

"I . . . I . . ." She sniffled. "Somebody give me t' drug."

"And who is that?"

"I ain't supposed to tell. Look, I 'ave no other way to support meself, miss, and me children will starve if I cannot feed 'em. Please don't make me tell ye —"

"Someone *pays* you to give Mr. Frith the drug?" Ivy said. "Oh, Miss Smith, this is a dreadful thing. Can you not see that you will be viewed as the guilty one by a court of law? You must tell us at once who gave you the powder. You must confess who employs you at this reprehensible task."

"But I . . . I shall 'ave no position . . . no wages . . . Johnny aims to marry ye, miss, and 'e will turn me out of t' 'ouse, for I am naught but a burden to 'im. I'll 'ave to go on t' streets, and me wee ones will —"

"No, indeed, for I assure you that nothing evil will befall you or your children."

"Ye canna say such a lie!"

"It is not a lie. You know I am to inherit a great fortune. Even now, I am planning to put it to use on behalf of people in your very condition — women with no legitimate means of support, debtors in peril of gaol, orphaned children, the ill and hungry. Even if Mr. Frith turns you out, your family will be cared for. Please trust me, Miss Smith."

Sniffling, the girl rubbed her grimy cheeks. She swallowed several times before looking up into Ivy's face. "Trust ye?"

"Yes, for I am a Christian and my words are true."

Veronica gulped down a sob. Then she nodded. " 'Tis Nigel Creeve wot pays me."

"Mr. Creeve?" Ivy exclaimed in horror. Turning to Mr. Richmond, she saw no surprise on his face.

"I suspected as much," he said. "Creeve is a reprehensible man, and he will stop at nothing to enrich himself. He pays you to act on his behalf, does he, Miss Smith?"

"Aye, 'e gives me enough of t' sleepin' powder that I should kill Johnny . . . 'e wants me to do 'im in . . . but I canna do it, so I give 'im only a wee bit. I tell Mr. Creeve t' powder ain't strong enough . . . I lie to him . . . and each time that 'e gives me more powder, I fear poison may be mixed into it. So I been puttin' that new powder away, and only usin' a bit o' what I 'ad left. And I ain't got much more, and I fear Johnny will come awake, and Mr. Creeve will find out that I been cheatin' 'im!"

Bursting into tears again, she allowed Ivy to draw her into a comforting embrace. Mr. Richmond knelt beside them and laid his hand on the woman's arm.

"Miss Smith," he said in a far more gentle voice than Ivy had expected. "If I guarantee your freedom, will you give all this information to the constable who waits outside the house? Will you turn over all the powders — including the ones you have hidden away? Will you testify against Mr. Creeve?"

"Ye canna promise me freedom. I done wrong!"

"The greater wrong belongs to Nigel

Creeve. He must be made to suffer the consequences. Agree to tell the truth, and I shall assure you that your consequences will be bearable."

The girl laid her head on Ivy's shoulder. Childlike, she trembled, sucking down the last of her sobs as Ivy stroked her tousled blonde hair. "Aye," she murmured at last. "I will speak t' truth. All of it."

"Very good, madam. And you will be cared for. I shall fetch the constable." Richmond rose and left the room. In moments, he returned with a uniformed gentleman, who led Miss Smith to a chair near the window and began to take her testimony.

Richmond beckoned Ivy to step aside with him. "I must bid you farewell now, Miss Bowden," he said in a low voice. "The constable and I shall go immediately to find Nigel Creeve, that he may be placed under arrest."

"Surely this information will serve to release you from accusation in the incident on the balcony," she said. "You will be free."

"I believe so."

"Then your urgency to return to India is not so great, is it? Perhaps you could stay in Yorkshire long enough to attend my birthday ball. It is but little more than a week from now, and I am sure we would all welcome you. My family . . . and Clemma . . . and, of course, I should like very much to have you there."

He looked down into her eyes, his own so deep and haunted that she sensed she could be drawn into them and held there forever. "Can you not see what this revelation means, Ivy?" he whispered, her name lingering on his tongue. "Creeve's claim on you is ended. Frith will recover. You must marry him."

No, she wanted to shout. *No! I cannot marry such a man!* But what right did she have to deny the hand of God? She had promised to help Miss Smith, and there were so many others like her. Such great need. The budding fortunes of her father must bloom into a rich harvest that would satisfy and fill the needs of those who could not fend for themselves. Ivy had been entrusted with that gift. What choice did she have but to use it for the glory of her heavenly Father?

"Once I am certain Creeve is in custody," Richmond said, "I shall return to Longley Park and finalize all my arrangements immediately. Your legacy lies securely locked away in my house, and I have entrusted my barrister with the keys. Once you are wedded to John Frith, it will be yours."

"I see." It was all she could manage.

"My ship sails within the week, and I must go to London at once to tend to legal matters of my own — matters regarding the future of Longley Park. I assure you, the house and grounds will not fall into disrepair again. You have taught me to practice good stewardship."

"I am happy to hear it, sir." Why did she feel as if she were going to cry? These were glad tidings. All would be well. All must be as it had been planned.

"I trust the conservatory will make a good setting . . . a suitable location . . . for your birthday ball," he continued, his words now faltering. "And that . . . peace and joy will fall upon . . . upon the Bowden family."

"Yes," she whispered. "Thank you."

"And upon you. I shall not forget you, Ivy." He took her hand and pressed it to his lips. "My dear lady, you have brought me the greatest challenge, the greatest delight . . . indeed, the greatest happiness I have ever known. In the conservatory, I once told you that I loved you. It was wrong of me to speak in such a bold fashion, but by now you surely know I am not steeped in proper behavior. I am hardly a gentleman, and I am worthy of neither admiration nor affection. My life has been one of sin and selfishness. Even as a Christian, I find myself behaving and thinking in a wrongheaded fashion. I wish you to know that you have shown me a nobler path; you have helped to set my feet on solid ground and my eyes on a higher ideal. I do love you, Ivy. Your memory will remain always in my heart."

He glanced up as the constable approached them. "I got all I need outta that lady," the man said. "She 'as vowed to stand up against Mr. Creeve in a court of law, and so we 'ave our case on solid ground. Me partner waits just down t' street, and 'e will take t' lady straightaway to t' 'ome office. They'll see she stays 'ere in Leeds until t' matter is resolved. And now, sir, you and I must 'urry ourselves to Nigel Creeve before 'e gets wind 'is goose is cooked!"

As the constable led Miss Smith out of the room, Richmond lifted Ivy's hand again to his lips, kissed it, and ran his thumb over the knuckles as if to memorize them. "Farewell," he said. "May God lead you and protect you always."

Struggling to hold back her tears, Ivy

tried to think of something she might say in response. Could she hold him back? Could she somehow express the depths of her love for him? Could she change the course of this downhill tumble on which she was falling headlong?

Before she could form the words on her tongue, he was walking away. She gazed at his solid back and broad shoulders. The dark curls in his hair. The strength of his deeply tanned fingers on the doorknob. The heavy weight of his boots upon the floor. He did not turn again to look at her. Instead, the door shut behind him, and the sound of his words faded into the darkness.

Seventeen

The familiar scents of salt water, drying fish, wet wood, and damp sisal rope filled his nostrils as Colin stood at the railing of one of his father's favorite ships. He had always loved the sea. In his childhood, this same journey down the Thames toward the open waters had always been one of anticipation and delight. It meant he was leaving boarding school, leaving musty textbooks, thick porridge, ink-stained fingers, damp mornings and shivering, lonely nights far behind. It meant he was returning home to India — to heat and mystery and adventure, to his parents and his friends, to freedom and fun and food heavily laced with sweets and spices.

But this time, Colin found himself gazing back at the shores of England instead of outward toward the ocean. Why did the morning mists that played across the water tug at his heart? How had William the Conqueror's castle towers grown so tall and majestic? When had they become so white, gleaming like fine alabaster in the sunrise? At what moment in the past three months had Colin fallen in love with England?

As the ship slid silently past the wharves, he listened to the cries of the fishmongers. He had always thought English a dull language. Now it rang like music in his ears — a myriad of dialects and magical phrases and singsong imagery. He reflected on the Yorkshiremen, who at this moment must be rising to sip their mugs of strong, hot tea and eat their blackened bread beside the fire.

Later, some would slip into wooden pattens and clatter down the cobbled streets of Otley toward the worsted factories and woolen mills. Others would tug on leather boots and trek up the fells to tend their sheep. A few, like Mr. Hedgley, would trudge across the dales in order to look after the great houses of the landed gentry. He would direct his apprentices to trim hedges and sweep walks. Then he would unlock the large old conservatory and toddle inside to continue preparations for the large ball soon to occur there.

Unbidden, Ivy's smiling face and bright brown eyes flashed into Colin's thoughts. What color of fine silk gown would she wear to celebrate her birthday? How would she braid and curl her hair? He had to smile at the thought of Ivy's futile efforts to make her locks behave in a stylish fashion. Had she any idea how magical he found her flowing mahogany tresses as they tumbled over her shoulders and down her back? What he would give to touch that mass of gleaming hair.

John Frith would be in attendance at the ball. As the constables had led Nigel Creeve into their headquarters on the day of his arrest, word had come that Frith was stirring already from his drugged stupor and was beginning to speak. Colin had made a point of stopping in to see him on the way to London and had found the fellow weak and pale but starting to regain his former boyish charm and impudence. Frith was still very eager to marry Miss Bowden, of course, and he was determined to see that any charges against Colin were dropped at once.

So, indeed, all was well. Colin could report to his father that his instructions had been fulfilled to the letter. The process had not been without detour, but Miss Bowden was soon to be securely wedded to Mr. Frith, and the fortune left to her by Justin Kingston was in her hands. Colin sensed he should have stayed in Otley to observe the wedding firsthand, but he had used every excuse to flee before that ceremony could occur.

How could he bear to watch a minister place Ivy's hand into the grasp of John Frith? How could he tolerate the moment when that man leaned forward to kiss a woman he did not love? How could Colin allow himself to think of beautiful, pure, and noble-minded Ivy in the arms of someone who was so unworthy of her?

Slamming his fist against the ship's rail, Colin turned from the fading sight of London and strode across the deck toward the east. He would not think about Ivy — a woman too perfect for any man to deserve, let alone someone as flawed as himself. What made him any better than John Frith? Or even Nigel Creeve, for that matter? Nothing!

Colin knew he was not pure. He was not noble or gentlemanlike. He was headstrong and stubborn and willful. His thoughts were wayward, his actions often uncontrolled. Only his surrender to God had changed him. Only that complete and total submission had given him the faith that he was a new man — learning and growing, holding out the hope that one day he might kneel in the Lord's presence and offer to God some small evidence that the life of Colin Richmond had been of value.

Certain that in Christ was his only hope for recovery from this consuming agony of loss in his heart, he pulled from his coat pocket the Bible the missionary had given him long ago. Ivy had challenged him to find Scriptures on marriage and to understand God's plan for man and woman. Now he began to search for a passage he had discovered in the sixth chapter of the book of Corinthians.

This chapter and the ones preceding and following it contained words so powerful that Colin had spent many hours poring over them and praying for guidance as to their meaning in his own life. The apostle Paul had admonished Christians not to keep company with those who were fornicators, idolaters, drunkards. He made it clear that those who regularly practiced such behaviors — along with adulterers, the effeminate, thieves, extortioners, and many others — would not inherit the kingdom of God. This passage was something that Colin had found hard to swallow, for he had certainly been guilty of some of those sins. Thanking God for his merciful forgiveness, he watched the ship ease farther down the Thames toward the sea.

Had John Frith turned from such ways? Colin wondered. Or would he continue in riotous living — perhaps with more resources at his disposal? Paul clearly instructed Christians not only to flee from those who made a habit of sin, but also to be aware that their own bodies were the temple of the Holy Ghost. Was it right, then, for Ivy to be joined in marriage to such a person?

Colin had turned the matter over and over in his mind. It was not his place to judge Frith. Yet Colin *had* been the instrument by which Ivy was forced into a union with the man. For so long, he had believed — as had Ivy — that this marriage was God's plan for her life. It was, wasn't it?

Verses in the seventh chapter instructed Christian women who were married to unbelieving husbands not to leave them. "The unbelieving husband is sanctified by the wife," the verse clearly stated. Did this mean that John Frith would go to heaven by virtue of marriage to Ivy? Was that not a good reason, then, that she should marry him? That she *must* marry him? For that matter, why should Christians everywhere not actively seek out unbelieving spouses in order to bring them into God's kingdom?

It all seemed too confusing. Colin leaned on the railing and glanced down at the passage he had located. But as he read the words, they were somehow completely unfamiliar. This passage beneath his fingertips spoke of finding God's approval as his minister in all afflictions that must come one's way. A *minister?*

But where were the words about marriage? Colin studied the passage again. Had he dreamed all that? Paul was indeed speaking to the Corinthians, but his message was something Colin had never read before in his entire life. As the words filled his heart, he found himself struggling to breathe.

Be ye not unequally yoked together with unbelievers: for what fellowship hath righteousness with unrighteousness? and what communion hath light with darkness? And what concord hath Christ with Belial? or what part hath he that believeth with an infidel? And what agreement hath the temple of God with idols? for ye are the temple of the living God.

Colin gripped the pages of the Bible, trying to make sense of this. Where had the previous words about marriage gone?

How had they been transformed into this? Such a passage! Such a message!

He turned the pages of the Bible back and forth, looking for answers. Was this some kind of magic? Did the holy words of Scripture actually fade and reform themselves in order to allow God to speak to Christians? Colin had never heard of such a thing. And yet he had been so certain that he had been reading in Corinthians. . . .

The pages flipped one by one in the sea breeze until the first book of Corinthians appeared in his hands. Colin stared down at it in bemusement. Were there *two* books? Two letters from the apostle Paul to the church at Corinth? Two passages about marriage . . . in two chapter sixes? Laughter filled his chest as he turned back and forth between the books, devouring the words again and again. As his eyes scanned the final message in the sixth chapter of the second book, he felt a peace spread through his heart.

Wherefore come out from among them, and be ye separate, saith the Lord, and touch not the unclean thing; and I will receive you, and will be a Father unto you, and ye shall be my sons and daughters, saith the Lord Almighty.

★ ★ ★

Ivy had seen enough of Leeds to last a lifetime. But the Bowden sisters were all aflutter over this latest journey to town to pick up their ball gowns from the seamstress and their new bonnets from the millinery shop. Ensconced once again at the inn, Ivy found it was all she could do to keep from whiling away every spare moment in the sitting room, on the settee where she had spent precious time with Colin Richmond. In fact, she had forced herself to walk past that place, to push every memory of him from her thoughts, and when she could not, to keep her damp handkerchief tucked well away from view.

Oh, she had prayed and read hundreds of passages of Scripture in an attempt to find some sort of peace about her future. But instead of leading to a clear understanding of why she must marry John Frith, all her efforts were in vain. The words swirled before her tear-filled eyes. Her head pounded with the effort of trying to focus on heaven instead of on an earthly love that was not meant to be. Though Colin had elevated her to a position of purity, and the Yorkshire countrymen considered her to be an angel, Ivy knew how very full of flaw and error she was!

She did not want to do God's will. She did not want to marry John Frith. She did not wish to have a fortune at her disposal. And she did not even really, truly care about building hospitals and almshouses to tend to the poor and hungry. Sometimes, at her most willful and angry moments, she informed God that she did not even care about orphans. She had been orphaned, after all, and look where she had ended! If this was God's will for orphans, then perhaps they were better off fending for themselves.

Letting out a sigh as she hurried down the steps and into the street before the inn, Ivy offered up a prayer of remorse and repentance. No, she did not really mean that. God had given her a full and abundant life. She did care very deeply about the needy. And the loss of Colin Richmond should not distract her.

She must turn her thoughts to her objectives and stop this senseless mourning. By now, the man she loved was already at sea again, sailing toward India, the ocean waves rising beneath his feet and a fine mist filling his lungs. Ivy must make do with cobblestone beneath her feet and the odor of Leeds's open-sewage drains in her nostrils. But such was the stuff of life. She trusted heaven would be far better.

Though the Bowden women were all gone off on their shopping adventures, Ivy had determined to visit Veronica Smith and to make certain that her condition was secure and her children were not starving. It did not take long to find the squalid flat in which the poor woman dwelled. The door hung loose on its hinges as a small child with bright blue eyes drew it open.

"Mummy, a fine lady is 'ere to see ye," the boy called over his shoulder into the darkness. "Shall I let 'er come inside?"

In a moment, Miss Smith's face appeared in the doorway. With a baby on her hip, she pushed the little boy back behind her skirts. As she recognized her visitor, a wariness flooded her face.

"What ye be wantin', Miss Bowden?" she asked. "I told me story to t' constables."

"Is she the one?" the child asked, pressing back through the doorway again. "It is 'er?"

"Get inside, Wills! Ye canna talk to 'er."

"It is quite all right for your son to speak to me, Miss Smith," Ivy said. "I have come to make certain that you and your children are faring well. Have you enough to eat?"

"Aye."

"No, we don't!" the boy cried. "Mummy 'as no work now that ye will marry —"

"Shut up, William, or I'll beat ye on t' backside! Get over to t' fire, boy. Stir t' broth!"

Ivy stared at the woman . . . at the blue-eyed baby on her hip . . . at the little boy who still gazed out from behind his mother's skirts. And something serene crept quietly over her. Something calm and certain and right filled every corner of her heart. She felt the tension slide out of her shoulders as tears of peace flooded her eyes.

Without speaking another word, she reached into her purse and drew out a pouch of coins. Pressing it into the woman's hands, Ivy tried to muster the words she wanted to say. "Do not be afraid any longer, Veronica," she whispered through trembling lips. "All will be well."

As the door fell shut behind her, Ivy made her way down the alley and back into the street. For the first time in many months, she knew where she was going and what she would do. First she must pay a visit to the barrister who kept the keys to her father's fortune. And then she would pen a note to John Frith.

Please come, she would write to him, just as she once had beckoned Colin Richmond. *Please come to the inn at once. I must speak with you.*

Eighteen

"Many happy returns of the day!" Clemma cried, setting a beautifully wrapped gift in Ivy's lap. "How old you must feel to be *twenty-one!* How very grown up! And to think you are to marry Mr. Frith in less than a fortnight. I shall miss you so dreadfully! Will you come and visit us often at Brooking House? And may I clean the ponds in the gardens at your home in Leeds, as you said I could? Oh, I cannot bear to think of our house without you!"

Ivy ran her hand over Clemma's pink cheek and leaned forward to give the child a kiss. "Calm yourself, dearest. I am certain we shall never be far apart."

"But you will marry and have children!" Clemma scanned the crowd gathered in the candlelit conservatory. "Where is Mr. Frith? Is he not coming? Everyone said he behaved very badly at his own party, and I want to see how he comports himself tonight. If he is horrid, Ivy, you must not marry him. Not even for all that money.

389

And then you may go on living with us at Brooking House!"

Ivy leaned back in the wicker chair where Colin Richmond had once told her he loved her. How strange and empty she felt to be here — surrounded by those she loved, enmeshed in gaiety and celebration — and yet so lonely.

"I do not know where Mr. Frith has kept himself all these days, Clemma," she said. "I wrote a letter to him when we went to Leeds to fetch our party gowns, but he did not answer me. I wished to speak with him on a matter of great urgency. Yet he did not come to call on us at the inn."

"Perhaps he was still recovering from his wound."

"I had received word that he was quite himself again." She tried to make herself smile at the guests who had come from Otley and the nearby villages to wish her well. Of course, some of them had come in hopes of converting an acquaintance into financial gain. She had learned that much about the realities of possessing great wealth.

"Oh, there he is!" Clemma said, pointing out across the boxwoods and hanging ferns toward a figure in the distance. "At least, I believe it is Mr. Frith."

Ivy rose from her chair as the man made his way past a cluster of bright red geraniums. His golden hair gleamed in the candlelight as he performed a gallant bow.

"Miss Bowden, how delightful," he said, taking her hand and pressing his lips to it. "May I wish you all the happiness in the world on this grand occasion? And may I say how lovely you look this evening?"

"Thank you, Mr. Frith." Ivy managed a curtsy, aware suddenly that all eyes in the room were trained upon the two of them. "I am pleased to see you so healthy again."

"Indeed, much of my recovery is due to you, dear lady." His smile radiated from cheek to cheek, and Ivy imagined that she heard a sigh arise from the gathering of females in the conservatory. "Not only did you tend me during my long convalescence, but you are due all the credit for uncovering the dastardly plot engineered by Nigel Creeve."

"Very true," Papa said, appearing at the table. "Mr. Frith, how delighted we are to have you join us. I trust that all will be well between us as we unite in great anticipation of your future bliss. For, as Mencius wrote — in a work translated by James Legge, I might clarify — 'The root of the kingdom is in the state. The root of the state is in the family. The root of the family is in the person of its head.' And it is a thought with which I could not agree more!"

His blue eyes suddenly glazed, Frith stared at Papa. "I beg your pardon, sir. What were you saying?"

"That you are to become the head of a new and great dynasty, a family that will strengthen the very foundation of this kingdom!"

"Ah."

"Sir," Ivy said softly, laying a hand on the man's arm. "I wrote a note to you asking if we might speak. I feel a great urgency to communicate with you —"

"This beautiful young lady is to become your wife!" Papa continued, proudly indicating to all the crowd the woman he had brought up as his daughter. "Milton might have been speaking of our own Miss Ivy Bowden when he cried out, 'O fairest of creation! last and best of all God's works! creature in whom excelled whatever can to sight or thought be formed, holy divine, good, amiable, or sweet!' Ah, indeed, this dear girl of ours —"

"Papa, please," Ivy said, her voice rising to a high pitch in her panicked urge to stop him from going on in such a manner. "I must speak with Mr. Frith, Papa, and I beg you to allow us a moment of privacy."

"Privacy!" Mama made her own appearance among those gathered around Ivy. Her face broke into a smile and she began to giggle. "Privacy!" she cried, clapping her hands. "Silence all, for our lovebirds require a moment of privacy!"

Horrified, Ivy wished she could sink straight into the earth, never to emerge again. But to her dismay, John Frith linked his arm through hers and escorted her away toward a copse of potted palms.

Oh, this could not be worse! Ivy had hoped and prayed that the focus of the party might be her birthday. But now she knew that everyone had one object in mind — the celebration of upcoming nuptials. Why had Mr. Frith failed to call on her? Ivy fumed as he led her into the candlelit clearing. And how on earth was she to —

"My darling!" he said, gathering her into his arms. "How dearly I love and admire you. How can I endure the endless days until we —"

"Please, Mr. Frith!" Ivy pushed out of his embrace and fluffed the crumpled fabric of her sleeves. "Goodness gracious, sir! What are you thinking?"

"I am only feeling," he said, falling on one knee, "feeling the depths of emotion that pour through my veins each time I —"

"Get up, Mr. Frith," she cried. "Get up at once and listen to me! I have a great many things to tell you, so kindly leave off this nonsense."

"Nonsense? But dear lady —"

"Why did you not come to me at the inn?"

"Well, I . . ." He gulped. "I was busy with matters of business. I had been ill for such a length of time that my . . . well, I thought perhaps you were . . ."

"You did not come because you did not consider my message to be of any great importance. Just as you do not consider my person to be of any value save for the fortune which —"

"That is not true! You are a delightful young lady. I am very eager to become your husband and to spend many hours at your side, lost in deepest admiration of your beauty."

At this, Ivy did not know whether to laugh or cry. Instead, she rolled her eyes and shook her head. "Come, Mr. Frith, let us speak honestly together. I must begin by telling you that I have been to the home of Miss Veronica Smith."

"V-Veronica . . ." He paled. "But why?"

"To see to her welfare, as I had promised."

A sharp cry from the gathered crowd cut off any further conversation. Ivy glanced at Mr. Frith as a collection of gasps was overshadowed by angry shouts.

"What has happened?" she said, stepping out of the copse to see what was occurring in the conservatory. "Come, Mr. Frith, we must —"

"What must you do, Miss Bowden?" Nigel Creeve stalked toward her, his hands at his hips. "What new mischief do you create — hidden away in the palm trees with your paramour?"

"I beg your pardon!" Confronted by Creeve's sneering visage, Ivy found it hard to breathe. "John Frith is not my lover. And you, sir, were not invited to my birthday party!"

"But I have come anyway."

"You should be in gaol."

"I am not wholly without profitable connections," Creeve said. "Indeed, my complete freedom is certain to be recovered within a short time."

"I am sorry to hear that," Ivy said, "though I doubt you are quite so far above the laws of England as you would have us believe."

She glanced to her side as Papa and several other men surrounded them. Swords had been drawn already, and she greatly feared a repetition of the disastrous events that had so plagued all their lives. Aware that Mr. Frith stood trembling beside her, she held out her hands in a placating manner.

"Gentlemen," she said, "I am sure there is no need for violence. It is a birthday party, after all. Mr. Creeve, do tell us what you have come to say, and then please depart our company, that we might resume our celebration."

"What I have come to say is this!" He pointed at Frith and turned to face the gathering. "That man cannot marry Miss Bowden, for he already has a wife!"

A collective gasp went up. Papa stepped forward, his hand on the hilt of his saber. "Renounce that statement, sir!" he cried. "I supported your claim to my daughter's hand until I saw you for the villain you truly are. And now I know that John Frith is the rightful man —"

"Papa," Ivy interrupted, "Mr. Creeve speaks the truth."

"What?"

"Indeed, Mr. Frith is the father of two children, and his marriage to me is quite impossible."

"That is not true!" Frith stammered.

"Only *one!* Only one of them is mine."

Ivy shook her head. "The baby favors you, as does his brother."

"Perhaps, but everything that man said about me is a lie!" Frith leveled a finger at Creeve. "I am not married, and I have every right to . . . to . . ."

"Miss Smith's baby is your child," Ivy said softly. "She loves you very dearly."

"She tried to kill me."

"She tried to save your life. Without her watch care over you, sir, Mr. Creeve would have succeeded in his attempt to remove you from the competition for my hand."

"Are you accusing me of trying to kill him?" Creeve cried.

"Of course I am, sir, for that is exactly what you did. And it is quite beyond me why you have disrupted my birthday party with news that I already knew and was attempting to relate to Mr. Frith. Your future was determined the night you stole Mr. Richmond's knife and used it against your enemy. Nothing will alter the evil you have done, Mr. Creeve. Just as nothing will alter the bright blue eyes and sweet smile of your baby son, Mr. Frith."

"But I am not married to the girl," Frith said again. "Truly, there is no record in any church —"

"There certainly should be, should there not? And if you are any sort of a gentleman, you will see to the matter at once." Ivy laid her hand on his arm. "Veronica loves you deeply. Marry her. Care for her children. You are not an evil man, Mr. Frith, but you have spent your life in pursuit of utter emptiness. Become the man God meant you to be."

Lowering his eyes, John Frith stepped back as Ivy walked toward Nigel Creeve. "You have given the information you came to deliver, sir. Will you please do me the courtesy now of returning to Leeds and never setting foot near me again?"

"But if Frith is wedded, then by rights you should still marry me!"

"Of course not," she said, brushing past him on her way back to the wicker chair. "I shall not marry you nor any other man."

"But Ivy, the fortune!" Papa cried, coming to her side. "You have to marry in order to get it. And . . . and you were meant to marry one of these two —"

"I do not have to marry anyone, Papa." Ivy settled into the chair again and looked around at the stunned crowd. "It is quite true that I was to marry Mr. Frith in order to receive my inheritance. Due to his circumstances, however, I cannot do that. It is also true that Mr. Creeve once held a legitimate claim to my hand — a claim which the courts might have declared valid enough to allow me to collect the fortune. But it is very clear to me now that I am not to marry either of these men."

"What will happen to all that money?" Clemma cried, stepping forward. "Is it going to sit in boxes and chests inside Mr. Richmond's house at Longley Park forever and ever?"

"No, indeed, Clemma." Ivy drew the little girl onto her lap. "The moment I realized that neither Mr. Creeve nor Mr. Frith could ever become my husband, I realized that God must have another plan for me — and for the legacy my late father entrusted to me. In the hope of discovering what other paths might be open to me, I went to speak to Mr. Richmond's barrister. While it is quite true that I shall never own a farthing of that fortune, I am happy to tell you that provision can be made for its use."

"It can?" Mama asked, her fingers knotted and white. "I mean to say . . . are you . . . are you quite certain?"

Ivy took the dear woman's hand and drew her close. "All is well, Mama. Mr. Kingston wished that his fortune might continue both to grow and to be put to good use. And so it shall. With the barrister's help, I have set up an array of funds and provisions to assist the needy." She paused. "*All* the needy."

"Ah!" Mama's face brightened. "All the needy."

"Indeed. And along with that, a small hospital is to be built in Leeds, and an almshouse will be set up to care for the poor and hungry. As the only living relative of Mr. Kingston, I am to oversee the administration of all matters concerning his legacy. I wish to assure everyone in this room that not only shall I put that money to work for you, but I am determined to see that the wealthy families of this region join me in contributing to its growth."

A general murmuring arose from those very same families, but Ivy did not care what they thought. She would be knocking on their doors soon enough, and they might as well be prepared to open their purse strings.

"The remainder of the fortune," she continued, "will be invested into local mills as well as into industries and developmental schemes. These will benefit England while producing a continued increase in the amount of money that can be used by

Kingston Ltd., the organization I have founded."

A moment of stunned silence was punctuated by the sound of a single pair of clapping hands. "Good girl!" Papa cried. "You have worked it all out better than any of us! Bravo! Bravo!"

Ivy laughed as the crowd erupted into cheers and rounds of applause. "Bless you all," she said. "And now, lest we forget we have come here to celebrate, let the music and dancing begin again!"

With a general sigh, everyone returned to their previous activities in an air of much relief. The band struck up the strains of a familiar waltz, and Ivy let out a deep breath. Mr. Creeve had been escorted from the conservatory by two of Mr. Hedgley's brawny gardeners. Ivy thought she caught a glimpse of Mr. Frith slipping away amongst the rhododendrons. Caroline and Madeline, wearing their new pink and yellow silk gowns, floated like lovely blossoms from partner to partner among the dancers. Even Mama and Papa slipped their arms around one another and twirled happily to the music.

Ivy ate a bit of cake and opened her birthday gifts one by one as the hours of celebration drifted by. Such lovely things emerged from the pretty papers. A silver necklace. A bottle of perfume. A length of damask that would make a lovely shawl. Mr. Hedgley, who was dancing with his merry little wife, had brought Ivy the stem of forsythia he had started so many weeks ago. She assured him she would plant it near the wall upon which her thriving vine now crept.

Ivy realized that she had done exactly as Mr. Hedgley had instructed. Like the spray of ivy she carefully tended, she had clung to the rock of her salvation, following God's path each step of her life. It had not been easy. She had not seen the way ahead of her until the moment she had gazed into that baby's blue eyes. But now she knew what her future held. Now she felt completely secure that she understood at last what God had been planning for her all along. Though it was not what she might have chosen for herself, by trusting in him one day at a time, she would move forward in peace.

"I do wish Mr. Richmond had stayed in England a bit longer," Clemma whispered, rubbing her eyes as she stifled a yawn.

At nearly two in the morning, Ivy wondered how the child had managed to stay awake so long. Many of the celebrants had gone home, yet the band continued to play and it appeared the festivities might continue until dawn.

"Mr. Richmond would have liked to see the conservatory all lit up again," Clemma continued. "Everyone looks so lovely and happy."

"Oh yes, he would have thought it marvelous," Ivy said in a low voice. She had tried to keep her thoughts from him all night, but as the hour grew late and her weariness increased, she found it harder and harder. "He is a fine gentleman."

"Indeed, he is. Did he tell you that he is making Longley Park into a school?"

"A what? Are you serious, Clemma?"

"Yes, a school for artists like Mr. Turner, who painted the Chevin and made it look like the Alps. Artists will be able to stay at Longley as long as they like, and there will be teachers and galleries and everything."

"I am all astonishment. Who told you this?"

"Mr. Hedgley. Everyone wishing for a position will have the opportunity to be employed at Longley House, and the income from the sales of paintings and sculptures will help to pay for it all. Is that not a wonderful idea? I think it is. I think

Mr. Richmond is brilliant, and I miss him very much."

Ivy leaned her head back on the chair and allowed her eyes to drift shut. She missed him too. Missed him dreadfully. But now she was resolved to go on with her life as God had unfolded it before her. Why had she doubted the plan of the Almighty? Had he not cared for her always?

Everything was so clear now. Ivy wondered that she had not seen it all along. She was not to marry, but she was to follow in her late father's footsteps by increasing his legacy and using it to help others. She was to become a patroness of all things good and beneficial.

As Ivy listened to the music, she envisioned herself many years hence — a white-haired spinster with a large array of assistants at her fingertips. They would hurry about at her beck and call, building new sewers and cleaning the floors of the worsted mills and transporting soup from cottage to cottage. And there would be a comfortable old settee upon which she would recline. And lots of little children would climb onto her lap, and she would braid their hair. And soft silk would brush past her face . . . drifting against her cheeks . . and the sweet scents of cinnamon and cloves would swirl around her . . . and a voice would murmur in her ear . . .

So, jao . . . so, jao . . .

And the scent would emanate from the skin of a man, strong and brown, whose deep voice filled her heart, whose warm arms held her gently, whose dark eyes gazed into hers as he spoke her name.

"Ivy . . . Ivy . . ."

How very real those eyes seemed as she looked longingly into them. How black the lashes. How mysterious the smell that clung to his white collar.

"Ivy?" The dark eyes blinked. "Are you awake?"

"Oh!" With a muffled cry of shock, she shrank back into the wicker chair.

"I do not mean to frighten you, but —"

"Mr. Rich . . . Richmond . . . you are . . . you are . . ."

His mouth curved into a grin. "I am the man who loves you, dearest sleeping beauty."

"But I . . . but you are on a ship . . . to India . . ."

"No longer. We had not sailed even as far down the Thames as Canterbury when I realized I must return to you at once. It was almost as though God spoke to me!"

Uncertain whether she was asleep or

awake, Ivy stretched out her hand and stroked her fingertips down the dark stubble on his cheek as he knelt before her. Had he come back? Was he really here? Oh my, how could this be happening?

"I rode day and night with hardly a pause because I knew I must carry this message to you," Colin said. He took her hand and held it so tightly there could be no doubt as to the reality of his presence here in the conservatory. "You cannot marry John Frith!"

"Oh," Ivy said. "Well, I —"

"I know you mean to do it, and I admire you greatly for your determination to do what is right. But I have discovered that such a marriage is *not* right."

"No?"

"No, indeed. You see, if you were already married to this sort of a man, then you must stay married to him, for that sanctifies him — a word which I am not quite clear on, but at the moment it really does not matter. But if you are not married to him — which I hope to heaven you are not?"

"No."

He let out a breath. "Good. Then you must not marry him, for as Christians, we are not to be yoked unequally with unbelievers. And though it is not my place to judge Mr. Frith, I must admit that his behavior leaves no doubt at all as to the state of his soul, which clearly cannot be surrendered to God. I say this with the greatest of trepidation, for I know that my own behavior is far from perfect, and yet it is the *striving* to do right which bears the fruit of the Spirit and which reveals the character of the —"

"Do stop talking, Mr. Richmond," Ivy said, laying her fingers over his lips. "I am not to marry Mr. Frith. It is all decided."

"It is?" He swallowed. "You decided this before you heard my reasoned argument?"

"Indeed I did, for God has been speaking to me too, you see. Well, he has been trying, though I have had a very difficult time listening."

"Ah. Then you are not to marry Mr. Frith."

Ivy giggled a little at his inability to comprehend. "Not at all. Nor am I to marry Mr. Creeve. In fact, I am to be the patroness of a benevolent fund which . . . which . . . why are you looking at me like that, Mr. Richmond?"

"Because I cannot believe how beautiful you are."

"Oh, but I —"

"And how very much I love you."

"But I think God intends me to be a spinster —"

"And how passionately I long to make you my wife."

Ivy stared at him. Then she lifted her head and gazed past him at the few friends and relatives who were still in the conservatory. She did not understand God. Why had he given her this life? These people who had brought her up with moral fiber and deep love? And why had he given her parents who had died and left her a fortune? Why was she led down a path of believing she must marry one of two unappealing men . . . led all the way to complete surrender, only to be shown that she was free of that obligation?

"And why," she whispered, "why was I so certain only moments ago that I would never marry anyone?"

"I cannot imagine," Colin said, running his knuckles down the side of her face. "I only hope you were wrong."

"I cannot understand how to follow God's will, for I cannot see it." She laid her cheek against his hand. "I have tried so hard to do what is right. And all is for naught, because I am still completely uncertain as to what God wants of me."

"I think you know quite well what he wants, and I think you are doing it each day of your life, dearest Ivy. You are trying very hard to do what is right . . . giving up your own will in surrender to his — whatever it might be . . . and walking with God each moment of each day."

"Then I am not to know his will for my future?"

Colin smiled. "I certainly hope not. That would take away the adventure that awaits us, would it not?"

Ivy turned her head and kissed his palm. The scent of sandalwood and leather filled her nostrils. She shut her eyes as tears spilled down her cheeks. How could it have come to this? Did God love her so much that he would give her the desire of her heart? Oh, how could she comprehend such blessed joy?

"Say you will marry me, Ivy," Colin whispered, drawing her up out of the chair, gathering her close, and laying her head upon his shoulder. "I must hear the words, for I cannot live another moment in the fear that you will live out your life as the spinster patroness of a benevolent fund. . . ."

"Yes," she said, as his lips covered hers. "Yes, my darling love. Oh yes."

To the fading strains of music in the conservatory, he turned her slowly among the flowers, his strong arms supporting her as she drifted in utter happiness.

"*So, jao,*" he whispered in her ear. "*So, jao,* my love."

Ivy lifted her head and looked into his eyes. "I have heard those words before. I now remember where. . . . They were spoken by the Indian ayah who looked after me when I was a little girl."

"And I shall be the one to say them to you from now on." He stroked his hand down her hair, and she could hear the beating of his heart. "*So, jao* means 'go to sleep.' *So, jao,* my darling . . . rest in the knowledge that I shall love you forever."

A Note from the Author

Dear Friend,

Like Ivy, I find myself constantly seeking to do God's will. But what is it? What does God want of me? And why won't he just send me a nice little letter or even an e-mail!

As I've walked along on my own faith journey, I think I have learned two important lessons. One is that God's will for us is basically always the same: He wants us to know and love him more, and he wants us to reach out to others with the good news of salvation. God created people to have fellowship with him, didn't he? And that is what he wants most from us.

Second, I believe that the process of seeking God's will in a specific situation may be more important than finding the answer! Seeking means we spend time with him in prayer and Bible study, we spend intimate time with family and friends in search of answers, and we spend time examining ourselves. What does the Bible say? What do our friends think? Where does our heart lead us? It is the process of seeking that helps us grow. And eventually, when we do make a decision, we must step out in faith that it's the right one.

Dear friend, remember that God can use everything you do — right or wrong — for his glory. But before you act, seek him. You will find that his will is really quite clear. I take these lessons to heart as I search for direction in my writing. More than anything, I want to write words that will please and honor God. Thank you for your letters sharing with me how often God uses my books to touch your heart. May we both grow in him!

Blessings,
Catherine Palmer

About the Author

Catherine Palmer lives in Missouri with her husband, Tim, and sons, Geoffrey and Andrei. She is a graduate of Southwest Baptist University and has a master's degree in English from Baylor University. Her first book was published in 1988. Since then she has published more than twenty-five books and has won numerous awards for her writing, including the 2001 Christy Award. Total sales of her novels number more than one million copies.

Catherine's first hardcover novel, *The Happy Room*, has just been released by Tyndale House Publishers. She is also the author of the suspense novel *A Dangerous Silence*. Her HeartQuest books include the series A Town Called Hope (*Prairie Rose*, *Prairie Fire*, and *Prairie Storm*); *Finders Keepers* and its sequel, *Hide & Seek*; and novellas in the anthologies *A Victorian Christmas Keepsake*, *Prairie Christmas*, *A Victorian Christmas Cottage*, *A Victorian Christmas Quilt*, and *A Victorian Christmas Tea*.

Her original HeartQuest series, consisting of *The Treasure of Timbuktu* and *The Treasure of Zanzibar*, have been rereleased as the Treasures of the Heart series. The first two books are now titled *A Kiss of Adventure* and *A Whisper of Danger*. Also look for the never-before-published third book in the series, *A Touch of Betrayal*, winner of the 2001 Christy Award.

Catherine welcomes letters written to her in care of Tyndale House Author Relations, P.O. Box 80, Wheaton, IL 60189-0080.